C000170618

Death Duty

An Inspector Mowgley Mystery

George East

A La Puce Publication
www.la-puce.co.uk

Other Books by George East

The Mill of the Flea series:

Home & Dry in France
René & Me
French Letters
French Flea Bites
French Cricket
French Kisses
French Lessons

French Impressions series:

Brittany
The Loire Valley
The Dordogne River

also

150 Fabulous Foolproof French Regional Recipes
by Donella East

The Naked Truth series:

How to write a bestseller
France and the French

The Mowgley Murder Mysteries:

Death Duty
Deadly Tide
Dead Money

A Year Behind Bars

Home & Dry in Normandy
French Kisses
(compilations from Orion)

LA PUCE PUBLICATIONS www.la-puce.co.uk

Death Duty

Published by La Puce Publications

website: www.george-east.net

© George East 2012

ISBN 978-1-908747-05-1

Typesetting and design by Nigel Rice

e-pub version ISBN 978-1-908747-03-7
mobi-kindle version ISBN 978-1-908747-04-4

About the Author

While trying out a number of life options, George East scraped a living as a private detective, film and TV extra, club bouncer and DJ, demolition worker, brewer's drayman, magazine editor, pickled onion manufacturer, snooker club owner, publican, failed rock god, TV and radio presenter, PR and marketing supremo, seamstress and the world's first and probably only professional bed tester. He gained his knowledge of police procedure and attitudes as a result of a number of arrests for violent behaviour in his extreme youth. In the 1980s, he gained an understanding and liking of plain-clothes policemen while running an inner-city pub which acted as a local (and once as a murder room) for a whole station's-worth of C.I.D. officers. This is the first Inspector Mowgley Mystery in what his publishers trust will be a series almost as long as the list of the author's past endeavours to turn a mainly honest crust.

It's 1999 and the world is on the brink of a new millennium. Detective Inspector Jack Mowgley is on the brink of enforced early retirement. Or worse. Attitudes are changing, and senior officers think people like Mowgley have no part to play in the Modern Police Force. For sure, Jack Mowgley is caught in a time warp with regard to policing policies and procedures, and PC he most definitely ain't. Divorced and dispossessed of his home, we find Mowgley sleeping on a redundant lightship in a scrapyard near the ferryport which is his patch. A colleague arrives to inform her boss about a dramatic event in mid-Channel, and Mowgley applies his own very distinct form of policing to solve an increasingly perplexing case...

The Players

Detective Inspector Jack Mowgley:
Officer notionally in charge of the city's intercontinental ferryport.

Detective Sergeant Catherine 'Melons' McCarthy:
Mowgley's colleague, conscience, confidante and drinking companion.

George The Dog: A dog.

Detective Sergeant Dickie Quayle:
Able but generally unloved member of Team Mowgley.

Margaret Birchall: The Overboard.

Yvonne McLaughlin: Witness to the overboard incident.

Two-Shits: Ferryport pub landlord.

Mundy The Younger:
Most junior member of Mowgley's team, and son of Mowgley's boss.

Linda Russell: Sister of Margaret Birchall.

Robert Birchall:
City solicitor and husband to Margaret Birchall.

Chief Superintendent Sidney 'Gloria' Mundy:
Mowgley's boss.

Detective Inspector Cyril 'Cyrano' Byng:
Bag-carrier to Chief Superintendent Mundy.

Capitaine Guy Varennes:
French police officer, friend and admirer of Mowgley and his attitude to police procedures.

Dodger Long: Scrapyard owner and Mowgley's landlord.

Eddie Barnes: Influential and dodgy City Councillor.

Offender Profile

Name:	John ('Jack') Mowgley
Rank:	Detective Inspector (just)
D.O.B.:	31.1. 50
Height:	5ft 11 inches
Weight:	16–17 stones (depending)
Body shape:	Lumpy
Distinguishing features:	'ACAB' tattooed on fingers of left hand. Scar on right temple. Frequently broken nose. Right earlobe mislaid
Eyes:	Yes
Teeth:	Mostly
Hair:	Dark, copious and untended
Facial type:	Lived-in (as if by squatters)
Favourite haunt:	Proper pubs
Favourite activity:	Drinking in proper pubs
Favourite drink:	Any cheap lager
Favourite smoke:	Any duty-free rolling tobacco
Favourite food:	Indian/fry-ups

Favourite film star:	Paul Newman in *Hombre*
Favourite film:	See above
Favourite film theme:	'The Trap'
Favourite music:	Country & Western
Favourite song:	'Ring of Fire'
Favourite singer:	Johnny Cash
Heroes:	Father & mother, Winston Churchill, Margaret Thatcher, Dennis Skinner MP, Cassius Clay/Muhammad Ali.
Politics:	Left, Right and Centre (depending)
Ideal woman:	Modest, demure, caring and companionable, with really big tits

Fact:

A team of police officers with Special Branch connections is based at each UK intercontinental ferryport. Their brief is to investigate all criminal matters taking place within the port and detain British and foreign nationals who have committed crimes and are passing through their patch.

Fiction:

Although based in part on real people, places and events, the characters and events and places featuring in this story are all works of complete fiction.

Dedication:

Thanks are due to the local C.I.D.'s finest during the 80s and 90s, especially Dougie, Floodie, Hoppy, Nick-Nick, Bingabong, Ace, Jock and most of all Big John M for all the inside info. And, of course, the fun we had during all those memorable (or not) drinking sessions.

Talking in tongues

Portsmouth is a treasure trove for anyone wanting to sample a whole range of dialects, slang and other alternative uses and abuses of the Queen's English. We Pomponians talk so funny for a number of reasons. To start with, the city has been a premier Naval port for many centuries and the Royal Navy has a language of its own. Also, generations of naval ratings arriving in Portsmouth from all parts of the British Isles have left their regional linguistic mark. Then there is the picaresque linkage with London, and Portsmouth has long been a popular stop-off point for travelling folk. All these elements have combined to create an often impenetrable argot (even to some locals) which blends rhyming slang, Romany, naval patois and all manner of regional dialects.

I have steered clear of giving full rein to my extensive repertoire of traditional Pompey street-talk in this book, but have included the odd word or expression which might give someone not of my area and upbringing a problem of interpretation. To that end I have included a brief glossary of some of the more esoteric examples of Portsmouth *lingua franca* at the end of the book.

One

The ship circled in the grey waters of the English Channel for almost three hours. The captain, crew and amateur sailors amongst the passengers knew it to be a pointless exercise, but propriety and standing orders required that the search be seen to be thorough and prolonged.

The car ferry had steamed on at fifteen knots for more than ten minutes before the alarm was raised. Even had the searchers been looking in the right place, it would have been near-impossible to spot a small white face amongst the rolling, spume-topped waves. Besides, as captain, crew and sailors amongst the passengers knew, survival time in the English Channel in mid-winter is mercifully short.

It would, they also knew but did not care to say, have been more than a small miracle to have found the woman and taken her alive from the cold, dark sea.

Two

When Melons arrived, Mowgley lay dreaming.

He dreamed often, or thought he did.

Mostly, his dreams seemed to be disjunctive fragments of events and places and people he knew. Taken together they made no sense and nearly always turned out badly. A bit like his waking life, really.

Invariably, the pace and progress of the events and characters streaming through his dreams were completely beyond his control. But now and then, he would know he was dreaming, and if he tried hard enough he could influence the outcome. He could make things happen and get what he wanted and ensure a happy ending. That was certainly not like his waking life.

His head was starting to hurt, so he gave up the struggle, yawned, opened an eye and looked blearily up at his visitor.

"Bugger me," she said, "what a state."

Knowing not whether she referred to him, his surroundings or both, he grunted neutrally and wondered yet again why he did not fancy her. Short hair, long legs, big tits, and not a bad face. Perhaps if she wore her old Plod uniform it would help, but he thought not. As far as he knew, policewomen and nurses didn't wear suspender belts and stockings nowadays. With some high-ranking male officers he knew of in the Modern Force, it was a different matter.

When Sergeant Catherine McCarthy had been wished on him, he had suspected it was a plot by those above who considered he did not grace a modern-thinking, inclusive and socially responsive police force. They thought they knew what he thought about women in general and women in the Force in particular, and probably thought he would react to her arrival in one of two ways. Either get pissed and try to get a leg over, or give her a hard time and an excuse to claim mental or sexual harassment, or both. Either outcome would have given them safe grounds for giving him the elbow.

But neither reaction, to their and his surprise, had happened. From the start and in spite of himself, he had liked her. This was mainly because although she was a woman, rarely used her weapons and wiles except on a job - and then usually only when he persuaded her to use them.

At first, she had been so unlike what he expected of a modern woman officer that he had thought she was a dyke. She did not scream, sulk, pout or whinge when she did not get her own way, even when she had the painters in. Most surprisingly for a woman, she even took the blame when she fucked up. Other points in her favour were that she always bought her round, thought in an almost logical pattern most of the time, and, most surprisingly of all for a woman, had a sense of humour and could laugh at herself. Well, sometimes. Best of all, she didn't compete with or try to control him. Or seemed not to. If she did, she was very good at disguising it.

He scratched his belly, yawned and continued to regard his sergeant. People who thought he didn't like women were wrong.

Once while they were both sober enough to exchange fairly coherent sentences, a wise old Super had said Mowgley was not so much a misogynist as a misanthrope. It wasn't that he didn't like women; he didn't like the human race.

After working out if he should feel offended or flattered, Mowgley had thought the judgement a tad harsh. He quite liked some members of the human race. The reason he didn't like most women was because of the power they had and how casually they often used it. It scared him in the same way he would be scared of a panther, elephant or poisonous snake. It was not the species he objected to, just the harm they could do to him. Perhaps it was true that, as many of his fellow ex-husbands thought, women were born without a conscience, and had been programmed at the start of it all to help them survive in a world where strength and not guile was all. Things had changed since then, which made them even more dangerous.

Mowgley yawned again, stretched and then took a comforting hold on his tackle as he continued to consider why Melons did not appeal to him sexually. In their early days together he had tried to fantasise about her, but it had never worked. From the beginning, she was almost one of the lads. He had never had a sister, but it must be the same sort of thing. For normal people, anyway. He had read somewhere that the average man thought about sex every ten seconds. But how did the surveyors know? Was there proper scientific research, or did they just ask a few blokes to make a note every time they thought about a bunk-up? The trouble with all these claims was that people believed them if it suited their prejudices. Mind you, he did believe that most women rarely thought about sex, and, whatever they said nowadays, they didn't really enjoy it. Well, none of the women he had done it with had enjoyed it, for sure.

Feeling his head hurt again, Mowgley struggled to an upright position and reached instinctively for his tobacco tin.

He had read somewhere that, if you smoked a cigarette within half an hour of waking up in the morning, you were addicted to nicotine. Fucking brilliant. The team of scientists who came up with that one were probably even now conducting an exhaustive research programme to prove that bears shat in woods.

After saying good morning to his posters of Johnny Cash and Muhammad Ali in his Cassius Clay days, he looked for his clothes while Melons told him about the overboard.

It was their first for nearly two years, she reminded him, and their first ever woman. It all seemed pretty straightforward, but with it being a French boat there would be the usual complications.

"Technically, it's all down to the Frogs, but they're more than happy for us to get involved. From their point of view, it's only a British woman, and not as if it's one of theirs."

"Charming." Mowgley found his right sock hanging from a broken light socket on the starboard bulkhead, then asked: "What about the Coastguard?"

"They told all ships to stop looking after the standard three hours. No point at that time of night and in those conditions, but they had to go through the motions." She shivered. "Poor woman, what a way to go."

Inspector Mowgley grunted assent, sniffed at the sock to test its wearability factor, then went in search of its mate. "Any forecasts on the body?"

"Because of where she was when she jumped, their best bet is three days and anywhere between Shoreham and Brighton."

"Nice surprise for a metal detectorist or dog walker, then."

"Yes, I suppose so."

Some comfort came with the information that D.S. Quayle had been on board the French ferry, having a jolly while pretending to be tracking the latest acquisition of an enterprising steal-to-order car ring.

For whatever reason he had been on the crossing, his presence on board was good news as all the paperwork would be down to him.

According to Quayle's call to the office earlier, someone could go ahead and notify the next of kin as there was no possibility of a mix-up this time.

Mowgley harrumphed at what was obviously a little dig, harking back to when he could find nobody else to break the news to a woman that her husband had died following a heart attack on a crossing to Bilbao. When he arrived and invited himself into the neat apartment on the seafront, he had been careful not to mention that the heart attack had happened while the man was trying to keep up with the demands of his very personal assistant. The young woman had had to ring a friend on her mobile and ask him to call the ferry company so they could tell the boat to send a couple of husky deckhands to enter the cabin and haul the twenty stone corpse off her. As one of the men had enjoyed telling Mowgley and the rest of the office, it was the leg irons, chains and other restraints which were the real problem for the woman. The keys were in the dead man's trousers, and they were in a pile of clothing by the door.

It was not until after Mowgley had told the alleged widow her husband was dead that he saw a wedding photo of a very slim man on top of the television, checked his facts and discovered he was at the wrong address. From then on, he determined never to go on a similar mission after a pub lunch. As he took lunch in the pub most days, the nause-up at least gave him a good excuse for lumbering someone else with the job.

Returning to the present, Mowgley learned there was a witness to the incident. She would be asked to wait at Cherbourg if Mowgley fancied making the trip to speak to the woman while it was all fresh in her mind.

Knowing it had been at least a month since he had been over for booze and baccy supplies, Melons had checked with Eastleigh and there was a plane available, if not exactly standing by. If he wished, she would come too. He might want someone to talk to the French authorities in French and without upsetting them, and she too was running short of fags. Either way he would need to phone Superintendent Mundy to clear the trip.

Mowgley nodded absent-mindedly, then yipped in triumph as he found his left sock.

Shuffling around on one foot he remembered reading that the standard daily test for President Reagan's physical competence had been his ability to put his socks on whilst standing up. The article hadn't mentioned any sort of mental test.

Properly clad, he lowered his freshly-socked left foot and felt a warm softness where there should have been cold steel decking. He groaned and asked Melons to fetch a butter knife from the galley. It had been a dirty night, but he must persuade the bloody dog to shit outside rather than inside the cabin whatever the weather.

*   *   *

Outside, oily water washed over the deck of the World War II German submarine. As it was lashed securely to the redundant lightship that was his current home, Mowgley had recently asked Dodger Long about the vessel's disturbing tendency to settle ever lower in the water after rough weather. His old classmate and now landlord had merely shrugged and pointed out that that was what submarines were designed to do. Mowgley had been unsure if the scrapyard owner had meant that submarines were designed to settle in rough conditions, or generally to submerge in any conditions.

While Melons tempted George The Dog out on to the deck with a Kit-Kat, Inspector Mowgley stood at the rail of his temporary home, sighed heavily and looked at his surroundings.

On the foreshore, a rat was investigating the exhaust of the American-made tank with Argentine army markings and a bent barrel. Beyond the waterside scrapyard, a couple of clearly dispirited figures in white coats were trying to persuade an assortment of tatty-looking dogs to run after a bundle of rags. The greyhound track was obviously gearing up for the evening meeting, and most of the dogs - or at least the ones he regularly backed - would need to start running soon if they were to finish by closing time.

Alongside the port basin, the flyover was choking up nicely with early morning traffic. In the middle distance, the cranes and funnels of the ferryport broke the skyline like rotten teeth. And it was raining.

Mowgley sighed again. "What's it all about, Melons?"

His sergeant walked to where he stood and handed him the neatly folded wrapper of the Kit-Kat.

"What's all what about?"

Mowgley took the wrapper and tossed it over the rail. They watched as it bobbed across the greasy water before coming to rest alongside the jetty, next to a somehow depressingly large condom.

"Here's me," he said, "a senior, experienced and particularly intelligent police officer, dossing on a dead lightship in the shittiest part of what visiting American sailors so justifiably call Shitty City. As we stand at the dawn of a new Millennium, I'm nearly fifty, with piles like a bunch of grapes, toothache, a bad back, a rapacious ex-wife, an old and incontinent dog, a psychotic boss and as much future as that French letter. I thought I was a pretty good copper, but everyone else seems to think I'm a dinosaur who should be put out to grass. If dinosaurs eat grass."

"I think they did," said Melons, then: "It is better to deserve honours and not have them than to have them and not deserve them."

"Who said that?" he asked testily as his roll-up smoked itself in the offshore breeze.

"I just did."

Mowgley tried to hit the condom with his soggy cigarette end and missed. "Har de har. I mean who said it first?"

"Mark Twain."

"Oh," said Mowgley heavily, "that's all right, then. Funny how it's always the people with lots of money and fame who tell us we don't need them and it's not much fun having them anyway."

Melons tried again. "When it's dark enough, you can see the stars."

Her superior looked up at the grey skies. "Not when it's bloody cloudy you can't. Come on, take me away from all this."

Mowgley shivered as he walked down the gangplank and between tall columns of rusting metal objects to where Melons had left her car alongside a trackless half-track troop carrier. His courtesy car from Dodger was not where he thought he had left it the night before. He made a mental note to check with the scrapyard office and find out if the crusher was working again. He had quite liked the hand-painted Ford Fiesta. At least, he thought as they drove towards the motorway, Eastleigh airport and the Cherbourg peninsula, he could always get another one from the same source, and some of Dodger's motors were so old they were coming into fashion as retro rides. Perhaps if he hung around long enough, the same might become true of him and his ideas of proper and effective police work. Or not.

Three

The day was not on the up.

Mowgley had refused the offer of Melons's company and Anglo-Franco diplomatic services, and sent her to tell the overboard's husband it was highly unlikely he would see his wife again. On reflection, his subordinate had had the better deal. He hated flying, and especially in planes with outside toilets.

At this time of day there was no scheduled flight to Cherbourg, so Melons had fixed him up with a charter company which usually took business people with a death wish to Alderney. It was not that the small Channel island was a dangerous place to be, just that the size of the plane did not inspire confidence that it would complete the journey in a head wind of more than a knot or two. He had honestly thought the company rep was joking when she led the handful of passengers past the relatively huge Channel Islands aircraft to a small delivery van with wings. He had known that she was serious when he and the other five people with a desperate reason to be in the Cotentin peninsula that morning were lined up alongside it. This, she said, was so they could be allocated the correct seats to keep the plane in trim.

Without actually poking anyone with a stick or looking at their teeth, the veteran pilot still gave a passable impression of a horse meat butcher on a buying trip as he selected who would sit where. Mowgley was left to last, then asked cheerfully to take a central position amidships and try and spread himself around a bit.

He did so, and thought the most disconcerting aspect of the journey was to see the pilot not in a proper, sealed-off cabin of his own, but sitting in the front seat like a coach driver.

At least, Mowgley thought as they bumped down the runway, he hadn't come round to collect the tickets and would hopefully not be serving their in-flight drinks.

*   *   *

Unsurprisingly, it was raining as the plane touched down at Maupertus airfield, but there were no cows on or near the runway. This was always a bonus.

The drive to Cherbourg ferryport went without major incident. This was not the driver's fault, but because the bucketing old Peugeot encountered only three cars on the journey, and all were travelling in roughly the same direction.

Mowgley patted the cabbie's shoulder as they pulled up at the terminal, and then nodded encouragingly to where a stream of British-registered vehicles was rolling off a P&O boat. There were sure to be some confrontational opportunities there, he pointed out, especially if the driver could get in amongst the first-time caravan-towers. His sarcasm was wasted, as he had constructed the dig in his version of French. His idea of the *lingua franca* could usually be decoded by French friends and contacts who were long used to what he did to their language, but never by strangers. In fact, most French people seemed to take a perverse pleasure in pretending not to understand what he said. In this case and apart from a scowl at the lack of a tip, there was no reaction to his jibe but a bemused grunt and Force Five Gallic shrug. Mowgley often wondered what the French made of the sound of a Briton speaking their tongue and why it seemed so painful to them. Neither could he understand why so many British women went weak at the knees when hearing the Queen's English mangled by a French singer or actor. He never got that sort of response when he made an effort and spoke to French women in their language.

Shouldering his bag, he set off across the small ocean of car park between where the cab driver had dropped him and the entrance to the terminal building. As he turned his collar up against the wind-driven rain, he considered how much shorter the hike would have been had he given the man a tip with the up-front fare.

As he would have expected, the custom post was deserted. This was due to the weather and the onset of the sacred lunch break, so any mass murderers, drug smugglers, illegal immigrants or other general fugitives from justice would be free to enter France without let or hindrance until after the cheese course.

Approaching the concrete and glass creation, he reflected as usual on how a nation with such a reputation for fashion, style and design could breed such crap architects. Replacing a majestic art-deco building which had welcomed American liners in the heady days when only people with lots of money went on cruises, the new terminal had been unveiled a couple of years ago by the head of the *Chambre de Commerce*. Mowgley suspected that as the sole Briton at the function, he had been invited to attend the ceremony not so much out of professional courtesy, but so his French opposite number could show off his posh new offices and superior facilities.

Although the responsibility for being in charge of all matters concerning illegal activity at the ferryport required Inspector rank and Special Branch accreditation, Mowgley warranted not much more than a boxroom as an office and an open-plan area for his colleagues, housed in a tired old building overlooking the docks. The location for Team Mowgley did have its saving graces, though, and one was being not much more than a stagger from his favourite boozer.

Although three million people passed through his

terminal every year and amongst them would be a large number of undesirable, he also got very little assistance or even acknowledgement from the commercial interests at the port. In effect, he was the sheriff of quite a sizeable and potentially troublesome town, but did not seem to be treated with the sort of respect, recognition or rewards accorded to Wyatt Earp. Even his sobriquet of the King of the Ferries was used more in mockery than acknowledgement of his status.

On the day of the official opening of the Cherbourg terminal and after the usual long lunch and speeches by everyone from the mayor to the chef who would be in charge of the filled baguette counter, the architect had explained how the building had been designed to 'echo its environment and usage'. While mentally agreeing that it was a novel idea to build the terminal in the shape of a boat, Mowgley could not help wondering if the structural requirements of building it in the shape of an upturned boat would prove a suitably reassuring symbol for the ferry passengers who would be passing through it.

A few years on and the concrete exterior was already looking grim. Inside it looked, smelled and felt like every other airport or ferry terminal in the fairly developed world. Perhaps this was because anywhere that people had to use on their way to where they wanted to go and could not wait to get away from could not be expected to have much of an atmosphere. At best, the punters hoped they would be processed through with no major delays, hang-ups or contentions. At worst, the most modern and well-appointed airport or ferry terminal could be an open prison for hours.

Today the ambience was especially depressing. The weather and season did not help, and the sprinkling of Britons waiting for the return trip looked like survivors of Dunkirk rather than patrons of a Bargain Winter Breakaway. At the bar, a collection of British lorry drivers were enjoying trying to upset the French staff, while a solitary booze cruiser was being sick on the juke box.

Mowgley sighed, stepped over a pool of vomit and the

drunk, who had by now slid to the floor. The Ferry King looked up and sighed again as he read the new sign above the main entrance: *Welcome to the Gateway to Europe*.

Yeah, right.

Four

At the Port Authority office, Detective Sergeant Dickie Quayle was doing his best to foster Anglo-Franco relationships with a representative of the ferry company on whose boat the overboard had been travelling. Thankfully, the young woman spoke little English. She also seemed less concerned with the tragedy and its potential negative PR impact than with escaping from Quayle, and left after giving Mowgley a bored smile and a cup of acrid black coffee.

After ditching the coffee, Mowgley ignored the no-smoking signs and rolled his fifth cigarette of the day while listening to Quayle's report.

As Mowgley would already know, the incident had taken place at around two o'clock that morning. The captain had gone by the book, and three ships in the area had been called in to help with the search before the coastguard had decided to call it a day. The overboard, a Mrs Margaret Birchall, had thoughtfully left her handbag on the deck at her departure point, and it had contained her passport as well as a well-used bottle of good quality brandy. As his boss would also be aware, her details had been phoned in to the office so someone could tell her relatives. Her car had been taken off the boat and was being looked at by a local scratch 'n' sniff team.

The good news was that a passenger had seen most of what had happened. Along with the witness, Quayle had also detained the steward who had looked after the jumper (Quayle had obviously already decided it was a suicide and not an accident) in the overnight lounge. The steward had said that she was a regular passenger, always travelled at night and booked a reclining seat which she hardly used. In recent times, she had preferred to drink rather than sleep the journey away.

Also waiting to be interviewed were two youths who said they had attempted to exchange pleasantries with the woman at the rail shortly before the incident. She was, they said, very drunk and abusive. Quayle had taken statements from and details of everyone else who seemed to have been anywhere near the scene. On such a rough crossing and at that time in the morning, he concluded, they were lucky to have anyone who saw anything.

Mowgley considered complimenting his sergeant on a concise and comprehensive report, then thought better of it. The little shit knew how good he was.

"Alright" he grunted while trying to blow a smoke ring, "let's have a look at the steward."

*   *   *

The job was proving much more difficult to crack than he had thought.

However he pursed his lips, ingested and exhaled, he could not produce a single smoke ring.

Mowgley inhaled deeply and gave some thought to the case.

As expected, the steward had repeated more or less exactly what Quayle had said he had said; now it was time to talk to the witness who had more or less seen the woman go over the side.

After a final failed attempt, Mowgley coughed and looked irritably across the room as D.S. Quayle slithered back through the door. Even the way his sergeant walked annoyed him today. If he were honest, the man annoyed him in every way on nearly every day. Quayle was good at what he did, but there was something reptilian about him, and especially about his ability to adapt to the requirements of the game modern policing had become. Quayle knew exactly what to say and what not to say and how to react to every situation and appear to be concerned, when he did not really give a stuff about anything but progressing up the ladder. He was a bigot and a racist and just as much of a chauvinist as a lot of coppers in the old days. What he had learned was how to adapt and hide the truth about the way he really felt. Mind you, that applied to most of the officers now clambering up the greasier-than-ever pole. Hypocrisy was the key, along with how to look as if you were feeling the family's pain at a press conference when announcing the death of some young pratt who had tried to deal drugs on someone else's patch.

Mowgley knew that Quayle was the face of what was to come, and that he himself was no more than an echo of the past. At one of the few Gender and Race Awareness courses Mowgley had been unable to avoid, Quayle had been asked by a man with a concerned look and a pony tail how he saw the role of the Force in today's Britain. Without missing a beat, Quayle had said that he thought the police should see themselves as an arm of the social services rather than just a blunt instrument of the State. Obviously, they had to maintain law and order as a given, but there was much more they could do for society by attacking the causes as well as the results of crime. At this point, Mowgley could bear no more, had feigned an asthma attack and headed for the nearest pub.

Overall, Quayle was very much not the sort of bloke you would want to get pissed with. That, in Mowgley's experience, was the real test. And apart from anything else, nobody was entitled to have such white and even teeth.

Mowgley concentrated on rolling another fag as a device to keep Quayle waiting. When he had licked the edge, created a near-perfect cylinder of just the right diameter, tamped one end on his tin, lit up, inhaled and blew a long stream of smoke at the sergeant, he said:

"Just the eyewitness to go then. What's she like?"

Quayle looked as offended as he dared by the smoke, then shrugged. "Bit of a lump. Do you want me to wheel her in?"

Mowgley nodded, watched Quayle leave and thought how punchable his face was. The sergeant would not have been so casually dismissive of a woman in reply to or in front of any other officer, and had done so as he knew Mowgley would know why he was doing it and how irritated his boss would be to see him coming clean. Despite his carefully-honed politically correct stance, Quayle judged a woman's character by her looks. If a woman wasn't what he thought of as fanciable, he would show little interest in what she might have to offer. It was a surprisingly common attitude in police procedural circles, even nowadays. When Mowgley was still in uniform, a very promising young D.C. had arrived at the fun factory. She was there for a month before discovering why she had been dubbed "Deefer". When some kind soul told her it meant "D for dog" she left. Being an unattractive woman in the force then was almost as reprehensible as being black. Or not a drinker and freemason.

As he waited for the witness, he looked at the passport photograph of the dead woman. She was or had been a cracker if you went for big hair, a tan like an overdone chicken tikka and bags of make-up. Not exactly tarty, but definitely new money, and probably someone else's. The photograph also looked more like a studio shot than the usual booth snap.

He closed and put the passport on the table as the door opened, then stood up as the witness came in. As he apologised for keeping her waiting and gestured to a chair, he thought how composed she looked. That was good, as it would mean she would not have a problem recalling events exactly as they happened. He also thought that she was hardly a lump.

He had learned little from the two youths about the incident, but a good deal about the overboard from the

French steward. All the yobs could contribute was that they had seen her on deck some time after midnight and offered her a drink in their cabin. Ironically, they had clearly been quite shocked when she told them to fuck off.

The steward had been on more cordial terms with the woman, and was obviously upset at what had happened to her. He said that she was a regular traveller, going over at least once a month to her *pied-à-terre* in Normandy, and always at night. She was a person of habit, and he always tried to give her the same seat with extra blankets and pillows and look after her, as she was polite as well as generous. Like some passengers, she liked to talk, and had often shown him photographs of the old and isolated cottage and explained her plans for restoring and updating it.

But she had changed over the past couple of months. She had begun drinking heavily, and instead of being content with a brandy in her coffee before sleeping, would buy a bottle of duty-free and take it outside, where she could smoke and drink while looking out over the waves. Sometimes she would spend most of the night on deck. More than once in recent crossings he had seen her in tears at the rail.

From what she had said, he knew that she had not been married long. From what she had not said but implied, there were already problems with the marriage. By her clothes and her manner and other things, he thought it would not be money problems, but who could say nowadays? Last night, she had really hit the brandy, and gone on deck in spite of the weather and his protests. He had tried to persuade her to stay and sleep, but she had said that there would be more than enough time to sleep later.

She had not returned, and the first he had known of the tragedy was when the witness had raised the alarm and the captain had turned the ship around. He did not know what had happened but he could not believe that it was more than an accident. In his opinion, the woman was not the type, and anyway, who would choose to go into the sea, especially on a night like that? He could think of much easier and less painful ways to leave a life.

Five

"Can I get you a coffee?"

"No thanks, I've already tried it. Just a cigarette to take the taste away, please, if it's alright to smoke here and you can spare one. I've run out."

Yvonne McLaughlin had had quite a night but was handling it well. She looked like she would handle most things well. He could see why Quayle thought she was nothing special, but guessed she would not care much what people like him thought about anything. And anyway, Quayle was well wrong. She had an intelligent and what people who wanted to sound clever called an animated face, framed with short hair which was worn naturally and unconcernedly grey. She also wore a half-smile as she watched him roll her cigarette, and had clever eyes behind plain, rimless glasses. When she spoke it was with a soft, cultured Scottish accent, and Miss, Mrs or Ms Mclaughlin was obviously anything but a fashion victim. As far as he could tell, she wore no or very little make-up, and no earrings, though her ears were pierced. A loosely fitting plain topcoat of good quality, and sensible rather than sexy calf-length boots. She carried a big and similarly sensible handbag, and her strong-looking fingers were clear of rings. She also had a small, fresh cut on her right cheek. One of the few bonuses of being a policeman was that you had an excuse for taking a good look at people and trying to work out who and what they were. It helped with the job sometimes, or perhaps he was just a nosey bastard.

Over the next hour, she smoked two of his roll-ups while telling him she was from an unpronounceable place in the Trossacks, where she had left a husband and a farm and a dog. She clearly regretted leaving the dog and the farm much more than the husband. She was renting a house in the city near to the Continental ferryport so as to be close to it, and had joined the boat as a foot passenger. She was going no further in France than Cherbourg for this trip, and she had an appointment with an estate agent later that day. With the money from the divorce, she planned to buy a smallholding from where she would introduce the locals and eventually the rest of France to the delights of Highland beef. She knew all about the French prejudice against English beef, but thought that would not apply to any meat produced by their old allies, the Scots. Apart from the opportunities of growing the product where she was sure she could sell it, she had heard the grass in the Manche department was as sweet as in Scotland, and the land and property was clearly much, much cheaper. Normandy was also a long way from her former husband.

Her account of the tragedy was as concise and clear as he had expected. She had not been able to sleep in her cabin as it was oppressively hot and stuffy for a Scot who worked in the open air, and the walls were far too thin for the most broad-minded of unintentional eavesdroppers. Tiring of the thumps, bangs and groans, she had gone to the bar for coffee and an hour with her personal stereo and French language tapes.

Deciding to take a turn around the deck before trying her cabin again, she had seen a woman leaning over the railing next to a lifeboat station. The woman was standing on the bottom rail. She was apparently not much of a sailor, as she had chosen the windward side of the boat, and was vainly trying not to be sick on herself. The witness had gone over to see if she could help, but had been told to go away. She had then tried unsuccessfully to persuade and help the woman to come down from the rail, and caught a glancing blow to her face in rebuff. She assumed the small cut had been done by a ring.

Having turned away to go in search of a crew member to help, she had reached the door to the stair landing when she heard a scream. She had not seen the woman go over the side, but there was nowhere else she could have gone. After returning to the rail and seeing nothing, she had run to the crew cabin. She felt dreadful, but could not see that there was much else she could have done.

Mowgley agreed.

He checked that Quayle had taken her details and said he would call in a few days to let her know what had happened and when the inquest was likely to be. As they shook hands, he thought about asking her if she might be interested in an impressive if near-derelict manor-house in the heart of the Cherbourg peninsula with great potential and thirty acres of perfect grazing land for small Scottish cattle. He contented himself with a warning about French estate agents and their tendency to inflate prices for foreign buyers, and a mental note to broach the subject of *La Cour* and its immediate availability when Mrs McLaughlin had less on her mind.

Six

Being French, the bus for Varengebec left Cherbourg spot on time. It was, Mowgley had observed, curious how French buses and trains were invariably punctual, but people always reliably late.

He waited till the bus struggled up the hill to the Auchan hyperstore roundabout before calling the office. He reckoned Melons had almost forgiven him for leaving her to do the dirty work, and would pretend to believe him when he said he was staying on for a couple of days to pursue his enquiries.

After reminding him of her fags and booze order and in which of his pockets she had put the list, she seemed anxious to tell him about her visit to the overboard's husband, so he let her.

Margaret Birchall had been the wife of a middle-range solicitor of whom little was known, so who was presumably not too successful or bent. In spite of that, the family home was on one of the better parts of Nobs Hill. Mowgley grunted and thought that the steward might be right or wrong about the deceased and her husband having money problems. Nobs Hill had acquired its local sobriquet for two reasons. One was the price of the big houses which overlooked the city, and the other was the nightly activity taking place in its panoramic car parks. A common euphemism for getting a leg over in this location was to have been on a visit to The Starlight Club on Nobs Hill.

Melons said she had taken young Mundy with her to break him in on bereavement calls, and that he had handled the situation well. In spite of his tact, though, the husband had, she added, been somehow more than distraught.

"What do you mean, *more* than distraught? You mean he cried, or what?"

"Not really. He was sort of… strange. He was shocked and upset, like you'd expect. But there was more. He was totally gone. It was like there was more to it. You know what I mean…"

Mowgley looked out of the bus window at a roadside field, in which a small man in brown overalls was hitting a large cow with a scaffold plank. The cow was taking little notice.

"No, I don't know what you mean. What else?"

"He wasn't alone. After we told him, I went to make a cup of tea, and a woman came into the kitchen. She was wearing a man's dressing gown. I asked her if she knew the wife."

"And?"

"And she said she should do. The overboard was her sister."

Seven

Unusually obliging for a bus driver, particularly a French bus driver, the small man with the big moustache dropped his foreign passenger off at the top of the track leading to *La Cour*. As Mowgley stepped from the platform, the driver asked him in surprisingly good English why he was going to such a dump. Hearing that the Englishman owned it, he made that irritating little cluck of fake sympathy the French are so good at, then offered to return his fare.

The Ferry King ignored the jibe, and gained a measure of revenge by complimenting the man on his sensible driving.

Even in daylight and through the rain, the Disneyesque towers and spires of the overblown farmhouse looked just as impressive as the day he and Madge had arrived to view it. It was only when you got closer that you saw the truth. His excuse for agreeing to buy it was that he had been pissed at the time, and that he liked the name. It was his only chance, he remembered thinking, of ever being known as Mowgley of The Yard.

As they toured the rambling buildings, his wife had said in a not-really-joking voice that she would leave him if he didn't agree to buy the place, and he had missed the golden moment. She had buggered off anyway, and what made it worse was that she had gone with the previous owner of *La Cour*. As well as the Frog stuffing her, they had both stuffed him.

In the way of some Britons who owned a house in France with more than four bedrooms, Madge - or Maggie as she now styled herself - had liked to call her second home a *château*. In truth, it was just a very big farmhouse with all sorts of embellishments and twiddly bits.

Once upon a time it must have been an impressive monument to landed power, but neglect, time and parasitical local builders had humbled the property over the years. Abandoned by the original owners, then ignored by wealthy Parisians in search of a more sophisticated weekend retreat, *La Cour* had sat patiently waiting for somebody rich, optimistic or stupid enough to take it on. Its patience had been rewarded with the arrival of Mrs Mowgley and her mug of a husband.

Pausing for breath, Mowgley reflected on how, in spite of or even because of the part *La Cour* had played in the death of his marriage, he liked the old place, and even occasionally felt at home here. Like him it was big, tired and battered and had been given a bruising by life. Unlike him, it had a bit of class. Also and for what it was and what it was worth, it was his. Or rather, it was mostly the property of the *Credit Agricole* mortgage division for at least the next ten years.

This was because, adding further insult to injury, his wife's parting shot had been to leave him lumbered with *La Cour* and the mortgage while she took the house in England. He could have fought her terms for the settlement, but after more than a decade as his sleeping partner she had enough on him to certainly cost him his job, and more than likely his liberty. When she left, he had been naive enough to ask her why, and she had told him. She had made a big mistake when he had persuaded her to marry him, and this was her chance to put it right and make something of herself and what was left of her life before it was too late. He was oafish, crude, had no taste, no consideration for her, and no ambition. It was only her pushing that had got him to Inspector level, and he was obviously going no further. It would be downhill all the way from now on. He was also an inverted snob, and a standing joke with decent people in the city. She might still have made something of him if he had had any class. Her new 'partner' had real class, knew how to treat a woman, and was much, much better in bed.

Amongst other things, she particularly hated Mowgley's filthy underwear and his equally smelly old dog. And, while she thought of it, he was grossly overweight, smoked and never put the toilet seat down after use (if he had bothered to lift it first). Worst of all, he had not shown a trace of regret at the death of Princess Diana. That alone showed exactly the sort of man he was.

It was strange, he thought as he trudged up the track, how you just can't please some people. He had to agree with some of what his wife had said, but she had not mentioned a single one of his good points. And he definitely did not understand her stance on The Queen of Hearts. Personally, he had always thought Diana a malicious, neurotic hysteric who had done more damage to the monarchy than Oliver Cromwell, and in a much shorter time.

Reaching the top of the drive, he saw that the massive oak door was ajar. Perhaps one of the locals he was paying not to work on the place had forgotten they were French artisans and actually turned up. Perhaps it was a break-in, or perhaps even squatters. That would be good news, as they would have to tidy the place up a bit and do some basic repairs to make the place liveable.

Eight

It was market day at Varengebec, so Mowgley had had no trouble in getting a lift to the nearest town to *La Cour*. One of the things he liked about rural France was how drivers would invariably stop for hitchhikers. In Britain those days were long gone, but if you thought about the potential dangers of giving someone you did not know a ride or getting into a stranger's car, you could see why.

In the square, the livestock had long changed hands and the farmers moved location to one of the bars for lunch and to indulge themselves in the traditional post-haggling activity of telling each other about the bad deals they had made and the money they had lost.

Now the market was in full afternoon swing, and husbands took a glass of rosé wine or *café-calva* and enjoyed looking at the barmaids while their wives did the serious business of finding the bargain food buys of the day. Smoke from the coals beneath lamb joints and herbed chickens carried the enticing scent across the square, and the air was also charged with the diverse aromas of freshly ground spices, locally cured hams and sausages, baked bread, strong cheeses and the piles of cow, goat and sheep shit not yet cleared away.

Paradoxically a typical and yet unique (like all the others) Normandy market town, Varengebec sat in the bosom of a gentle valley in the heart of the Cotentin peninsula. It was a local saying that all roads led to Varengebec, but then, in Mowgley's experience, all Cotentinese roads led to everywhere on the peninsula if you stayed on them long enough. The Romans had seen to that.

The focal point of the town was the market square, said by residents to be the largest and most impressive in Normandy. This was a common claim throughout the region, but Mowgley reckoned the one at Varengebec would certainly be in the running.

Dominating the square was what was left of a once very grand castle. Like the square, it was big and impressive, and its ownership had been variously ascribed to any number of historical figures, especially William the Conqueror. In this part of Lower Normandy, William was claimed to have lived, grown up, slept, slaughtered or ravished a local maiden in just about every commune.

The list of guests reputed to have spent at least a night in the castle was unusually long, even by Norman standards. Across the centuries, the Queens Victoria and Elizabeth (both First and Second) had allegedly rested at the castle while on royal progresses through the region. Other famous visitors were said to include Richard The Lionheart, Henry VIII, Winston Churchill (twice), President Kennedy and Lord Lucan.

Nowadays the remaining walls and tower were scrupulously maintained and preserved by a rolling Eurogrant via Paris, so there was never a moment when work was not progressing slowly on some corner or crenellation. As a regular visitor, Mowgley was fascinated by the length of time and number of artisans involved in any project, in particular an outhouse which had been re-roofed at least twice in the past six years.

Today, all works in the castle had ceased in honour of the fact that it was market day.

Inside the Bar Normande, Madame Gilbert was effortlessly coping with the table service while her husband Claude dispensed drinks and pronouncements from his position at the pumps.

Having gone through the customary hand-shaking routine on his way to the bar, Mowgley ordered a drink, exchanged a few words with the patron, then contemplated the similarities and disparities between his two local drinking haunts. They could not be much more disparate, though a little more than a hundred miles apart as the crow was incorrectly said to fly.

Across the seventy miles of English Channel or *Manche* ('sleeve') as the French would have it, The Ship Leopard would be half as full and take ten times the money during this session. Drivers, loading stewards, tarts, amateur and professional smugglers and others who made an official or unofficial living from the docks would now be mixing business with pleasure. Here at the Bar Normande and apart from those attending a session in Speakers Corner, customers mostly kept their own council and certainly bought their own drinks.

Conspicuous consumption was the house rule at the Leopard, and that was how mine host Two-Shits liked it. In Varengebec, a visit to the Normande was an expensive occasion to be slowly savoured, and serious drinking was done at home before arrival and after departure. Another cultural difference was that it was highly unlikely that there would be a fight in the Normande before closing time. Mowgley loved both pubs and what went on in them. Sometimes he almost thought he was a lucky man for having the life he had.

Alongside him at the bar, he saw La La Ted was trying to hold a glass steady in his palsied hand. The oldest English resident in Varengebec, Ted had earned his nickname at the Ship by being roughly the same shape as a Teletubby, and also from his love of choral music. He had become a late convert to Catholicism, partly, it was alleged, because of the free wine at Holy Communion. As a result of a misunderstanding over the church social club funds and a choir boy the previous year, he had opted for an exchange visit under the twinning scheme that Mowgley had set up between the two licensed premises, and had never returned. Now he was ensconced in a bed-sitter above the veterinary practice across the square, and survived by giving music lessons to the children of local parents and walking their dogs. Sometimes after a heavy session in the Normande, he confused the two activities, but the locals took a very relaxed view of his occasional lapse.

As he was thinking about the pros and cons of paying for a room for the night, smuggling himself into the nearby monastery to share Ted's cell or getting a lift back to *La Cour*, Mowgley was pleased to note the arrival of his friend *Capitaine* Guy Varennes, a reasonably big fish in the area's section of the national military police force, or *Gendarmerie*.

Much to the confusion of and sometimes the cost to foreign visitors and particularly visiting motorists, France has two distinct law enforcement agencies. In general, the *Police Nationale* - formerly much more evocatively known as the *Sûreté Nationale* - holds primary jurisdiction in large towns and urban areas. Smaller towns and rural areas are in the hands of the *Gendarmerie*. The menacingly spit-and-polished high boots, blue overalls and caps (to say nothing of their weapons-heavy belts) of its foot soldiers are enough to inspire caution and respect if not fear in the civilian population, and particularly road users; the arrogant manner and general attitude when dealing with members of the public is more than enough to inspire general loathing. Mowgley had no proof, but much observation of and encounters with members of the *Gendarmerie* had convinced him there must be a special school where rookies were taught to be nasty to the public. Sometimes he thought a little more of the French way and less of the touchy-feely empathy in fashion across the Channel would have a positive effect on crime figures in Britain.

But as a plain-clothes officer at a relatively elevated rank, Guy had no need for arrogance or aggression in his demeanour. The young Norman was an ardent anglophile, constantly bemused by English culture and attitudes in general, and British police methods as exampled and recounted by Mowgley in particular. The English detective liked him and found the Gallic approach to peacekeeping in a mostly rural area equally interesting.

Following a companionable hour of exchanging news of their respective activities, the two left the table and the bar, and set out for *La Cour* in Guy's unmarked car.

Apart from a missed opportunity with a slow-moving hare, the journey was uneventful until they came up behind a BMW with Berlin plates, travelling sedately along the coastal road.

"Ah," observed the young officer, adroitly flicking on the siren, "a blatant case of drink-driving."

"How do you know?" asked Mowgley.

"It is obvious. He is clearly travelling within the speed limit, so he must have something to feel guilty about."

Mowgley thought about this example of French police logic, then watched as the detective walked to where the car had pulled over. Guy exchanged a few words with the driver, then returned. Reaching into the glove box, he unsnapped a folded parcel of plastic, and invited his friend to blow into the exposed tube. The German, he explained, had admitted having a glass of wine with his dinner, but it was best to be sure he would be over the limit.

Re-folding the bag, Guy returned to the car, and Mowgley reflected on the ill-luck of the traveller. At this time of year, to be the only German visitor in the area to come across a policeman who had lost his inheritance when his grandfather's pig farm had been blown up on D-Day was misfortune indeed.

*   *   *

Arriving at *La Cour*, Mowgley invited his friend to take a nightcap in the annexe. This was an ancient caravan which had been abandoned on the car deck of a ferry, then sequestered by Mowgley as a home from home in the grounds while work was allegedly progressing in the main house. It was not the most spacious or comfortable of billets, but free, and the money from the fake expenses claims for hotel accommodation while on official business in Normandy came in very handy.

In the midst of a tranquility which the citizens of Shitty City could but dream of, the two men sat in the gentle light of a gas lamp as they compared their philosophies, and it was well after midnight before the police captain left.

As he watched the car bucket up the track, Mowgley considered calling Melons, but decided against it. There would have been no developments in the overboard case, and he would have heard if anything of major note had happened.

Less than a hundred miles away and in another world, a ferry boat would be slipping away from the linkspan and into the Solent waters. On board would be a few hundred passengers, all with their own reasons for crossing the Channel at this time of night and year. Some would be on booze cruises, some on cheap off-season mini-breaks, and others visiting their properties for a few days of escapism and bad DIY. There would be at least a dozen people up to no good at some level of iniquity, and most of them would get away with it.

About now, the passengers would be claiming their cabins or taking command of a seat for the night before heading for the cafeterias and bars and duty-free shop to buy or steal their requirements. Over the coming hours, some would get drunk, some would have sex with their own or someone else's partner, and a few would sleep the miles away. Together, they represented only a fraction of the millions who would pass through the port this year, but they would be of the same overall mix of humanity.

Reluctant to retire, Mowgley took a pee against a blackthorn bush and smiled as he heard the resident owl hoot an announcement of its presence. The air was almost breathtakingly sharp, and overhead the big Normandy sky was full of stars. It was at moments like these, he thought, that a man was able to grasp an inkling of the full significance of the cosmos and his relative insignificance and unimportance in the grand scheme of things.

Realising he was pissing down his left trouser leg, the Ferry King swore, shook and zipped, then walked reflectively back to the almost welcoming light of his caravan.

Some time, he thought, it would be nice to live at *La Cour*, but retirement was not an option yet.

Well, not voluntary retirement, anyway.

Nine

"Got thirteen across?" asked Mowgley.

"I haven't got the paper yet; what's the clue?"

"Rubbish in a Chinese harbour. Four letters."

"Bollocks."

"No, I said four letters. Bollocks doesn't fit."

Melons groaned theatrically, stepped aside to let Mowgley enter, then made a grab for his *Daily Telegraph*. It was a Thursday, so a bad crossword day for her. Mowgley seemed to get on with the Thursday compiler, and invariably finished first. Having completed it, he would annoy her for the rest of the day by making obscure references to the clues she hadn't solved before finally doling out the answers as if speaking to a backward child. Standing Orders (which he made up and quoted whenever it suited him) ensured she could not turn the tables on him when she finished first.

Catherine McCartney did not have a brother, and had never known her father. At this stage of her life (which probably meant at any stage of her life to come if she were honest with herself), she had no plans for having children. Sometimes, it seemed all the variety of male characteristics and relationships could be found in the lumpy shape of her superior officer. Except, of course, a lover.

She shuddered at the thought as Mowgley lumbered into the basement flat and dumped two carrier bags on the coffee table. Looking round the tidy room disapprovingly, he sniffed loudly and asked: "Where's George The Dog?"

Melons reached into one of the bags and took out a carton of cigarettes. "He's fine, just sulking in the kitchen. You know he gets upset when you leave him behind. But he's been a good boy, more or less - and he's even had a bath."

Mowgley sniffed again. "Obviously. Why?"

"Why what?"

"Why did you give him a bath?"

Melons lit a cigarette. "If you need to ask, there's no point in telling you."

Mowgley pursed his lips and opened his eyes wide in mock-perplexity: "That's a non-sequitur."

"No it's not. A non-sequitur is when you say something that has no relevance to what the conversation is about."

D.I. Mowgley opened his eyes even wider, then said: "You mean like rubbish in a Chinese harbour?"

"No, the technical term for that is a load of bollocks. Why do you do that?"

"What, do the old rubbish-in-a-Chinese-harbour-junk routine?"

"No, open your eyes wide like that. It makes you look like a surprised hippo."

"I'll have you know," Mowgley looked over her shoulder at a mirror and curled his upper lip, "that I was runner-up in the Wimborne Road Youth Club Elvis Presley Moody Eyes Lookalike Contest for 1961."

"Dare I ask who won?"

Mowgley lowered his upper lip and frowned, then sat heavily on the sofa: "A bloke with a hare lip, actually. He had a natural advantage with the sneer. So, what's been afoot during my absence?"

"Not much to report, really. Dickie Quayle has got everything under control with the overboard. He'll tell you all about it at the office."

"I'm sure he will, the smug little tosser." Mowgley took out his baccy tin. "So tell me again about your visit to the husband of the more-than-certainly deceased, then I'll tell you all about my trip."

"As I said, it was all very strange. We arrived before he went off to work, and he answered the door. When I said who we were, he looked really shifty…"

"Well he would, wouldn't he? He's a solicitor."

Melons leaned forward and pushed an ashtray across the coffee table. "Yes, but he looked extra shifty when he found us on his doorstep. As if he thought we had called about something else. When Stephen told him about his wife going over the side, he literally collapsed. We had to help him into the living room."

Mowgley pointedly ignored the ashtray. "Believe it or not, Sergeant, some people actually love their other halves. They could be forgiven for being more than a tad upset to hear that their loved one has almost certainly gone to a watery grave."

"Of course, but …I still think there's more to it than that. He's got something to hide."

"Haven't we all? And the fact that he'd probably just been playing the two-backed beast with his dead wife's sister might have added to his burden of guilt and remorse a touch, don't you think? Anyway, what did you make of her?"

"As I said, she came flaunting down the stairs as I made a cup of tea. She asked me who I was, and I told her and asked her who she was."

Mowgley reached over and took the silver foil from Melons's cigarette packet and began to fashion it into an hour-glass shape. "And what was her reaction to the grim tidings?"

"Different from Robert Birchall's."

"How different?"

"A bit…practised."

Mowgley spat in the cup he had formed at the end of the foil dart: "What do you mean, 'practised'?"

"You know how it is with a bereavement call. When you tell someone that somebody close to them is dead, they either don't understand for a moment, or don't believe what you're saying. Then, just for a split-second before they react when it has sunk in, you can get to see the truth about how they really feel or will feel later. Sometimes it's devastation at the loss, sometimes shock at the thought of being left alone; sometimes it's even a sort of relief you see in their eyes."

Mowgley grunted as if unconvinced by her analysis and tossed the foil dart at the ceiling. "So what did you get to see for that split second when you looked into the windows of Linda Russell's soul?"

"Absolutely nothing. It was as if she knew what was coming and was ready for it, but had worked on not being ready for it. I got the feeling she would have liked to have given a good performance by throwing herself around the room a bit, but she couldn't lower herself to do it for me. She might have done for a man, but not me. So she just gave me a cool stare and sat down and did her best to look shocked. She's a very cool customer, I reckon."

Mowgley picked up the dart from where it had fallen on to the coffee table and tried for the ceiling again. It fell back on to the table. "Is she also a tasty one?" he asked.

Melons looked at the dart and then the ceiling. "How do you mean 'tasty'? And what are you doing?"

"I mean why do you obviously dislike her so much? Moral outrage that she's been shagging her sister's husband, or was it just that she's a bit of a corker to look at?"

"I don't know what that's got to do with it, but I suppose some men would say she was attractive - if you go for the expensive tart look. And I asked you what you were doing with that thing?"

Mowgley squinted up at the ceiling and threw the dart. It bounced off. "Robert Birchall obviously does. Go for the tarty and expensive look, I mean. His wife was all big hair and lip gloss." He stood up, steadied himself, took aim and threw the dart at the ceiling for the third time. It bounced off again and fell on Melons's lap. "I haven't done that for years," he said. " I used to be really good at it. My spit must be weaker nowadays."

Melons picked the dart up and dropped it in the ashtray. "Like your sperm count, probably."

Mowgley stood up and instinctively put a protective hand to his crotch. "What's my sperm count got to do with it? You're at the non-sequiturs again, aren't you?"

"No, just talking bollocks, as you like to say..."

Ten

"You don't seriously expect me to get into *that*?"

Melons prodded the rusting wing of Mowgley's latest courtesy vehicle with a disdainful toe, then looked round to see if her neighbours were watching.

"Careful," Mowgley cautioned as a hole appeared in the hand-painted bodywork.

"What is it?"

"It's a car."

"That's a matter of opinion. I mean, what sort of car is it supposed to be?"

"It's a rare Lada convertible. Dodger sold my last grace-and-favour motor, so he came up with this one for me to use till he does it up and flogs it on."

"It's convertible," observed his sergeant, "because the top bit fell off and somebody stuck a tent on it; it's certainly rare because all the others made in this year are dead."

"Not at all," said Mowgley defensively, "I was reading that, since the unification of Germany, they can't get enough of them in what was the Eastern bloc. Dealers are snapping them up and selling them like hot cakes over there."

"Have you ever bought a hot cake?" asked Melons as she attempted to wrestle open the passenger door, "…or tried to drive one?"

"No, but you know what I mean."

*   *   *

Situated on the top of the Port Authority building, the C.I.D. office offered panoramic views across the harbour and was, as the hand-made notice on the door informed visitors, a compulsory smoking area.

A stickler for leading by example, Mowgley lit up as he entered and looked briefly at the incidents board. He was pleased to see there were no All Ports Warnings relating to escaping murderers, IRA escapees or Mr Big drugs dealers, though the previous night's National Lottery numbers were in clear evidence. He noted with little surprise that the office syndicate had failed to scoop the jackpot or even win a fiver consolation prize. As he had not paid his dues for a month, he was actually quite relieved.

Two of the five desks in the outer office of the fun factory were currently occupied; one by Detective Sergeant Dickie Quayle, the other by Detective Constable Stephen Mundy.

Mundy was the son of Superintendent Sidney 'Gloria' Mundy, head of the city C.I.D. The better educated members of the ferryport team believed the local supremo's nickname was a surprisingly good Mowgley pun. It was common belief in and around the fun factory that Mowgley kept a dark secret about his superior officer, as how else had he kept his rank and job after a series of high-profile cock-ups. It was also believed in some quarters that Mundy junior had been detailed to the port office as an *agent provocateur*, but generally agreed that he was far too green to get the goods on his wily boss. Mowgley was, it was further acknowledged, hard on the lad, but someone had to be the official office whipping boy.

Seeing his boss loom large, Quayle finished his call to a port barmaid whose deckhand husband was on the overnight ferry to Bilbao and joined them to report on progress with the overboard.

The Coroner's officer, he said, had been informed and would be contacting them about an inquest date. As reported by Sergeant McCarthy (Mowgley was the only member of the team allowed to call her Melons), the victim had been married to Robert Birchall, a local solicitor. In the line of duty, D.S. Quayle continued, he had taken Birchall's receptionist out for a drink. At the ripe old age of forty three, she had said, her boss had married the overboard only a year ago. Previously, he had been regarded, as a bit of a sad old loner, but had changed for the better since the marriage. His new wife had sorted him out from haircut to fashionable footwear, and even made him change his boring Ford for a flash BMW. The couple had gone on frequent holidays to exotic locations, and if you hadn't known him, you would have found him almost fanciable now. He had also started drinking at lunchtimes, and had once even commented on the size and quality of her breasts as he passed through Reception after a long session. She had fleetingly considered the chances of a sexual harassment charge, but with him being a solicitor and it being common office knowledge that she got her tits out and photocopied them as the traditional finale to the Christmas party, had decided against it.

She also suspected that her boss was at it with his wife's sister, who was a frequent caller and lunch companion, especially when his wife was away at their place in France.

Quayle concluded his bulletin with the information that the dead woman had worked part-time at an upmarket estate agency in the city, and seemed well-liked by the rest of the staff. Quayle had not yet checked out the insurance situation or discovered any other reasons why the accident could have been anything but an accident. Or, of course, a suicide.

Resisting the urge to thank Quayle, Mowgley looked through the pile of paperwork on his desk for a full minute before deciding it was time to go up the pub.

Eleven

For Mowgley, The Ship Leopard was a truly local local. Confusingly for foreigners and non-drinkers, local pubs can be near or far, and the designation depends upon a complex variety of qualifications. It may be as simple as proximity, though some locals can be many a mile from the customer's home or place of work. Other aspects of the premises to be weighed in the balance before awarding the pub local status include size, structure, type, décor, what marketing people call the customer profile and the appeal of the licensee, or his wife or any of his barmaids.

Perversely, it can be the very lack of appeal of the licensee which appeals to the customer. Deconstructional theses on the Great British Local have probably already been written; if not, they should be as it is a fast-disappearing species. It would be fair to say that Mowgley, if asked to take part in a survey, would have ticked most of the boxes in the list of pros and cons qualifying The Ship Leopard as a local. As it stood less than half a mile from the fun factory, it also qualified on the locational parameters, which was an altogether happy circumstance.

Although the only remaining pub in that part of the docks was so close to hand, Mowgley as usual drove to take his luncheon at The Ship Leopard. In a reflective mood, he took the scenic route to survey his small area of influence and mourn the loss of what it used to be.

Once upon a time, the commercial area of the waterfront had been an interesting collection of decrepit warehouses surrounding a quayside from which rusting vessels would stagger along the narrow channel and past the naval dockyard to the open waters of the Solent. In its heyday, the area maintained more pubs to the acre than the most enthusiastic matelot on a runashore could manage a pint in, and that made no allowance for the bagshanties and other unlicensed drinking dens. Together with two hamburger vans and a black man who dealt in a variety of noxious substances, at least a dozen prostitutes did all their business in an area of less than a square mile.

Nowadays the docks were, like Blair's Britain, New. Like the Prime Minister's politics and persona, they were also bland, far too neat and tidy and obvious to be credible. They were also aesthetically unsatisfactory to anyone with any sense of the value of continuity and an understanding of history. It had probably not been much fun living and working in the old docks area, but people liked reminders of the past in which they were not unlucky enough to live. If not, Mowgley conjectured, why did so many thousands queue up for a tour of the old ships and restored buildings on display in the nearby Naval dockyard? He couldn't see future day trippers paying to wonder at the design and décor of the Customs & Excise administration block or the site of a Costa Coffee Express. There were a lot of new 'facilities' and signs welcoming visitors to The Port That Cares About People, but during the process of modernisation, it had surely lost its soul. Every year, the ferryport processed millions of sullen travellers who in the old days would have been taking their fortnight in Bognor Regis or Bridlington, but, who nowadays thought nothing of laying out a fortune in a foreign country where they spent most of their time looking for an English pub or curry house.

After an interesting exchange of hand signals and the consideration of booking a cyclist who was committing the double offence of wearing Spandex tights and a pointy plastic helmet, Mowgley wondered why so many people thought something new must be better. 'Old-fashioned' was used as an insult, and the tosser on the bike really thought he looked appealing. People would wear or eat or drink anything if they were told it was fashionable. What he found most risible was how people would mock the fashions of the recent past and not see how they themselves would be mocked in the future for what they were wearing now. As he had worn the same style of clothes (and sometimes the same actual clothes) for at least a decade, he was at least consistent. And as all things were cyclical and there were only so many things you could do with a pair of trousers, perhaps he would be in the vanguard of fashion when hipster flares became all the go again.

*   *   *

The Ship Leopard was a relic of those harder but more character-full times for the city and its people.

Once it had stood provocatively on the quayside, offering warm and often watered beer and a ribald response to any expectations of speedy and polite service, food, heating or inside toilets. Now it was surrounded by rows of identical warehousing units, vast lorry parks and soaring office blocks. Not having enjoyed the benefits of a brewery makeover, The Ship was shunned by those in search of pastel colours, exotic drinks and foreign foodstuffs, but was a popular haunt for a cross-section of the port's dodgier inhabitants. It was also a handy fuelling stop for lorry drivers from all over the country, who could get legless before making the short off-public-highway drive to the ferry linkspans and, hopefully, on to the right boat to take them to their continental destination.

Mowgley loved The Ship and sometimes fantasised about taking a pub when he was retired or found out. But he was a realist and knew that running a pub was not all beer and skittles.

To the majority of respectable people with business to do at the ferryport, The Ship Leopard was simply a blot on the landscape; to Mowgley and a host of other social misfits, it was a reminder of how things used to be and could or should have been, and as such a haven from an unforgiving and uncaring world. It was also a convenient location to buy and sell anything from duty-free goods to brief and sometimes even dangerous sexual liaisons.

Arriving in the car park, Mowgley observed that the White Van Quotient was low, even for the day and time. Only three anonymous hire vehicles were either on route for or returning from a shopping expedition to Cherbourg. Inside the pub, the drivers would be taking orders or delivering their goods to private individuals or shopkeepers in the area. There would be no undercover customs officers in evidence, as they would all be busy waving proper smugglers through the checkpoint.

As usual, the single bar was heaving, and, as usual, Two-Shits was on duty behind the jump. Arriving there from his native Yorkshire with his wife's sister and other urgent needs to re-locate, it had taken the new landlord less than a week to earn his nickname. As the clientele soon learned, if a customer had been on holiday to Spain, his host had run a bar there. If a customer recalled his time in a branch of the armed forces, the new landlord would relate adventures in all of them. Two-Shits had won his scatological nickname when a fork-lift driver had returned from the toilets and reported on a particularly satisfying bowel motion. As the new licensee opened his mouth to comment, the man had held up his hand, taken a swig of his beer and then said "Yeah, I know. I've just had a good shit, and you've just had two."

Mowgley ordered a pint of driving lager and checked that his own consignment of booze and baccy had been delivered to the cellar and his slate adjusted accordingly. Taking the top off his drink, he surveyed the day's offering on the blackboard menu without enthusiasm. As usual, the customers proved more interesting.

At the bar, Billy Woolworths was working on his fourth superstrength barley wine of the session, and trying it on with the senior barmaid. He had already passed lightly over his property interests in the city and beyond, and was moving on to his plans for a solitary Christmas somewhere in the sun. Given his overall appearance and that he was paying for his drinks in taxi tokens, it was unlikely that the barmaid would take seriously his intimation that he got his pub nickname from a family association with the chain of retail outlets. At this stage of the session, Billy had also forgotten that she knew exactly how he had come to national fame some years before. After a late lunchtime session, he had somehow contrived to become locked in the toilets of the city centre Woolworths on Christmas Eve. From there, he had been forced to forage for survival until his release. By the time he was discovered by a security guard, Billy had worked his way through a frozen turkey, four tins of fancy biscuits, three boxes of chocolate liqueurs and at least a case of pure malt whisky.

Emerging on Boxing Day from what he openly acknowledged was the pleasantest Christmas he could remember for many a year, he had sold his story to the local paper's investigative reporter for a week's worth of Final Selection barley wines, and the reporter had put the tale of Billy's ordeal on the wire. For a week or more, Billy Woolworths had become a national celebrity and had lived high on the generosity of visiting media folk from as far afield as The United States. The story had inevitably come down with the Christmas decorations, and Billy was left with no more than a new name and the faint hope of compensation for the torment he was later persuaded he had suffered. A defrocked lawyer with even more enthusiasm for strong barley wine than his client had suggested that the mental trauma of his false imprisonment was worth many hundreds of thousands of pounds, and Billy was now living on hope, taxi tokens and a modest retainer from Mowgley in exchange for unspecified services.

Next to Billy Woolworths at the bar was Pompey Lil, or rather the current holder of the title. There had been a Pompey Lil on duty in the seedier pubs of the city for at least three generations. This incarnation's party trick was to leave her prosthetic eye in her glass while visiting the unisex toilet facilities. She claimed it was to dissuade anyone from finishing her drink, but the locals knew it was also a none-too-subtle way of advertising a special service no dual-eyed prostitute could offer. It was probably a pub myth that she thought of the extra service when saying farewell to a regular naval client bound for the Far East. The story went that she had promised to keep an eye out for him on his return, and that had given her the inspiration.

Next to Lil was a friend and sometimes competitor, Wild Willy Wally. He was a small man permanently clad in a large mohair sweater, who never had quite enough pancake makeup on his face to completely disguise his permastubble. Self-advertised as The Fleet's Delight, Wally was said to perform a fascinating trick with Pompey Lil's glass eye on invitation, but Mowgley had always taken care not to be present when the performance took place.

The Ferry King contemplated his friends and fellow customers, smiled contentedly, then turned his attention to the heated display cabinet as he summoned Twiggy the barmaid. In the way of these things, her pub name had come about because of the abundance of her breasts.

Swaying gently, Twiggy approached, rested one hand on the cabinet and regarded him with much more interest than she had shown in Mr Woolworths. She liked Mowgley, and as she had once told him, had he been ten years younger, four stone lighter and a bit less scruffy and a bit more better-looking, he would have been welcome to a slice of her bread and butter pudding anytime.

Remembering the compliment and giving her what he considered an especially winning smile, Mowgley looked at the day's bill of fare again before asking for the *plat du jour*.

"I thought, Jocasta," he asked politely as she placed a weary-looking pie upon an even more tired pile of chips, "that it was Cornish pasty and chips today?"

Without pausing in her duties, Jocasta - whose given name was actually Dawn, smiled patiently and said. "That's what it is, my lover."

Though already knowing he was on to a loser, Mowgley pointed an accusing finger at the plate. "I am a detective," he announced haughtily, "and in my professional opinion that is a meat pie and not a pasty from Cornwall."

"No," came the practised rejoinder. "Yesterday it was a meat pie. Today it's a Cornish pasty."

"Oh. Well that's alright then, isn't it?" The ritual exchange completed, Mowgley picked up his plate and crossed the bar to his reserved seat.

He had barely begun to excavate for any traces of meat in his pasty/pie when Melons arrived. Mowgley gave up his search, pushed his plate to one side and ordered his D.S. a drink before they set to wrestling with the crossword.

*   *   *

As his sergeant left to ferry the fourth round back to their table, Mowgley thought it was time to make room for what was to come.

At the urinal, he encountered a stevedore known locally and understandably as King Dong. Dong was demonstrating his party piece with a cigarette and the eye of his gargantuan penis for the benefit of a group of awed drivers who were not regulars at The Ship Leopard. As they settled their wager with WingCo, Mowgley noticed that the aged potman had lost his dentures and gained a black eye.

A small man of indeterminate age and an inexhaustible fund of stories of his exploits as an officer in the RAF during the War, WingCo lived with a cross-dressing window-cleaner called Ramon in a bedsitter close to the port. Their relationship was purely platonic, and co-habitation enabled both to claim the full rental on the room from the Department of Health and Social Security.

The building they lived in was being bought on mortgage by Social Tony, a local entrepreneur who was also the proprietor of a second-hand furniture shop next door to the former hotel. The shop specialised in providing basic domestic items to unemployed couples bearing vouchers from the DHSS, and as the beds, fridges, televisions and cots were destined for the unfurnished apartments owned by Tony next door, the rents for which were also paid for by the Social Security office, the arrangement was a convenient one for all concerned. As the rate of break-ins and burglaries at the block was inordinately high even for that part of the city, there was a constant demand for re-furbishment courtesy of the Social, with Tony's shop naturally supplying the replacement items. It was said by admirers that one ancient gas stove had moved between the shop and the accommodation block more than a dozen times, costing the taxpayer more than a luxury fitted kitchen.

Enquiries as to the cause of his injuries established that WingCo - who had actually served his country in wartime as a cook in the Naval Dockyard - had sustained them the previous evening at closing time. Under instructions from Two-Shits, he had insisted on collecting the unemptied glasses of a group of strangers about to depart on a combined golfing weekend and booze cruise to Cherbourg. On leaving the pub, WingCo had found them waiting, and their leader had set about him with a golf putter. It was not so much the beating, he said, but the humiliation of having to apologise for getting blood on the bastard's club.

After listening to his story, Mowgley gave the old man a twenty pound note that he insisted he had borrowed when WingCo was flush as well as pissed, then went in to the lavatory cubicle to make a couple of phone calls. This would give him a modicum of privacy as he enquired as to the return time of the golfing excursion, and also avoid having to stand next to King Dong at the urinal.

Back in the bar, Mowgley paused to make a complaint about the door of the toilet cubicle.

"What about it?" asked Two Shits.

"I would have liked one, that's all."

"Must have been that stag night yesterday," said the licensee of The Ship Leopard, phlegmatically sucking his teeth, "that's the third one I've lost this year."

Twelve

Pacific Village was the love-child of a Channel Islands property company and an award-winning American architect. As the brochure proclaimed, the development had been designed to bring a new kind of living to the City. It was also, the over-excited copywriter had continued, an *homage* to a typical Californian concept. A place where the sun would always shine in the hearts of residents and visitors, no matter what the weather

The collection of skimpily-built houses, apartments, restaurants and bars surrounding an exclusive (by virtue of the astronomical mooring fees) marina had proved an immediate success. The fact that Pacific Village had been built on a former rubbish tip, was within a mile of a notorious sink housing estate and mere yards from a permanently busy motorway had not deterred people who knew, as the brochure also said, where and how to live Life to the Full.

Mowgley parked close enough to a fluorescent sun 'n' fun jeep to give its owner the fun of trying to open the driver's door, and walked towards the marina with George The Dog following at his own pace. In the distance, some of the gently-bobbing luxury motor cruisers and yachts had probably cost even more than the houses surrounding them.

After pausing for George to investigate the contents of a

well-matured rubbish sack, Mowgley walked along the boardwalk and into Pacific Heights, an apartment block from where those willing to pay upwards of £200,000 for a penthouse had almost as panoramic a view of the coastline as the residents of the tower blocks on the nearby council estate.

Arriving at the top floor, the Ferry King thumbed the doorbell and winced as the tinny strains of *La Mer* announced his arrival. The door opened and he put on his bereavement face.

"Miss Russell? Detective Inspector Mowgley. Thanks for seeing me."

Linda Russell looked at Mowgley as if thinking about asking him to use the tradesman's entrance, then down at George The Dog with even less enthusiasm. Finally, she turned and led the way into the apartment. Mowgley and George exchanged eyebrow-lifting expressions, then followed. Right on cue, George farted squelchily as he crossed the threshold.

As she walked ahead of them in the sort of carefully contrived, hip-swinging steps used by models on catwalks, Mowgley thought how the sister of the dead woman suited her setting at Pacific Village. She looked very expensive and very artificial, and was obviously continuing the family tradition of orange permatan and big hair. She was packaged in a dress that must have cost more than his Christmas slate at the Ship Leopard. Overall, she reminded Mowgley of the doll he had bought a friend's daughter for her tenth birthday. It, too, had seemed a lot of money for what it was. Having said that and to quote Dickie Quayle, all things being equal he would rather be in Ms Russell than in prison.

Inside, the apartment looked just as he knew it would. It was a classic example of bad taste by people who were convinced that money had magically endowed them with good taste. The sort of people, he thought, who have onyx-topped coffee tables with magazines they never read carefully fanned out on the glass top.

In seconds he had spotted the onyx-topped coffee table, and the copies of *Vanity Fair* and *Cosmopolitan* on it, and without realising he was thinking aloud, said "Bingo."

"What?"

Mowgley thought quickly, then smiled inanely and said weakly: "Bingo. I was just thinking it's bingo night …at the Police Social Club."

"Oh." Linda Russell regarded him and then George as if she were thinking he might be a better bet for a sensible conversation. "Don't worry about it."

"About the bingo?" asked Mowgley, then saw that she was looking at the trail of muddy paw prints George had left on the mushroom soup-coloured carpet. "It's not mine," said Linda Russell, "I rent the place and somebody else cleans it."

"Ah," said Inspector Mowgley, "that's alright, then."

"Would you like coffee?"

"Only if it's instant, please," replied Mowgley. He cleared his throat messily, reached for his baccy tin and hoped that George would fart again before too long.

As she went to the kitchen, he looked at the framed photographs on a reproduction Sheraton cabinet with the wrong legs. There were at least a dozen pictures of the sisters, and one was obviously recent, showing them at some sort of function. Margaret Birchall was looking directly into the camera. In a surprisingly restrained blue dress and caught unsmiling and with a thoughtful expression on her face, she looked somehow apart and distant from the scene. Mowgley picked it up and wondered if she had had any sort of inkling that she would be dead in a few weeks. The flash on the camera had made her eyes look red, like a tiger in the night, he thought.

Alongside, her sister was falling out of a red dress and toasting the photographer with what looked like a glass of champagne. Leaning towards her with an arm possessively draped round her bare shoulders was a man who Mowgley knew very well.

He looked out across the harbour to the distant ferryport

and thought about people and life and his place in it all until Linda Russell returned with his coffee.

For a while they talked uncomfortably, both knowing what each thought of the other. She said that Margaret had met Robert Birchall when he had attended some sort of legal conference in Doncaster. They had married within a month of the meeting, and she, Linda, had moved down shortly afterwards to be near her sister and enjoy the delights of the South, an easy move as she was single and had no ties. She had been working for the council for the past six months, in the Planning Department. Margaret's accident had been a terrible shock, and she didn't know whether she would remain in the city or go back home. She felt she should stay on a while to be near her brother-in-law, who would need all the help he could get in coping with the tragedy.

Mowgley muttered sympathetically, and stood up. She rose to face him across the coffee table. He watched her eyes as he held out a hand and said: "We'll let you know as soon as we know more about what happened, of course. And whether it was an accident... or otherwise."

"Whether it was an *accident*? What else could it have been?"

Mowgley shrugged and carefully put his coffee cup on to the cover of one of the glossy magazines on the coffee table. "We don't know. That's what the inquest is for. To try and decide how it happened. Or why."

She lay a limp hand in his, then followed him to the door, walking in short, somehow angry steps.

Before she had quite closed the door, Mowgley turned as if in afterthought, and said: "Oh, I forgot to ask. Do you see much of your brother-in-law?"

Beneath the permatan, a flush to Linda Russell's cheeks would have been near-impossible to detect, but her eyes showed her quick anger. For a moment, Mowgley thought she would slam the door in his face, but she quickly gained control and asked coolly: "See Robert? What has that got do with anything?"

"Nothing much," replied Mowgley, "just wondered."

Nodding and smiling his inane smile, he turned away and walked down the thickly-carpeted corridor. He felt her gaze all the way to the lift, and thought how he would not like to have her behind him and in a bad mood if he were looking over the rail of a ferry boat in mid-Channel.

*   *   *

At the car park, the owner of the fun vehicle was attempting to squeeze into the driving seat without infecting his door by contact with the battered Lada.

As his female companion looked languidly on, the man weighed Mowgley's size and physical condition in the balance, and obviously felt emboldened enough to try to make himself look tough and say: "That was an arsehole bit of parking wasn't it?"

"I'm sorry, I don't speak a word of English," Mowgley said agreeably, and drove off after bestowing a manic smile on the long-limbed and uncaring girl.

Reaching the roundabout on the outskirts of Pacific Village where the price of properties dropped steeply in ratio to their distance from the marina and proximity to the motorway and council estate, he thought about Linda Russell, then reached for his mobile phone. He was still getting used to the idea of being able to make a call from wherever he was, and still not sure he approved of being contactable wherever he was and whatever he was doing.

After a near-miss with a cyclist, he fumbled with the buttons, made an early evening dinner appointment, then called Melons.

"You got out alive, then?" she asked as he tried to hold the phone to his ear, navigate the roundabout and change gear at the same time.

"I reckon she really fancied me," he said without a trace of irony. "And by the way, your trick with the eyes doesn't work."

"Perhaps you weren't looking properly."

"Perhaps." He paused, smiled at the driver of a patrol car parked in a lay-by, then spoke as if revealing a priceless punch-line: "I agree, however, that there may be more to Linda Russell than meets the eye. Ha ha ha."

After waiting for a comment which he knew would not come, then checking that nobody had disturbed the pile of papers on his desk, he threw the mobile phone on the back seat and settled down for the drive to the heart - if it had one - of the city.

Switching on the radio and finding a phone-in, he listened for a while and wondered why so many people were allowed to vote in elections, then hit the buttons until arriving at a book programme on Radio Four. The star guest for the afternoon was an American woman, and, somehow unsurprisingly, the author of a work celebrating thirty years of feminism.

After agreeing that everything wrong with the world was the fault of the male gender, the guest and interviewer moved on to what dominant bastards men had been, and how useless and feeble they were nowadays. If only, was the consensus, they could be gentle and strong, loyal, considerate and yet sexy and sometimes even masterful and always do what they were told. After cranking down the window to get more of the sea air and less of George, Mowgley turned over to Classic FM and concentrated on rolling a cigarette with one hand, which was much harder than the cowboys made it look.

At least, he thought as he spilled the tin of tobacco on his lap, the women hadn't mentioned about blokes pissing on toilet seats.

Thirteen

As it was early evening, the tablecloths at the Midnight Tindaloo (or, to give it its proper name, the Midnight Tandoori) were relatively unsullied.

Mowgley liked the owner, but also his restaurant because it was very traditional. This traditional-ness included the misspelled menu, the once-plush red seating and neon-lit posters of rural sub-continent scenes framed by Indian-style arches cut badly from sheets of plywood. At this quiet time, the tatty flock wallpaper and sticky carpets gave the place the tacky air of a nightclub visited during sober daylight hours. In all, the Tindaloo made Mowgley feel very much at home. The place also conformed with a universal mystery applying to this type of catering establishment, and one which defied even Mowgley's deductional powers. Why was it, he often wondered, that with tens of thousands of Indian-style restaurants nationwide, all with different owners and different chefs with their own styles and signature dishes, every Bombay, Calcutta and Taj Mahal had exactly the same signature smell.

Taking his seat while debating inwardly on the immediate pleasures of a fiery chicken phal and the later penalties of experiencing a rectum like the rising sun, Mowgley pondered on the symbiotic relationship between the city's drinkers and those who ran the dozens of curry shops around the docks area. It was claimed that there were more Indian (actually and as the owners were keen to point out if anyone bothered to ask, they were all Bangladeshi) restaurants per head of population in the city than anywhere on earth, including Birmingham. It was also claimed that the only sub-continental Asians living in the city were those who owned or worked in the restaurants and their families.

For local enthusiasts, an evening's drinking without a curry to round it off was like a day without wine to a Frenchman. Probably because of the city's naval heritage, the unwritten rule *vis-à-vis* a visit to a curry house was that at least ten pints of lager had to be consumed before sitting or falling down to eat. In Indian restaurants in more sophisticated places like Brighton and Bognor, people ate early then went on to see a film or have a leisurely drink. In this city, the cooks would not get into top gear until well after the witching hour. The tradition of drinking before eating had the advantage of ensuring that those on a pub crawl would get the full effect of the alcohol on their empty stomachs. It was almost a point of honour amongst naval ratings that they had never tasted a curry while sober.

Mowgley's reverie was interrupted by the arrival of his dinner companion, who was followed in to the premises by a party of men who had obviously set a lunchtime start to their run ashore. Having made a nuisance of themselves on a dozen licensed premises, they would now top the evening off by rehearsing the staff of the Midnight Tindaloo for the torment to come at pub closing time. But there would be plenty of opportunity for revenge, Mowgley thought. The detective looked at the door to the kitchen and the faces peering resignedly through its porthole window, and wondered not for the first time at the stupidity of people who were rude to waiters about to serve them with a dish in which anything from a dash of urine to a fair-sized turd would go unnoticed.

"How's it going then, chief?"

Dougie Skase was senior investigative reporter and

chief sports correspondent for the local paper, and looked it. He took himself and his work very seriously, though critics said that he was the senior staff member because anyone with a modicum of talent soon deserted the Evening Post and moved on to a real newspaper. Dougie, they said, was still with the Post because their star investigator would not be able to find the railway station, and also because he would have had to pay for his own fare to London.

But Dougie was actually a contented man. With 3.4 murders a year amongst the 150,000 people living cheek to jowl in an island city less than three miles square and a football team that tottered from one crisis to the next, he did not have to look far to find a story. In a small but densely crowded pond he was a big fish and a frank and fearless hero to those fans of the city team who could read.

This was because he had an intuitive ability to know exactly when to be supportive, and when to join or lead the regular baying for the resignation of the manager, chairman, captain or - in one memorable piece of comment journalism - the whole team.

As if in homage to the glory days of the team, Skase was stuck in the Seventies in attitude, speech and fashion. The belt on his calf-length trench coat was extravagantly and tightly knotted, and this may have been the reason he never seemed to take it off. If he had so done, revealed to the world would have been a widely-lapelled and severely waisted pin-striped 'Italian' jacket of a style that no clothes-conscious Italian had ever worn in any decade. Elsewhere and always on show were the lurid kipper tie and the almost painfully flared bottoms of his half-mast trousers, from which protruded highly polished Cuban-heeled boots. Mowgley had not decided if Skase wore the boots to add three extra inches to his height, or as another nod to his chosen style era. The hugely-kippered tie seemed as much a practical measure as a fashion statement, as Skase was a very messy eater and Mowgley knew from previously shared meals that it doubled as a bib. Topping off the ensemble, the Beatles haircut and long sideburns sat oddly on the head of a man with a severely balding crown and who would not see sixty again.

Overall, then, Skase was as badly and sadly clad as Mowgley. The difference was that Skase believed himself to be a sharp dresser.

But if his sartorial standards were extravagant, his fiscal standards were ultra-conservative. The chief reporter allegedly managed to exist almost entirely on a combination of expenses and free drinks and meals and the odd cash dropsie from those who wished to gain a few inches of free publicity. Sometimes, the brown paper envelope would be handed over by those who wished to keep their names out of rather than in the public domain.

Though not spending a lot of time reviewing his view of the newspaperman, by and large Inspector Mowgley thought that Skase was a pompous little wanker. He was, though a useful wanker. What the reporter thought about him he neither knew nor cared.

The two men studied the menu, and Mowgley made his order while exchanging sympathetic looks with Bombay Billy, the owner of the Tindaloo. The detective knew that Billy would have his hands full with the headaches on the other table, and Billy knew that Mowgley would rather have enjoyed his chicken phal alone. As always, Mowgley thought about Billy's strength of character and what it had taken for the young man to leave his home and come to a land of barbarians, working countless hours and enduring endless abuse as he struggled to make a success in a strange and godless culture. One day he would have the last laugh when he went back home a wealthy man as a result of serving half a million so-called Indian meals which were unheard of in his own country, and he would have earned his retirement.

Above the noise from the nearby table, the two men competed for control of the poppadoms and pickles, then talked about recent events of mutual interest. Skase was currently investigating the latest allegations of murky business activities at the city football club. The team was on its third owner and ninth manager in ten years, and the activities off the pitch were invariably more dramatic and interesting than those on it.

In the days of savage haircuts, well-dubbed yet still unyielding boots, baggy shorts and self-discipline, the Blues had held a regular position at the middle of the old first division table. The players had come to work on bicycles and earned about the going rate of the skilled craftsmen they considered themselves and were seen to be.

Nowadays, rather than reporting on the matches, Skase's stories were more likely to be about crisis management, loutish behaviour in local night clubs and the constant threat of relegation. Yet in spite of their dismal performances, the players earned pop star money. The perception was obviously that they should be paid huge salaries even if they didn't earn them by results or attendance figures. The club was losing a not-so-small fortune a week, and a good gate these days would be about the same numbers as the old team would have attracted for a reserves friendly. The only time the star players performed with any enthusiasm and energy was in the bars and city night-spots where they preened and posed around, scoring much more frequently with football groupies and knickerless slappers than they ever did on the park

At the moment, the club was in the process of shedding its latest manager and chairman, and the process was so familiar that Skase, had he had the imagination, would need do no more than change the names and file the same report. As usual a saviour with no connections to the city and less track record of success but a high publicity profile had been appointed, with the club giving him a huge salary and the keys to the gates of the club in return for promises of a golden future and a good cup run as he got the team in shape for promotion.

Whatever was hoped for and promised, the sequence of events was unvarying. First would come a sudden change of key figures on the staff as the saviour surrounded himself with his allies; in spite of the butchery the supporters club would gather at the ground to chant their messiah's name and pledge undying loyalty and confidence in his ability to regain past glories. An occasional win would be met with euphoria and city-wide celebrations, and new players would be bought in at almost incredible transfer cost and wages. Home draws would be claimed as victories, and trouncings explained away with what should have been laughable excuses. Then the rot would set in. Gates would fall as defeat followed defeat. The die-hard supporters would re-visit the ground on a weekday evening to demand the sacking of the manager and the public execution of their former saviour. From being a saint he would become an arch-villain, and the fan mail would become hate mail. After a flurry of bulletins from the ground denying rumours of boardroom battles, the chairman would declare complete confidence in their coach and his aides, and everyone would know that this signalled the beginning of the end. The coach would depart with a huge pay-off, and the game would begin all over again. The star players' houses would be put up for sale and they would depart for a fraction of what they had cost, and the rumours of a new messiah or mystery millionaire would begin. Dougie Skase would have yet more material which would write itself, and his newspaper's sales would increase sharply. Only the team and its long-suffering supporters would continue to lose.

As Skase explained the background to the latest drama, Mowgley nodded regularly and tried to appear interested. Soon, he would be able to get to the reason he had arranged the meeting.

"The best little story this week," Skase concluded, "is about the supporter who chinned the club owner when they met in the street outside the ground."

"I suppose," said Mowgley, brightening considerably, "that you could say it was a rare case of the fan hitting the shit. Ha ha ha?"

Waiting in vain for a reaction to what was probably his best pun so far that year and as his companion became preoccupied with a new stain on his tie, Mowgley thought about explaining the gag, then gave up and whet Skase's appetite with some low- level and harmless information on current events at the port. Mopping his brow and calling for another jug of water, he then steered the conversation to civic affairs and asked Skase if anything was happening of particular interest in the council chambers.

After sitting through another unwanted briefing on the controversy over traffic-calming measures and the recent installation of a one-way system with no-entry signs at each end of the road, Mowgley chose his moment and asked what Councillor Eddie Barnes was presently up to.

Skase grunted, then without pausing to empty his mouth, said: "You mean apart from lining his pockets, shagging his staff and doing favours for his builder mates?"

Skase was, as Mowgley knew, not a fan of the chairman of the city planning committee, but then not many people were. Eddie Barnes had a long and distinguished history within the civic affairs of the city, mostly distinguished by his ability to profit from his position without getting caught. Over the years, he had made a good living as a haulage contractor, and a fortune from the opportunities his position brought. Starting with one lorry, he now employed a dozen drivers and lived on Nobs Hill in a house allegedly built from materials earmarked for one of the new schools he had played an active part in bringing to the city. He had a special handshake and was said by insiders and enemies to have turned down the post of Lord Mayor as it would have got in the way of his real business of running the council as his own private company.

A clever man, he kept a low profile and seemed to Mowgley to be almost completely free of ego. His only interest was to accumulate money and the things that money brought. Like any powerful man, he was envied and hated by many, and mostly by those who would have been just as bent if they had had the balls and the brains. As far as the policeman was concerned, Barnes was no worse than most of his colleagues. He was just better at getting what he really wanted in return for the hours of officially unpaid effort he put in. Mowgley knew Skase despised Eddie Barnes. A small man in character as well as size, the reporter would resent Barnes on principle. The principle would not be that Barnes was bent; rather that he was better at it than Skase.

Mowgley watched his dining companion's open-mouthed chewing action with undisguised fascination for a while, then asked casually: "So who is Barnsie shagging these days, apart from the ratepayers?"

Skase concentrated for a moment on getting a new consignment of meat, rice and naan bread to swallowable consistency, then washed it down with lager, belched contentedly and said: "Some tarty bird. She only arrived last year, and now she's his secretary. He's set her up in a flat at Pacific Village, and according to my contacts she's getting more dick than dictation. And he's at it again with the old girl's place over the Hill."

Like most readers of the Post, Mowgley knew about the place over the Hill and its eccentric owner. Thanks to the efforts and enterprise of her long-dead husband, Mrs Cheshire-Norman had once owned the best part of a village in the now very desirable green belt where the city petered out and the countryside began beyond Nobs Hill.

From a wealthy Cotswolds land-owning family, Freddie Cheshire-Norman had been a rare example of old money with business acumen and a burning desire to make new money, and a great deal of it.

In the days before the car had made it fashionable and possible for the middle classes to live in the countryside while looting their inflated incomes from the city, rural property had generally been thought worthless. As country folk abandoned their unvalued homes to move into town, Freddie had quietly bought them up for, even in those days, almost laughable prices.

After his death, his wife had done her best to give away her millions to a series of increasingly rapacious property developers, and now sat looking mindlessly out to sea in a nursing home where the monthly charges would have bought almost a terrace of farmworkers' cottages in her husband's heyday.

Apart from a still substantial but rapidly diminishing fortune, the childless and sad old woman's only property asset was the manor house in which she and Freddie once lived. Like her, Didcot House was a once-beautiful ruin. Now inhabited by an extended family of New Age travellers who no longer travelled, the property featured in the Post at regular intervals as entrepreneurs tried and failed to launch schemes to buy and turn it into a golf course, leisure centre or hotel, or all three. All the schemes reportedly failed due to a lack of finance, will or planning permission, but mostly because Mrs Cheshire-Norman had no interest in saving herself or her home from a slow and undignified death.

As the chief reporter for the City Post explained, the latest rumours of choice concerning Didcot House were that it was going to be bought by a cult who believed that the city was built on the site of the drowned metropolis of Atlantis, or destined to become a privatised prison.

A more likely story was one concerning a bid by an unknown development company, who had given no explanation of what they would do with it if the owner could be persuaded to sell.

"And do you think it'll happen?" Mowgley toyed with the remains of his onion bhaji while giving the rowdy table a Paddington Bear stare which he knew would probably go unnoticed. The combination of the headaches' oafish behaviour and his companion's table manners were getting on his nerves. He lifted one leg to allow a fart to escape and ruminated on how he could not stand people who had no consideration for others' sensibilities.

Skase looked thoughtfully at his tie, then spat on his fingers and rubbed earnestly at an obstinate blob of mango chutney.

"Don't know, but something's going on. The old girl is totally gone, and people have been trying to do something with the place for years. If she did sell it as a private residence, it would cost more than it would be worth to make it liveable in. But that bastard Barnes is involved, you can be very sure."

Mowgley paid keener attention.

"So why would anyone want to buy it now?"

Skase looked at Mowgley as if he had asked why people robbed banks, then pushed his plate away and sat back in his chair.

"Because with planning permission to turn the house into flash flats and build luxury homes in the grounds, whoever got it would make millions."

Mowgley lifted his eyebrows slightly to express ongoing interest and concentrated on the flock wallpaper as Skase began to excavate remnants of sinewy meat from a hollow back tooth with the point of his reporter's pencil.

"But I thought you said they'd been trying for years to get planning permission on it and never would?"

Skase studied the pencil, sucked the point, then looked pleased to be able to show off his superior knowledge of current local affairs.

"Things have changed. The green belt areas used to be sacred, but not any longer. You must have seen all the crap about the rape of the countryside and the screams from the people who don't want anyone moving into their back yard. Besides, I know that someone has put in an application to build a hundred homes in the parkland around the house, and I got a tip-off that Barnes is involved. He must know something; anyway, he's denied any knowledge of it, so he's got to be well at it."

As Mowgley digested this information along with his curry, the noise from the headaches' table reached intolerable levels. They had grown tired of waiting for their meal, and one of their number was entertaining the rest of the table by teaching the waiter to talk proper English. As Bombay Billy arrived to calm the situation, Mowgley excused himself and went outside to check that he had not left his lights on.

Returning, he went over to the noisy table and politely asked if anyone owned the old Granada outside, and if so they might like to know that a group of kids were presently trying to remove the wheel trims. As a large man swore savagely, rose and hurried outside, Mowgley called for the bill and made the usual commitment to give Skase a call if anything interesting came up at the port. The reporter nodded, pocketed the curry-stained receipt and stood up. Adjusting the enormous Windsor knot on his tie, he asked as if in afterthought, "By the way, I forgot to ask, do you know anything about a bloke being found in the ferry terminal toilets with the handle of a golf club stuck up his jacksie?"

Mowgley did his best to look surprised then thoughtful, then shook his head.

"No. Do you know what sort of club it was?"

Skase shrugged. "A putter I think."

"Oh. Well, he certainly holed out, by the sound of it. Ha ha ha."

Skase looked blankly at him, then left, still working on his newly re-decorated tie. Mowgley wondered idly if he actually ever got kipper stains on his kipper tie, then went into the kitchen to pick up George The Dog's takeaway and have a word with Bombay Billy.

Pointing out the driver of the Granada through the porthole window in the door to the restaurant, he suggested that the owner of the Midnight Tindaloo apologise for the lamentable service and give the table a few drinks in compensation, making sure that the Granada owner had more than his share.

Outside, the sky was full of stars. The detective belched, farted carefully to avoid follow-through, then took his mobile phone from the back seat. From the boot he took a large spanner.

Calling the office, he instructed D.C. Mundy to pass on a message to the city central station that it might be a good idea to have a car outside the Midnight Tindaloo shortly. They should be awaiting the arrival of the driver of an E-registration, grey Ford Granada Ghia. He had been drinking heavily, and would certainly give a positive result if invited to take a breathalyser test.

The officer attending would have a good reason to stop the car as both the rear lights were broken. Or, Mowgley reflected silently, they would be in just a tick.

Whistling cheerfully yet already regretting the chicken phal, the King of the Ferries twirled the spanner like a miniature majorette's baton as he marched toward the Granada. It was a real example of *entente cordiale*, he thought as he arrived at the rear of the car, to be in such accord with regard to police procedures with his colleagues on the other side of the Channel.

Fourteen

According to the incident board:

1) Death had called in Mowgley's absence, and would return at a mutually convenient time.

2) The office syndicate still hadn't won the Lottery.

As Mundy the Younger had not needed to explain, it was not the Grim Reaper who had arrived for Mowgley, but the Coroner's Officer, affectionately known in the business as Dr Death. He would be returning within the hour.

Not written on the notice board was the message that Chief Superintendent Mundy (as his son was alone in calling him when he was not within earshot) would take it very kindly if Mowgley could spare a moment from his busy schedule to give him a call and let him know that all was well in his world.

Mowgley sighed. Sarcasm was not Mundy's strong point.

He turned to where Melons was struggling with the crossword: "What did Gloria really want?"

She shrugged. "I didn't take the call. Perhaps he thinks that it might be nice if you let your superior know what was going on from time to time. Oh and I think it would be nice if you could change the battery in your mobile a bit more often than your y-fronts."

Mowgley sighed theatrically again. Sarcasm was Melons's strong point. He summoned her to follow him into his office, looked gloomily at the neat pile of paper on his desk (in direct contradiction of Standing Order 69570/b, Melons had tidied it in his absence), then asked: "How was Doctor Death?"

His sergeant repeated her shrug. "You know Terry. He just wanted to know when you would be ready for an inquest date on the overboard."

Mowgley thought it must be his turn to shrug, so did so. "Soon. Anything else?"

"Not much. I checked the messages at your official residence and I think you should, too. Going by some of them, the students you've sub-let to seem to be using it as a central cannabis distribution point. I don't think the Police Authority would be so keen on paying the rent if they found out. It would also be nice if you could let us know where you are from time to time. Just in case something comes up that we think you ought to know about. And you're going out of order."

"What?" Mowgley slumped in his seat and stared fixedly at the stack of paper.

"The shrugging. You did it again when I said about your police apartment, and you knew it was my turn."

"Sorry," said Mowgley absent-mindedly then, "sit down and I'll reveal all."

"Alright, but only if you tell me why you're trying to hypnotise your desk."

Mowgley concentrated for a few more seconds, then gave up and reached for his baccy tin. "I was reading a book by this bloke who says that nothing is real."

"That was John Lennon, wasn't it?"

Mowgley looked quickly up at the frosted glass panel in the partition. "Where?"

His sergeant shook her head. "No, I mean it was John Lennon who said that nothing was real. *I Am The Walrus*, wasn't it?"

The King of the Ferries lit a roll-up, blew a plume of smoke at the ceiling and said thoughtfully: "I think you'll find it was *Lucy In The Sky With Diamonds*. And Lennon did admit at least once that Paul co-wrote it, so we cannot be clinically sure who did that line. Anyway, this bloke in the book said there is no such thing as karma or kismet or fate or luck, and we control our own lives and everything that happens in them."

"So?"

"So, as we are in control even if we don't know it, what happens to us is what we subconsciously *want* to happen, whether we think so or not. Are you with me?"

"Not really, but go on." Melons took Mowgley's cigarette, pinched off the wet end and took a drag.

"Well, his point is, if you *know* that you're making it up as you go along, you can do something about it, if you try hard enough. A bit like when you know you're dreaming."

"So?"

"So I was trying to make all this paperwork disappear. But it's not working."

Melons returned Mowgley's cigarette and frowned. "But surely, if you could make anything happen and solve your problems, the paperwork wouldn't be a priority?"

He nodded glumly. "I know. But it would be a start, wouldn't it? If I can't do something simple like that, how am I going to get on to the advanced stuff?"

"Why not do it the easy way and just spend a day sorting your desk out? When it was done it would become a self-fulfilling prophecy, enabling you to move on to the big stuff like making the world a better place and solving the Mephisto crossword."

Mowgley expelled a petulant breath. "That's typical of you. Always being logical. Now come and sit down while I tell you about my adventures."

Closing the door and perching above him on the corner of his desk, Melons listened as Mowgley explained about his meeting with the overboard's sister and his meet with Dougie Skase.

Taking her turn to shrug, she said: "So, what do you reckon to it all, then? What's the connection? Why are you getting so excited about Didcot House and a dodgy councillor? Eddie Barnes has been at it for years but it's not our problem."

"There was a photograph of Eddie with Linda Russell in her flat; the sister was in it too. And Skasey reckons that Eddie is shagging her."

"Who, the dead woman?"

"No, you pratt - her sister, Linda Russell. She works for Eddie."

"Big deal. Eddie shags all his secretaries, it's a well known fact."

"I know, but I've got one of my feelings. Margaret Russell cops hold of a solicitor and marries him inside a month, and her sister comes down to join them and gets a job and a legover with the chairman of the council planning department who everyone knows is bent as a nine bob note. The solicitor starts acting like he's found what his dick's for after forty years, and we think he's now at it with the sister of his dead wife, who obligingly gets pissed and falls off the overnight to Cherbourg. On top of all that, Big Eddie is up to something with an old house which is worth a fortune if it gets planning permission and which is owned by an old lady who doesn't know what day or year it is. Call me old-fashioned, but I think it's worth doing a bit of traditional detective work at this point."

Melons arched her eyebrows. "You mean like fitting someone up?"

"I mean I think you should go and see the old girl with celerity and, as we are supposed to say in the trade, pursue your enquiries."

"And what about you?"

"I'm going to take my calls, have a pint with Doctor Death, and go and tell the witness about the likely date for the inquest."

"Why don't you just call her?"

Mowgley stood up and began to undo his creased and

stained black tie as he walked to the bentwood hat stand in the corner of the office. "Because she has been through a great deal of stress and trauma, including the break-up of a marriage, the prospect of a move to a new country and a new life, and on top of all that, the involvement with a sudden and dramatic death. As any psychologist will tell you, the three most stressful events in a person's life are marital breakup, moving home and sudden death. I believe it is my duty to do what I can to ameliorate her distress by applying the personal touch and showing her the caring face of the Criminal Investigation Department."

"You mean you fancy her."

Mowgley hung his business tie up. "Not at all."

Melons pursed her lips and blew a raspberry. "Then why are you putting your special Johnny Cash string tie on? And you've combed your hair in the fairly recent past."

Trying to think of a withering response and failing, Mowgley tied his tie and nodded toward the door.

"That will be all, thank you Sergeant. If you want me, I shall be in my office."

Melons rose, crossed the floor and tweaked his tie. "You're in your office now, big boy."

"Well spotted."

As she opened the office door, Melons turned back and asked: "What about Mundy?"

Mowgley shrugged out of turn again. "No, he won't be in my office, and I don't fancy him at all. Any more questions?"

"Only one; who exactly is this Celerity you want me to go with to see the old lady over the Hill?"

Mowgley sighed for the seventeenth time that day. "As you well know, it means with all due speed, Sergeant."

*　　　*　　　*

After an unproductive hour of looking at the pile of papers on his desk, Mowgley left his office, gave D.C. Mundy a playful cuff with a rolled-up copy of *Country Music Times*, then line-danced to where Melons sat at her desk arranging a visit to see the owner of Didcot Hall. He amused himself with a little further light bullying of Young Mundy as he waited for her to finish her call, then asked where George The Dog was to be found.

"He's in my car. Why?"

"I thought I'd take him with me when I go to see the witness."

"Oh - is she an animal lover, then?"

Mowgley decided not to risk going out of shrugging turn and settled for a medium strength raised eyebrow. "Don't know, but the chicken phal I had last night is making its presence felt. I thought that if I take George-"

"You can blame him for the stink." She shook her head despairingly. "Apart from being unfair on George, it's not very original as a game plan, is it?"

Mowgley smiled in agreement. "No, but hopefully effective. You know what they say about giving a dog a bad name, ha ha ha. But to business. What's to do with Mrs Thingy-Thingy?"

"I'm off to see her now. What do you want me to find out - if the poor woman's capable of telling me anything?"

Fiddling with his string tie, Mowgley walked over to the window and looked out across the ferryport. "I want you to find out what's going on with Didcot House, Councillor Eddie Barnes, Linda Russell, Robert Birchall and the late Mrs Birchall, Sergeant. I want you to find out if the old lady has been having any dealings with any or all of our suspects. If she isn't capable of telling you, talk to the other residents and the staff. And while you're at it, you could see if she'd like to buy a nice ruin in Normandy. Blimey…"

Melons walked over and stood at his side. "What's up?" Mowgley pointed towards where a P&O ferryboat was loading.

"I reckon the bloke in the book might be right. I concentrated on making that car go over the linkspan and on to the boat, and it worked."

His sergeant nodded gravely. "Yes, so it did. See what

you can do with the other twenty lined up behind. I bet if you tried really hard, you could make them all go on that boat. I bet you could even make the ferry steam out of the harbour."

"Yes," said the King of the Ferries, refusing to rise to the bait, "I bet I could."

He adjusted his string tie again, waved as if to an adoring crowd, gave her a full-strength Paddington bear stare, then turned on his heel and was gone.

Fifteen

Following an enjoyable interlude at The Ship Leopard with Dr Death and a bracing exchange with a group of Visigoths warming up for a booze cruise, Mowgley was well fortified for the encounter when he arrived at the home of Yvonne McLaughlin. He knew that it was a sign of weakness to have to drink several pints before feeling confident enough to chat a woman up. He also knew that what he thought was witty repartee after several pints would probably not be seen as such by the sober recipient, but what was a man to do?

Apologising for having to bring his old and smelly dog, he followed the witness into the passageway of the terraced house and accepted her offer of a glass of wine. She left him in the small and pleasingly untidy sitting room and went into the kitchen, made some clinking sounds, then called out "It's okay for you to drink on duty, then?"

As she reappeared with two glasses, Mowgley stepped back and pantomimed a heart attack: "For old-fashioned coppers like me it's almost compulsory. You don't want to take any notice of what you read about policemen in books. Well, not all of it, anyway."

She smiled ruefully. "I'm not a great reader, and especially not detective stories. Mostly, it's just television, cop shows, I'm afraid."

"That's worse. They always make us look like deeply-caring yet flawed and outwardly cynical individuals battling single-handedly to put the world to rights while despairing at their inability to do so. Next you'll be asking if I have a sensitive soul buried deep beneath this flip exterior, and a shallow self-seeking boss who I'm in permanent conflict with."

"Well, do you?"

"Do I what? Have a sensitive soul or a shallow self-seeking boss?"

"Both, or either."

He gave her his best profile and tried to look sensitive and cynical at the same time as he accepted the glass of wine and restrained himself from drinking it in one go. "The shallow self-seeking boss bit is inevitable. They're the main qualifications for a senior position in any big company, aren't they?"

"I suppose so." She led the way over to a sofa and gestured for him to sit alongside her. He settled down, ensuring that George was nearby, and began to roll two cigarettes. It was all going very well so far, he thought. He sometimes amazed himself by how witty and entertaining he could be after a couple of drinks.

"By the way," she asked as she leaned towards him to accept a light, "is it Mowgli as in innocent in the jungle?"

"No." He lit his cigarette. "It's Mowgley as in cutting grass happily. It's an old Irish name. The Mowgleys were very big in Cork before the potato famine."

"I see," she said as if she didn't, then sipped her wine, sighed contentedly and blew a plume of smoke towards the ceiling. It was going even better than he could have hoped, Mowgley thought. She seemed relaxed and pleased to be in his company. For some reason, that was unusual for nearly every woman he had known except for Melons.

There was a surprisingly unawkward silence, then she asked: "What about the sensitive bit?"

He paused in mid-drink: "Sorry pardon?"

"Are you sensitive?"

Mowgley clenched his buttocks to forestall an

impending phal attack, then said: "That's a trick question, isn't it?"

She sipped from her glass. "It's not meant to be. Why do you think it is?"

"I generally find that people who claim to be sensitive usually mean self-obsessed. They're very sensitive about themselves and their feelings, which must make them insensitive about other people's, although they pretend not to be. A bit like the paradox of self-seeking and shallow people being the best qualified but least suited to being in charge of others."

She reached across him to tap her ash into the metal waste paper bin by his knee and he felt an unaccustomed stirring.

"Hmm. This is all getting a bit deep for me. I'm just a simple Scots farmer."

"I don't think so." Mowgley made a mental note to try to be less clever for the moment, then balanced his empty glass on the arm of the sofa and looked at it wistfully. He would have to be careful. He was entering that brief phase that all drinkers know. After a modest intake, the mind worked better and faster and the words came easier. Then after another few sherbets, you only thought you were on top form and it was downhill all the way. Brendan Behan had summed it up perfectly, but he couldn't remember how he had put it on account that he, Mowgley, had been pissed when someone told him the quote.

Apparently missing the empty glass signal, Yvonne McLaughlin stubbed out then dropped her cigarette in the waste bin, and said: "It was good of you to come and let me know about the inquest. Do you know when it's likely to happen?"

After this subtle reminder of the official reason for his presence, Mowgley told her about his meeting with Death and promising to keep her fully informed about the case, then looked wistfully again at his glass and made a half-hearted attempt to rise. Without speaking, his host went to the kitchen and returned with the bottle.

"So," he said, settling back down and easing his buttocks away from the cushion while she was still at a safe distance, "how's the hunt for the farm in Normandy going?"

"Not too well. All the estate agent in Cherbourg had to show me was a selection of ruins that would cost a fortune to restore, and all with very little land around them. Alright for Brits who want to have a stately home but can't afford one over here, I suppose. You know, the sort of people that fall for a lot of spires and winding staircases and stupidly convince themselves they can do a ruined castle up for next to nothing."

"Yes," said Mowgley heavily, "I was married to one."

"Oh. Am I allowed to ask what happened?"

"To her or the ruin?".

"Both, if you don't mind talking about it."

Mowgley did his rueful look. "It just didn't work out. Anyway, she stuck me with an impressive ruin. Actually, I was thinking of asking if you might be interested, but..."

She smiled. "Well, I'd like to see it. Perhaps..."

"Yes, perhaps."

*   *   *

For the next hour, they talked and smoked and drank, and laughed.

Apart from the problem with the phal escape committee, Mowgley felt more at ease in a woman's company than he had for years. It was almost like being with Melons, only different, as, after his fourth glass of wine, he felt bold enough to tell her. She smiled, but Mowgley noticed her eyebrows arched slightly. "Surely you're not telling me that you don't get on with women?"

Choosing to ignore the eyebrows, he ploughed on. "It's usually more of a case of them not getting on with me."

The eyebrows moved a little further upwards."Oh? Why do you think that is?"

"Don't know, really. But before you ask, I'm not frightened of women - well, most of them - and I didn't hate my mother. I suppose it's that they seem to feel threatened by me. Or say they do when it suits them."

She refilled his glass. "Are you sure it's not the other way around?"

"What is?"

"A lot of men feel threatened by women, don't they?" she asked.

"Do they?"

She sipped her wine. "You obviously don't agree."

Mowgley chose to ignore the slight trace of coolness in her voice and ploughed on.

"I agree it's what women say nowadays."

"But you don't think they mean it?"

"I don't think they know what they mean. They say they want to be treated the same as men, and that's what I try to do. But as soon as it gets a bit rough or it suits them, they come over all sensitive, cry, say you're a bully and that they feel threatened."

"But you work with a woman, don't you?"

Mowgley frowned and continued to ignore the warning signs: "Yes, but that's different. She's-"

"Like a man?"

"No. She's definitely a woman, but she thinks and acts like a man. Most of the time."

"And that's good?"

He considered his reply for a moment, then said: "It's good when we're on a job. It's certainly less bloody confusing and annoying. Look, whatever people choose to think and say nowadays, men and women are different, mentally and physically. If I'm going into a pub full of drunken yobs, I don't want to have to worry about looking after a five foot tall, seven stone policewoman with a fetching pony tail. If I'm talking to another officer about a job, I don't want to have to be worrying if anything I say will upset her and give her an excuse to accuse me of sexism or racism or any other bloody ism."

He fell silent, realising it was not going so well. She looked at her glass thoughtfully and half-smiled.

"Interesting. Do you know how to spell 'misogynist'?"

"Yep – but that doesn't make me one. I don't hate women, nor am I scared of them. I just don't like being blamed for everything that's wrong with the world now. That's what it's like to be a bloke nowadays. Especially a white heterosexual bloke who likes to read the Daily Telegraph."

She filled his glass, sat down and asked for another cigarette: "So I can take it you don't approve of equality between the sexes or agree that women have a bad time from men?"

"I don't think you can have equality because we are, like I said, different. I agree it's not much fun being a woman sometimes. I think you should agree that it's sometimes not much fun being a bloke. Some women have a wonderful life because they were lucky enough to be born with the looks and enough brains to use them. Some men have a great time because they are men. But lots of men and women have a crap life."

Warming to his theme and encouraged by her lack of frostiness and also the effects of six pints of beer and five glasses of wine, he pressed on: "If you think about it, nature planned it for men to be the superior species. It's all about testosterone. Man is designed to act as part of a team and go out and get the dinosaur for dinner - and yes, I know that Man and dinosaurs were not about at the same time. Woman was created to be a nurturer. That's why you get more men at the extremes, as geniuses or in nick. It's nobody's fault, it's just how it is. We can change the rules and the perception, but not the nature of what we are. Man is - or should be - the predator."

"And woman should stay at home and look after the children?"

"That's right."

She nodded, smiled again, then asked: "But if it's all down to nature, how do you account for the tarantula?"

He drained his glass and put it on the arm of the sofa. "What about the tarantula? You're not going to do that thing about the female being deadlier than the male and eating the male after sex are you?"

"No," she said, "what actually happens is quite interesting and keys in with what you have been saying about nature as against nurture. In the arachnid world, the male brings it all on himself. All male spiders are apparently obsessed with sex, all the time. Whenever they get in range, they try to attract the female by tapping their feet." Mowgley belched and had the presence of mind to turn it into a grunt: "You mean like Fred Astaire?"

"Quite. As long as it's a John Travolta and not a dad-at-a-disco type dancer, the female will often be attracted. Her way of showing it will be to tear off his leg. The funny thing is that the male will then keep on tapping with the remaining legs. Even after that, he'll go back for more. He just can't help himself."

Mowgley waved his arm in a dismissive fashion and knocked his glass into the waste bin. "There you are then, I rest my case."

He made to get up. Even after the drink, experience told him he was on the edge of the moment when it suddenly became hard to shape his lips around his thoughts, and even harder to form them. Anyway, this was also the time when any female he had given the benefit of his philosophy forgot logic and reasoning, and went all girly. By doing so they proved his point, but would not see it. Best to quit while he was not in trouble.

"No need to run now you've said your piece." She put her hand on his knee, then stood and rescued his glass from the bin before going to the kitchen. "It's rare enough I get any stimulating conversation. Especially with a man."

"Well, as long as you promise not to tear my legs off."

"Just make sure you don't start tap dancing, then."

"No chance, I'd only fall in the sink, ha ha ha."

Bemused as well as befuddled, Mowlgey sat and watched owlishly as she returned with a bottle and sat alongside him just as he broke wind. It was silent, but very strong.

Despite his condition, he had the presence of mind to push George The Dog away with his foot: "Sorry about that. He's got a bit of an upset stomach."

"I'm not surprised," said his host dryly as she reached out to refill his glass, "it smells like you've been feeding him on chicken phal..."

Sixteen

"Is there a law against shagging a witness? Something along the lines of tampering with material evidence, perhaps?"

Mowgley looked hurt."I haven't been shagging anyone; I was just telling you about how well I got on with her. If I didn't know better, I'd say you were jealous."

"Ho Ho. Or as you would say with your equally false laugh, ha ha ha."

They were convened in his office. He had asked for her report on her visit to the owner of Didcot Hall, but she had insisted on a detailed account of his meeting with Yvonne. He had said it had gone well and that he had enjoyed himself, but she had wanted more:

"She must be a very clever woman."

"What makes you say that?"

"I bet you went steaming in and did your rant about women and their place in the scheme of things and nature and all that old toffee."

"No," said Mowgley in a way that Melons knew meant 'yes'. "Why do you think that, anyway?"

"Easy-peasey. You looked really... smug this morning when you came in. I bet she played you just right, just like a big fat fishy."

"What do you mean, 'played me just right'?"

Melons picked a long hair from his shirt front, looked at

it speculatively, then dropped it on the desk. "If she'd have taken your argument to bits, you'd have had a ruck and buggered off. If she'd have played the little woman and told you how strong and masterful you were, you'd have hated it and buggered off. She's only known you for five minutes and she knows exactly how to handle you."

"What - you mean like you do?"

"Don't be ridiculous."

"So all this time when I thought we suited each other naturally, you've been playing me along like a big fat pollock to get the best results, and you don't like it when you think someone else can do it. How like a woman."

"Bollocks not pollocks. I just don't like to see The Great Detective being taken in."

"My arse. Now, what about the old lady?"

Melons looked as if she wanted to continue talking about his evening with Yvonne, but also wanted to tell him what she had dug up. "It was very interesting."

"Go on."

"As Skasey said, the poor woman is completely gone. It was very sad, really. She's sitting in the nursing home looking out over a part of the county her husband used to own, and paying a grand a week for the pleasure of being bullied by someone on a fiver an hour and unhappy about it. Because of the type of Alzheimers she suffers from, she has moments when she seems to know exactly what you're talking about, then off she goes back to her own, private world. When she was in a lucid state, she told me about when she and her husband used to entertain at Didcot Hall, and showed me some old pictures. She was really beautiful once. Now she's just waiting to die. In a weird way, I think people like her are better off when they are in their own world."

Mowgley nodded glumly. "Not much point in asking her about who's trying to buy her old home then?"

"Not really. I talked to the matron about who manages her finances, and she said everything is looked after by the old lady's solicitor. He comes to see her once a week and pays all her bills."

"So he'd be the one to ask about any plans for Didcot House, then?"

"Definitely."

"Who is he - do we know him?"

"You've not met him, but I have and I think you should. It's the overboard's husband, Robert Birchall FRISC."

*   *   *

They drove up Nobs Hill to the strains of the theme from *The Trap*, with Mowgley slapping his left thigh as if urging an imaginary horse up a steep incline.

As with *Shane*, *The Big Country* and *The Magnificent Seven*, it was the sort of simple, uplifting film music which made Mowgley's heart swell. Luckily for him, his grace-and-favour Lada from Dodger Long was old and out-of-fashion enough to be equipped with the sort of eight-track cartridge player upon which all Mowlgey's favourite Western themes were recorded.

Nobs Hill was defined by the way the houses got bigger, further apart and even more expensive the higher they were up the slope and above the city. If you had money, you either lived by the sea on one side of the city, or on the hill above it. Never anywhere in between.

As the Lada laboured gamely on, Mowgley looked down to where coming up for 150,000 people lived on a spit of land three miles long by a bit more than a mile wide. And that was the official figure, taking no account of illegal immigrants and those with other reasons for not wishing to appear on the books.

He had once tried to work out the acreage on which this huge mass of humanity lived and worked and took their pleasures. After a while he had given up but, whatever the size, it surely wasn't enough. With Melons's help, he had managed to calculate that, in the city, more than ten thousand people fitted in to the same ground area as the gardens and fields at *La Cour*. When you thought about it, it was amazing how they all rubbed along together and how relatively little murder and crime took place on that seething patch of humanity.

Territorial boundaries usually consisted of no more than a forecourt or, in the rows of workers' terraced cottages (as the former slum dwellings were now dubbed), just a wall with a door opening straight on to the pavement. Amazingly, and apart from the knee-tremblers against walls, the 347 yearly break-ins, the casually broken windows and the vomit in the milk bottles, the boundaries were mostly respected.

Unusually for a lot of officers he had known and what people would think his philosophy would be, Mowgley held a general view that the great majority of people were reasonably honest and just wanted to get on with their lives. They also did not want to be burgled, mugged, raped or generally frightened by arseholes, and would support stronger and stronger deterrent measures if any government had the bollocks to bring them in rather than just talk about it at election time.

When he was young and new at the job, a uniformed sergeant had told him that most of the burglaries and car crime in the city were committed by less than fifty people. If they could be rounded up and kept off the streets, the crime rate would be halved and the police would be able to get on with sorting out the real villains. When Mowgley had asked him why they didn't just round up the miscreants and bang them up for a night to prove the point, the man had smiled and said "If only it was that easy, son."

*   *   *

Robert Birchall lived in a house which seemed grand for a middle-range solicitor with an expensive wife to keep. Hilltop House had been built by a former Lord Mayor of the city who, after the war, had had the radical idea of taking poor people out of the bombed and otherwise uninhabitable properties in the poorer parts and shipping them out to a purpose-built estate. The new council houses boasted bathrooms, and gardens in which to grow vegetables.

Unfortunately, the bold scheme had also swept away any sense of continuity and community along with the rubble and rats, and the second biggest council estate in Europe was home to lots of unhappy people. They used the bathrooms, but a lot of the gardens were full of cars on bricks instead of vegetables. The progenitor of the estate had got his recognition and honours, and as he was the supplier of building materials in his day job, also a more than small fortune.

Steering the Lada defiantly through the wrought iron gates, Mowgley saw that Birchall had other visitors. Two unmarked police cars sat alongside a patrol car with its roof lights flashing, and an ambulance with its back doors open was backed up to one of the three up-and-over doors in a garage which was bigger than many houses in the city below. Near the reproduction Georgian front door with its mandatory brass dolphin knocker, a couple of uniforms were trying to look busy. That meant someone a bit important must be on the premises.

The door was ajar, and as Mowgley pushed it open. He felt an obstacle, pushed harder, then realised he was, as usual, giving his boss grief.

Detective Superintendent Mundy was a large, fleshy man with a face like an aged baby. Now he looked like an angry aged baby. He glared at Mowgley, then at Melons and then at the Lada, then spoke in the thick Northern accent which he maintained scrupulously to show his honest-to-goodness, no-nonsense roots.

"What the fook are you doing here?"

"Good morning." Mowgley thought of saying he had been just about to ask the same question, but decided against it. The Super was obviously in an even worse mood than usual, and Mowgley had been skating on some particularly thin ice of late. So he adopted what he thought of as his respectful but assertive look, nodded at the door and said: "We've come to have a word with Mr Birchall, sir."

"You're a bit fooking late," said Mundy as if Mowgley

should have known, "He's fooking dead."

Seventeen

They watched as two paramedics carried the shrouded figure on a stretcher out of the garage. Whatever Mowgley was going to ask Birchall, it would now not be possible. Instead, he asked Mundy what had happened.

"He's fooking killed hisself," said the angry baby, his accent becoming ever thicker, "What I asked is what you're doing here?"

As they were joined by an anxious-looking C.I.D. Inspector and an even more anxious-looking policewoman, Mowgley explained the relationship between the deceased and the overboard, hoping that Mundy wouldn't ask why he hadn't heard about the ferry boat incident for the best part of a fortnight. Even he was not likely to believe that Mowgley was waiting for the body to turn up before putting in a report.

After listening impatiently to a suitably edited version of the salient details, Mundy screwed up his face like a baby struggling to fill its nappy. His fiery red face then took on the satisfied look of a baby when it has done its business. In Mundy's case, it was because he had solved the case and reached the solution: "That's why he did it, then. Not long married, wife falls off a boat. Nothing to live for so tops himself in the garage."

"Mmm," Mowgley tried to make the noise sound non-committal and agreeable at the same time.

"Right," said his boss brusquely. "Nothing more for you here, then. Back to your little kingdom (it had been Mundy who had bestowed Mowgley's mocking kingship of the ferries on him). Oh, and give me a call tomorrow. I was beginning to think *you'd* fallen off one of your fooking boats."

Not acknowledging but probably enjoying the sycophantic titters of his two acolytes, he turned his back on Mowgley and his sergeant and swept back into the house.

"Well, there you go," said Melons, scowling at one of the uniforms who had had the temerity to smile at her, "case solved."

"Mmm," repeated Mowgley. "Makes you think, though, don't it?"

"Think what – how Gloria manages to keep his job? 'Nothing to live for', my arse."

"No. What it makes me think is why Gloria would turn out for a simple hose-up-the-exhaust-pipe job. He's not known for taking a keen interest in what goes on apart from a photo-opportunity or going on telly to announce a drop in the crime figures."

Melons shrugged: "Perhaps Birchall was in the same lodge and he's just showing a bit of respect. Perhaps he just fancied a run-out. Why should it be any more sinister than that?"

"Because he's a crap actor. All that huffing and puffing and the way he jumped on the excuse I gave him by saying about his wife."

Mowgley rolled a cigarette ruminatively, then asked: "What are you doing tonight?"

"Is that a proposition? If you're at a loose end, why don't you give your Yvonne a bell?"

Mowgley ignored the jibe, and nodded towards the house.

"He's always had a fancy for you, hasn't he?"

Melons looked horrified. "Mundy? You must be joking."

"No. Cyrano."

"Now I know you're joking. Apart from anything else, he's got a conk like a bottle-nosed dolphin." Inspector Cyril Byng had gained his nickname as a result of not only having a rather prominent nose, but of allegedly spending a lot of time trying to insert it in Chief Superintendent Mundy's rectum.

"Well, you know what they say about blokes with big noses."

"No, what do they say about blokes with big noses?"

"That they 'nose' how to make a girl happy, ha ha ha. Anyway, he's not bad looking in a low light or if he don't turn sideways."

Melons groaned. "Then *you* be nice to him."

"I'm not asking you to give him one. Just take him out for a beer and find out what it's all about."

"What do you want me to do, exactly? Go in and ask him if he fancies a date with possibilities of a legover later?"

"I hope you can be a bit more subtle than that. Why not tell him I've gone off in a huff and ask for a lift back. Then suggest a drink and..." Mowgley paused and gave her his puzzled Chinaman look "...what the devil am I doing? You are asking me how to pull a desperate bloke with a huge shonk and bad breath who can only get close to a bird by arresting her?"

Melons lit a cigarette after retrieving her lighter from Mowgley, took a drag and expelled a cloud of smoke. "Well... alright, but there will be a price. Two bottles of gin and four hundred fags next time you go over. Deal?"

Mowgley rolled his eyes theatrically and held his hand to his head. "There you are, typical bloody woman. All that indignation, and when it comes down to it, it's just a matter of price."

Eighteen

Mowgley hated going to see the doctor. Or the dentist, or anyone who was going to tell him how badly he was looking after himself. That also applied to his bank manager. The waiting room at the surgery was always overflowing with sick people, and he inevitably came away feeling worse than when he had arrived.

He took out his baccy tin and stared glumly at the opposite wall. In the old days, his GP had been a real doctor. A tall, naturally dyspeptic type with a pronounced cast in one eye, he had regarded his main function as bullying his patients into getting better. He had never actually said 'pull yourself together' in Mowgley's hearing, but it was obviously what he was thinking when he came out his den and surveyed with obvious distaste those waiting to see him.

Dr Creed had been a hunting and shooting enthusiast, with a row of framed photographs of dogs, a pair of shiny riding boots and a stack of fishing rods permanently on display in his surgery. This was probably, Mowgley thought, as a reminder of what he would much rather be doing and how the patient was preventing him from doing it. On the rare occasions Mowgley had visited him, the routine was unvarying. After looking up irritably at the source of his interruption, he would focus one eye on his unwelcome visitor, nod curtly at a seat in front of the desk and return to his furious scribbling. When Mowgley had been given enough time to reflect on the thoughtlessness of placing a further burden on such a busy man, the doctor would lay down his pen, look across the desk and ask "Now then; what do you think is wrong with you?"

In the twenty years Mowgley visited the practice, Dr Creed had never once volunteered any information about what he thought the problem was or how it could be avoided in the future. He would grunt impatiently as he heard the symptoms, ask a few questions, write a prescription as if he was paying for it personally, then stand up to show the interview was at an end. In other words, he had been a proper doctor.

Now, there were four GPs sharing the practice; they were much younger than Mowgley, and pretended to care deeply about their patients for the twenty minutes they were each allotted. Given the hours they worked, the pressures they were under and the sort of people who came in to plague them, Mowgley thought, they had to be putting on an act.

Instead of Dr Creed's rambling Victorian house with ivy-clad walls and a proper gravel drive which reflected the gravity of its function and his status, the medical 'team' (as it said in the English version of the thirteen languages on the welcome board) operated from a user-friendly, purpose-built and completely soulless square-shaped and single-storeyed building, the reception and waiting area of which looked like the set for a breakfast television programme. And Information Technology reigned unchallenged. The latest addition was a computer screen which was supposed to register your arrival for an appointment. The first time Mowgley had keyed in his initials and date of birth as instructed, the machine had mistaken him for a pregnant eastern European and begun talking to him in Serbo-Croat. The only human contact on entry was a line of permanently irritated women hiding behind the row of computer screens which helped them avoid dealing with the patients. Their main function seemed to be to intimidate patients and do their best to stop them being seen by a doctor for at least the coming calendar month.

Although there must have been at least a dozen dragons working on rota to cause a pall of despondency to settle over the waiting area, they all looked the same to Mowgley. Any visit made him wonder why, of all professions, dentists' and doctors' receptionists were so uniformly charmless and unfriendly. Perhaps it was a scheme to put people off going to see their doctor and saving the NHS money, with special training schemes and a NVQ in sour-faced expressions and unhelpfulness techniques. Or perhaps it was that the women were just irritated by all the sick people and fakers they had to put up with.

As he took a state-of-the-art designer seat which was as uncomfortable as it looked, he thought how the walls of the waiting room were almost as scary as the dragons at the gate. They were covered with posters aimed at alerting people that they might have or could easily catch some really unpleasant disease if they did not mend their ways, and most of which they had previously been unaware. In effect the literally graphic posters also made people who didn't have any of the ailments wonder that they might. When there was no avoiding a visit to the surgery, Mowgley would while away the waiting time by awarding the posters points for illiteracy, overkill and the graphic nature of any illustrations. So far the gloriously full coloured illustrations made the vaginal thrush poster a hands-down winner in its category, though for sheer irrelevance and impenetrability, the one with a red no-go circle informing patients that the surgery was a nuclear free zone was unbeatable. If someone in the Kremlin did press the button, Mowgley wondered, how would the missiles know that they were not allowed to drop on this particular place?

Another difference between then and now was that old Dr Creed and his like had never been judgemental. It was up to the individual how much he abused his health as long as he didn't whinge about the outcome of the self-abuse.

Nowadays, the message seemed to be that you could live forever if you behaved yourself, which made being told you had a terminal illness much more of a shock to the system.

Deep in consideration of this example of the Law of Unintended Consequences, Mowgley absentmindedly rolled and put a cigarette in his mouth. When he lit it, the reaction was more extreme than if he had got his dick out. No flashing lights or sirens went off and nobody made the vampire-repelling sign of a cross at him, but there were audible gasps as the patients on either side of him recoiled in horror and those opposite shrank back in their seats. As he exhaled in her direction, one middle-aged woman got up and ran from the room. She obviously considered the emissions belching from the hundreds of buses, lorries and cars grinding their way in low gear on the main road outside the surgery less of a health risk than his fag smoke. As he realised his mistake, one of the dragons materialised at his side without actually seeming to cross the distance between them. She looked at the fire extinguisher as if considering using it on him then snapped. "I must ask you to put that out immediately; the whole of this building is a smoke-free zone."

Holding his arms aloft in mock surrender, Mowgley stood and headed for the exit door. Funny, he thought as he filled his lungs with cigarette smoke and fossil fuel fumes, I would have thought dragons would have appreciated a bit of smoke.

*   *   *

Instinctively finding the smokiest pub in the area, Mowgley was ordering a pint of Dutch lager from Wales and a Cornish pasty from Dagenham as Melons arrived.

After asking what she was drinking, he emptied his glass and handed it to her. She remained standing at the table.

"How was the doctor - I assume you went to see about having your wallet surgically extracted?"

"Oh, sorry pardon." Mowgley produced a crumpled ten pound note and handed it over. "I didn't get to see him as it happens. I was thrown out for not being ill enough."

"Ah. You don't want to tell me, do you? Has the rash come back?"

"Mind your own bloody business and get the shants in, will you?"

She did, then sat opposite Mowgley and opened a pack of duty-free baby cigars.

They clinked glasses in their accustomed ironic fashion, and she handed over his change before asking: "Tell me something. Why do you always sit with your back to the wall?"

"What do you mean?"

"What I said. Whenever we go in a pub or a caff or anywhere public, you always sit with your back to the wall, facing the door."

"Ah, that's an interesting question."

"That's why I asked it. And?"

Mowgley shifted in his seat, took the top off his beer, and started to roll a cigarette. "Wild Bill Hickok was shot in the back when he changed from his usual seat facing the saloon door. Incidentally, he was playing poker and holding aces and eights, which is why that combination is known as 'dead man's hand'."

"But you don't play cards, and it's hardly likely someone is going to shoot you in the back, is it?"

"Why not?"

"If it was me, I'd want the pleasure of seeing your face when I shot you."

"Ah, but you're a woman, aren't you?"

"Last time I checked. But what's that got to do with it?"

Mowgley made an unsuccessful attempt at a smoke ring and shrugged. "Never mind. To business. How did it go last night?"

"Actually, it wasn't as bad as I thought. Cyrano isn't such a tosser after a few drinks."

"What, you mean when he'd had a few drinks?"

"No. When I'd had a few drinks. Boom boom. What I mean is he's just lonely, clumsy, low on self-esteem and awkward with women. I'm used to handling someone just like that."

"Bloody cheek. So, why were the heavy mob at Birchall's place yesterday?"

"You were right, there is something going on." Melons took a drink, then said: "Birchall was under investigation. The city C.I.D. got a tip-off he'd been up to something murky and were going to have him in for a chat when he topped himself. The cleaner found him in the garage."

Mowgley made a thoughtful face, then asked: "Did you find out who bubbled him?"

"Anonymous. A woman. She said he'd been using clients' money improperly to do property deals."

Suspecting he knew the answer already, Mowgley asked: "Whose money - and for what properties?"

"Our old lady's money. A couple of weeks ago, he lent half a million pounds of her money to a company called Fulcrum Developments. Nobody's heard of them or where they come from."

"That's dodgy, but not necessarily illegal. Didn't he have power of attorney or whatever they call it to look after her financial affairs?"

"Yes, but that's not the point."

"What is?"

"It looks like he lent the old lady's money to the company to buy her own property. The loan was to buy Didcot House and all the land around it."

"How do you know?"

"It's all in here." She took a folder from her briefcase-sized handbag and passed it across the table. "Harry let me take copies of the stuff he had. They think the memo came from the anonymous caller, and the other stuff came from Birchall's safe. The other news is that the poor bastard was in big trouble before all this happened. There was more owed on the house than it's worth, and the flash car was on tick. There was next to nothing in his personal account, and things must have got even worse when he started splashing out on his new wife to keep her happy."

"I know the feeling." Mowgley pushed the ashtray and his glass across the table and opened the file.

The first sheet bore the County Council crest and an extract from a meeting of the planning department. Stapled to it was a discussion document, outlining proposals to grant permission to an application for development of a large country property into eighteen apartments. The property was Didcot House.

"That would make the place worth a few bob more than the buying price, then, but not that big a deal, surely?"

"It gets better than that. They're also talking there about giving permission for fifty to a hundred houses on the land. 'A new village' is what they called it. With full permission, the place would be worth fortunes to the developers. And if the new owners didn't want to develop it themselves, all they would have to do is pass it on to a big building company and make a stonkin' great profit for doing rock-all."

"But what if the planning permission isn't granted?"

"The new owners would be stuck with it. But don't you see, they must have known permission was going to be given. They were on a safe bet."

"How?"

Melons stubbed her cigarette out. "Think about it. Birchall has the access to the old lady's money. She's got pots of it, and he's the only one who knows what's going where at any time. She mostly doesn't know what day of the week it is. On one of his regular visits and while she was lucid, he would have persuaded her it was a good idea to sell and that half a million was a fair price. All he had to do was loan her own money to this company, then they would just have to wait for the application to be approved and permission given and either develop it themselves or sell the package on. As soon as that was done, Birchall would put the money back into the old lady's account. They probably had a buyer lined up..."

"But it all falls to pieces if the buyers were worried that the planning committee would decide to refuse permission."

Melons snorted. "Oh come on. Doesn't it strike you as more than coincidental that Robert Birchall was knocking off his wife's sister, who also happens to be shagging her boss, who's a well bent councillor who happens to be chairman of the planning committee. It was all a set-up."

"Start again and go slowly and be gentle with me. Are you saying that Unsteady Eddie gave Linda Russell the nod about the planning application and she got Birchall to supply the money to this building company so they could get in and buy the place before permission was granted?"

"What do you think?"

"And then they would split the proceeds? But who would get what?"

"Don't know. But you have to admit something very smelly is going on."

Mowgley gave a 'maybe' shrug. "I notice you've carefully left out any reference to what all this has got to do with the late Margaret Birchall."

Melons rose to recharge their glasses.

"Too true. But you're the Great Detective, so start detecting..."

"Alright," said Mowgley on her return and after transferring his cigarette to the hand with his glass in it, then holding up his index finger: "When I do this, you've got to say 'check'."

"Why?"

"Because it's what we used to do when I was a cub and we were going camping and we were checking the kit. And it's what they used to do in mystery films."

"I see," said Melons as if she did not. "Check."

"No, not yet," said Mowgley irritably, "after this." He drew on his cigarette, sipped at his pint, then said: "One: Margaret either didn't know anything about it all, and just got pissed and unlucky."

He waited with his index finger pointing at the ceiling as he looked expectantly at Melons.

"Oh, sorry. Check, but doubtful, I reckon."

Mowgley held up another finger. "Or Two: Margaret didn't know about it but did know about her sister having it off with her husband and got pissed and unlucky, or just wanted out of it."

"Check. That's more like it."

Mowgley held up a third finger, awkwardly taking another swig of beer and puff on his cigarette before continuing: "Or, Three: Margaret found out about either her sister and the dodgy deal or both and was unhappy about either or both, started drinking a lot, and was a threat."

"Now you're getting warmer, I reckon. Oh, sorry: Check." Mowgley held up a fourth finger.

"Or Four: Margaret was in on it and got unhappy and pissed and was a threat."

"So you mean she was pushed rather than jumped or fell? Hmmmm."

Mowgley held up his little finger.

"You didn't say 'check', but never mind. There is of course the possibility that everything I have just said is a load of bollocks and you've got your deductive reasoning all wrong."

Melons made a wry face, then said: "Okay, but you still haven't mentioned why Birchall would go into his garage with a bottle of single malt whisky, a box of pills and a bit of hose pipe."

"I've run out of fingers. But, on the other 'hand' - ha ha ha - you're assuming he was full of remorse about Margaret's death, whether or not he had anything to do with it. Or that he found out that we or rather the C.I.D. were on to him..."

"Or that he didn't put the hosepipe up the exhaust pipe himself."

Mowgley groaned. "Oh shit. This is getting really messy. What else are you thinking?"

"I'm thinking that we have two choices. We either leave it all to C.I.D. and watch them make a nause-up while we get back to worrying about illegal immigrants, smugglers and all those headaches going over for the World Cup in France. Or -"

"Or what?"

"We go for it and risk the Wrath of Mundy."

Mowgley nodded glumly, then yelped and half-stood, his paunch rocking the table.

"What?" said Melons, steadying her glass. "Have you sussed it? Is this the Eureka Moment?"

"No, it's the bloody Pain Moment. I forgot to move me fag and I've burned my sodding fingers something rotten."

Nineteen

The Ferry King lay in his bunk, contemplating the rusty line of rivets above his head. Dawn was breaking over the scrapyard, and light was beginning to seep through the grimy portholes.

It had been a calm night in the basin alongside the ferryport, and the retired lightship had hardly moved at its moorings. Mowgley stuck his nose above the bedcover and sniffed the morning air. George The Dog had also spent a peaceful night on the galley table, and with luck there would be no unpleasant surprises waiting on the cabin decking.

So far, the day was going his way. At least and unlike Robert Birchall, he was still alive. He remembered how, towards the end, his father had said if he woke up breathing in the morning, he felt he had had a result. Of course, if he had not been breathing he would not have woken up, but Mowgley did not like to point that out and spoil the old man's philosophical observation.

He spent a few moments considering what could be called the plus points in his existence, then decided to get up. He had always found that keeping busy was the best way not to think too much and get really depressed.

*   *   *

Outside and in spite of the calm conditions, the submarine

alongside his home seemed to be riding even lower in the water.

Mowgley kicked one of the giant cables lashing the lightship to the rusting U-boat, and immediately wished he hadn't. He couldn't be sure, but the cable appeared to be getting ever more rigid. There was no plimsoll line on his vessel, but the distance between the water and the deck seemed less than when he had moved in. Perhaps it was something to do with the tides. As he picked his way gingerly down the gangplank, a rat emerged from beneath a heap of anchor chain and scurried past him off the lightship on to dry land.

"Oh no," he said aloud, "not you too."

Despite the early hour, Mowgley's landlord was already hard at work with an oxy-acetylene gun, cutting a giant bronze propeller into more manageable chunks. Mowgley stood and watched as Dodger Long leapt nimbly aside to avoid being crushed by a falling blade, then turned the gas off and pushed the mask to the back of his head.

"Some captain is going to be really pissed off when he tries to get out of the harbour this morning," observed the detective, nodding towards the propeller, "and shouldn't you have waited till the Royal Yacht was officially decommissioned?"

Dodger looked at Mowgley to see if he was joking, decided he was, and then led the way into the former naval destroyer gun turret which currently served as his office.

After being assured that the contents were truly no longer in working order, Mowgley took his ease on a crate of decommissioned WWII hand grenades while his host made tea.

Dodger Long was, Mowgley reflected, not a particularly unique character, though time was ensuring there were fewer of them. The city seemed to either make or attract the sort of people who were not frightened to have a go at life and could see an opening where a nice little earner was waiting to be exploited.

Awarded a charter in the 12th Century after Richard the

Lionheart had had a good day boar hunting on his way to crossing the Channel to kill as many infidels as possible, the city had a colourful history. Once the greatest naval port in the Empire, it had become a magnet for those with a good reason to go to sea, and those who figured they could make a good living from them.

Once the city had been known to have more pubs than lamp posts, and in Nelson's day there were said to be more gin and opium houses, gambling dens and brothels in the dock area than the rest of the county. The city had been bombed heavily in the War, and a lot of people had lost their lives and homes and livings. Others had made a lot of money from what came next, and Dodger Long was one of them.

Growing up in a family of ten in a one-bedroomed slum, he had seen the benefits that post-war waste could bring to those with a nimble mind and strong nerve. From the early Fifties, he had quietly collected the redundant bits of armaments that the Admiralty was allegedly anxious to dispose of, and sold them on as scrap or to those with an interest in what they had been built to do. As the years passed he moved on from relatively small items of destruction to bigger ones, and soon he was buying whole ships. The business had developed across the years, and it was now said that Dodger could have equipped a small country with weapons of war, as long as the customers weren't too fussy about their condition and effectiveness and the chance they might damage the users more than the intended victims. As his little empire made more and more undeclarable profits, he had extended his collecting hobby and invested in properties with sitting tenants paying shillings a week in rental. Each time a widow died or a family were shipped out to the new council estate, the house would be repaired and the rent adjusted. Nobody, especially the Internal Revenue, knew how many properties Dodger owned, and it was alleged that he too was ignorant of the extent of the true scale of his portfolio of increasingly valuable terraced houses. Mowgley knew a plumber who had been sent to work on one of Dodger's properties, and on arrival found a car park where the house had been. The owner had simply forgotten that he had sold it to the council and used the money to buy two other houses in the same street.

But it would be a mistake to think that Dodger was careless with his business affairs or money. Mowgley had observed that those with the trick of making big money seemed to have a habit of worrying about the pennies while being adventurous and even unconcerned with the thousands or even millions of pounds. To those who had dealt with him, Dodger was well named. He did not charge Mowgley rental, but the detective paid his dues by turning a blind eye to some of the lorryloads which arrived at the scrapyard, particularly at night. It was an arrangement of mutual benefit.

Also, Mowgley believed, the two men had a sneaking admiration for each other. Mowgley admired his landlord's work ethic, his understanding of human nature and greed, and his knack for making money. Dodger seemed to have an almost protective attitude to Mowgley, as a clever and rapacious man sometimes does for an honest fool.

At least, that's what Melons had said during an unusually intellectual late-night debate after a Two-Shits lock-in at the Ship. More likely, Mowgley said, Dodger thought it a good idea to have a policeman owing him a favour. And it seemed quite a few people in influential positions owed Dodger a favour. To many citizens, it was a mystery how a scrapyard was allowed to remain at the entrance to a city which was going all-out to become what the proposers like to call a Maritime Heritage Tourist Honeypot. Rarely a month went by without someone writing to the paper about the eyesore at the gateway to the city. But Dodger was still in residence. Because of his contacts and past dealings, he also knew a surprising amount of the fine detail of how planning permission was sought and gained, properly or otherwise. This was why Mowgley was consulting him.

Taking the mug of tea and closing his eyes whilst drinking it so as not to see what floated on the surface, he told Dodger as much about the situation with Didcot House as he thought necessary, then took the photocopy from the folder and passed it across a table made from an old cable drum.

"What do you think of that?"

Dodger shrugged and handed it back. "It's a bit of paper from the council."

"Yes, but what do you think about what it says?"

"Are you taking the piss, or what?"

Remembering that his landlord could count better than anyone he knew but had never bothered with a formal education, Mowgley apologised and read the contents out aloud.

Dodger absorbed the information, sniffed, slurped a mouthful of tea and gave his opinion: "It's a load of bollocks, isn't it."

"Why do you say that?"

"It's all wrong. To start with, Barnes is a city councillor, and the application for planning would have been made to the district council. It would have been fuck-all to do with Barnes. He'd have known about it, but he wouldn't have been able to do anything about it. Even Barnsey couldn't have that sorted. Besides, everybody in the city who fancies himself as a property developer has had a pop at getting building permission on that land at one time or another."

"So why would this lot try?"

"Just flying a kite I suppose." Dodger looked thoughtful. "Unless they do know something nobody else does. But I've never heard of them, and I thought I knew everyone in the game."

"But if they did know something and wanted to go through the proper channels, what would normally happen?"

"Nothing's ever normal, especially with this council, but they have to be seen to be playing by the rules. To start with, they'd put in an outline application and proposal which is considered by the planning committee. Whoever has put the application in may have had a deal with the owner to buy the place at the going rate when and if permission is granted, but the price would be very different with permission. Only a total pratt would agree to sell a place at the same price if they knew it was going to get permission, and only a total lunatic would buy a place like that on spec."

"What if they knew it was going to get permission because they'd had the nod from Eddie?"

Dodger pursed his lips, fished something from his cup, looked at it curiously then flicked it away and said: "Eddie Barnes can do a lot of things, but he couldn't swing this unless the whole district committee was in on it. Besides, like I said, they wouldn't give permission whatever the dropsie level was."

"Don't forget they've been told they've got to find space for a lot more houses in the area."

"Doesn't matter. There's all sorts of better places, and besides there's all those fucking trees on the land."

It was Mowgley's turn to look curious: "They can cut 'em down can't they?"

"No, of course not. That's the whole fucking point. It's all classified as ancient woodland. Every tree would have to be identified and listed, and left where it was unless it was real crap. Unless they were planning to have trees growing in the kitchen, it couldn't be done."

"Are you sure?"

"Sure I'm sure. That bit of paper is a come-on. Somebody wanted somebody else to think that something was going to happen for some reason. Why don't you ask whoever it was put together for?"

"I would" said Mowgley, shutting his eyes again as he drained his mug, "but he's a bit hard to get in touch with now..."

Twenty

At the fun factory, the messages on Mowgley's desk indicated that his life was about to become even more complicated.

Chief Superintendent Mundy was almost as anxious to hear from him as his bank manager, and Two-Shits had been on the phone to say that his Jack Russell bitch Mimi had just given birth to a litter of ten really ugly puppies.

"So what does he want from me - a congratulations card?"

"No," said Melons, "he says that George is the father and you are responsible for the puppies."

"How does he know it's down to George?"

"Apart from the resemblance, they're crapping all over the carpet just like George does, so he reckons it must be in their genes."

"Great. Anything else?"

"Yes, I want to know what you're up to. Stephen is muttering about going undercover and special observation duty, whatever he thinks that means. He says he can't tell me because it's all on a need-to-know basis."

Mowgley raised his hands in a placatory manner. "Don't get carried away. The boy's been watching too many cop programmes. I just asked him to keep an eye on Linda Russell."

"Am I allowed to ask why?"

"It's better than having him organise the Lottery pool and loitering around the office. Anyway, it's you who thinks she's up to no good, isn't it?"

"But he hasn't got a clue about obbo work. Why don't you at least let me go with him."

"Can't spare you. You're coming with me to call on the city's favourite councillor."

"Why do you need me?"

"As a witness for a start. Anyway, going by your success with buttering Cyrano up, you can always get your tits out if he won't co-operate. Better than beating it out of him, isn't it?"

Twenty-one

Mowgley ignored the vacant parking spaces and positioned the Lada across the rear of a brand new XJ40, then waited as Melons climbed across the gear stick to exit from the only operable door.

"What was that all about?" she asked as they walked towards the marina.

"What was what all about?"

"Blocking the Jag in."

"I think that's Eddie Barnes's new motor. We don't want him slipping away before we have a word, do we? He's an elusive little rascal, our Eddie."

"But what if it's not his car?"

"It's a brand new Jag, ain't it?"

"So?"

"You wouldn't understand."

"Yes I would. Bloody men..."

*   *   *

"The missus said we'd find you here. Permission to come aboard, Cap'n?" Without waiting for a reply, Mowgley walked up the gangplank to the gleaming deck of the Princess Starline 2000. He had forgotten how flash the boat was, and also that it was called *Wet Dream*.

The owner of the floating gin palace looked past him to

where Melons was standing on the pontoon. "Isn't the lady coming on board?"

"Don't think she would want to come on your boat, Edwardo. Besides, that's no lady, that's my sergeant. It's her turn to wear the high heels today, and I don't want her spoiling your deck."

"Don't worry about that, Jack. I'd rather speak to her than you."

"I'm sure you would, but you'd be wasting your time. She's a raging lesbian." Mowgley smiled and nodded at his sergeant, then shouted: "I was just saying you get a bit seasick."

The two men went into the cabin, and Mowgley watched as the councillor poured drinks from a large and ornate bottle of very expensive single malt scotch whisky. It was strange, he thought, how someone as short and ugly as Eddie Barnes surrounded himself with such beautiful, big things. Or maybe it was not so strange. Perhaps, like a lot of short and not exactly handsome men, he was compensating for his lack of natural attributes and showing he could still win the game of Life. Napoleon and Hitler and the boss of Formula One Racing seemed to have done alright for themselves in spite of their shortcomings. Eddie Barnes had a big beautiful home, a big and once-beautiful wife, a big beautiful car and boat, and spent his spare time trying to shaft every good-looking woman in the city, whatever their size. Psychologists would probably say it was all about compensating for a damaged self-image. Eddie would probably say he just liked shagging and showing people how well he was doing.

Mowgley looked around the cabin of the luxury cruiser, then ran a finger along a gleaming chrome handrail. "Looks like you're still doing alright for yourself, matey."

"Not too bad, Jack." He looked Mowgley up and down, then took a drink. "How about you?"

Mowgley followed his example with the drink, then shrugged. "Can't complain. I've got a boat too, and it's bigger than this one, with more lighting. And a big place in

France."

"Yeah, I heard. I was sorry to hear about Madge."

"Careful Eddie. You sounded like you meant that. Anyway, she calls herself Maggie now. That was another change she made to suit her new image. How's Joanne?"

"Better than nothing. What do you want, Jack?"

"Just coming to an old school friend for advice. Mind if I smoke?"

"If you must and as long as it isn't whacky baccy. I don't want you fitting me up."

"As if." Mowgley got his rolling tin out and opened it, then reached again into his inside pocket and took out a folded piece of paper.

"I wondered if you could tell me about this?"

Barnes took the paper and looked at it. Mowgley made a cigarette, asked for a light then said: "This is where you say you've never seen it before."

Barnes opened a drawer and handed him a book of matches with the name of his boat on the cover. "You're right, I haven't. It's a load of crap."

"You're the second person to say that today."

"Where d'you get it?"

"From a friend of a friend of yours. He's dead, and you're shagging his former sister-in-law. By the way, it looks as if he was shagging her as well. Does Joanne know about her, by the way?"

Barnes took a drink and put the paper on the table between them. "I'm telling you, Jack, I've never seen this before."

"I just knew you were going to say that."

"What do you want me to say?"

Mowgley lit his cigarette for the third time, then held his glass out for a refill. "I just want to know what this is all about, Eddie. Look, I'm stuck with this thing and I never asked for it to be put on my plate. I'm minding my own business and then a woman falls off a boat, and I've got all this shit to handle. So far, I've got a dead solicitor, an old lady being done out of her money and her property, a mickey-mouse memo, a building company that doesn't exist and a boss chewing my balls off. It's not you I'm after, just some help with the answers. How long have we known each other? You must be in the mix somewhere, and I just want to know where and why. Call me naive, but I somehow don't think you would want to be poncing around with this fiddle. You're definitely too smart to drop yourself in it and risk everything you've grafted for in the past. I want you to tell me what's fucking going on. If you're straight with me, that's it. If you ain't, the waves I'll have to make are really going to rock your boat. Am I being unreasonable?"

Barnes looked at his former schoolmate, poured himself another drink, then offered the bottle to Mowgley. "Look Jack, we've known each other for a long time -"

Mowgley did his groan and put his hand to his heart and rocked back on his heels: "Oh *perlease*..."

"Don't take the piss. You know it's fuck-all to do with me, don't you? I helped Linda Russell get a job, and she came on to me. I never started it."

"You sound just like the President of the United States. Next you'll be telling me you never had sex with that woman..."

"Fuck off. Anyway, I gave her the elbow weeks ago. She's too dangerous."

"What do you mean?"

"She started it all, and the funny thing is she seemed to want to drop me in it and shit in her own chips. She spread it around the office that we were having it off and even took me round to meet Birchall, It was like she was showing me off to him. I thought she was just trying to make him jealous or something, but there was more to it than that. She wanted something out of me and she got it."

Mowgley snuffled. "Are you telling me you feel used?"

"You know what I mean. As you said, do you really think I'd risk everything for a bit of cunt?"

Mowgley emptied his glass and stood up.

"No Eddie," he said thoughtfully, "I don't think you would."

"What was all that about? Why did you bring me if you didn't want me to go on board? What are you playing at?"

"Calm down, calm down. All will become clear. Just trust me."

"That's what people who are going to stitch you up always say."

They had reached the row of shops and restaurants alongside the marina, and Mowgley gestured at an empty table outside a shopfront which was busily pretending to be what people mistakenly thought the outside of a continental café bar would or should look like.

They sat looking at the huge menu cards and trying to stop them taking flight on the inshore breeze, then Mowgley said. "I thought it said 'coffee' on the window?"

"It does."

"But there's nothing about coffee on the menu."

"You are in a stroppy mood, aren't you? You know very well its on the list under 'Your Coffee Experience'. You can have mocha, latte, skinny latte -"

"There you are, then" said Mowgley triumphantly. "What do you ask for if you just want a cup of black coffee? Not espresso or in a cafeteria thingy - just a cup of bloody coffee. In a proper coffee cup, not a gallon mug?"

"I knew it. You just wanted to sit here so you could work yourself up into a frenzy and have a rant, didn't you?" Melons looked up, saw the waitress approaching and hauled Mowgley to his feet. "Come on, let's get out of here."

"Why, what's the matter? Where are you taking me?"

Melons steered Mowgley away from the table, across the boardwalk and towards the car park. "I am not in the mood for one of your confrontations, and that poor girl certainly doesn't deserve it. At least I get paid for you giving me grief. We are going to the Leopard for a pint and a pie, and you can tell me all about what your old school chum has been up to."

Three pints and two pastys later, and Mowgley was in a more benign mood. He had reported fairly faithfully the content of his conversation with Eddie Barnes, and they were now in the Lada and proceeding towards the city's main shopping centre.

Though the boundaries had long been overrun, the teeming city was made up of a dozen former villages. When Mowgley was a kid, each area would have streets of proper shops. If you wanted a pair of shoes, you went to a shoeshop, and if you wanted a beer at home you took the bathroom jug to the bottle and jug of the nearest pub. With a local on virtually every corner, you did not have to walk too far. In those days there were butchers' shops selling only pork products and wet fish shops with their stock on show laying on platforms of crushed ice. No salmon or trout, but you could always get a good bloater or a handful of sprats for a few coppers. Nowadays, punters bought all their food and a lot more from out-of-town supermarkets, and visited the vast, bland Fountain Mall for fancy goods and to worship at the altar of consumerism while they drooled over all the things they could not afford and did not need.

In the Seventies and before the cathedral of glass and steel had been conceived, the brave new world of shopping had taken the form of a gaunt and towering block of prefabricated concrete. Local legend claimed the project had been dreamed up and proposed as a spoof during the council Christmas party. Others said the monstrous edifice was a cover for a series of nuclear-proof bunkers earmarked for the city leaders if it all kicked off. Whatever the truth, the blackened slab-sided warren of commercial units topped with a multi-storey car park had won the title of Ugliest Building in Britain on several occasions, and that was against some pretty stiff competition.

But Mowgley, like many locals, felt somehow protective

of it. As with the football team, it was alright for the natives to criticise the monstrosity, but disparaging comments from outsiders were not welcome.

"So what are we doing here?" asked Melons as Mowgley pulled up outside a shop which seemed not to have changed its window display since opening for business in 1975.

"I just need to pick some things up." Mowgley passed her the keys as he began negotiating with the driver's door-locking system.

"What sort of things?"

"Umm, a new shirt."

"What's wrong with the old one? You seem to like it, and how are you going to get it off?"

"Very droll." Mowgley heaved himself out of the car and smiled at an approaching traffic warden.

"Come on, what's going on?"

"I'm going out tonight, that's all."

"You've got a date, haven't you?"

"If you must know, I'm just taking someone to dinner."

"'Taking someone to dinner?' You haven't taken *yourself* to dinner for as long as I've known you. People like you don't do dinner. You go for a curry when you're pissed enough not to taste it. You're going out with the witness, aren't you?"

Without waiting for an answer, Melons climbed from the Lada, tossing Mowgley the keys as the traffic warden arrived.

"You don't think I'd let you choose a pair of socks, do you? You wait and be nice to the warden, and I'll pick up some shirts - and some underwear in case you get lucky..."

Twenty-two

"That's a nasty rash on your neck."

"No," said Mowgley defensively. "It's just where my tie's a bit tight."

"For some reason, you don't look like a tie person to me. I rather liked that cowboy stringy thing you wore last time, though."

Yvonne McLaughlin smiled, leaned across the table and tweaked the knot, then patted his shirt front. "Is all this new?" she asked. "If so, I'm flattered."

"No, I buy a new tie and shirt every few years or so whether I need them or not. Is your fish alright?"

"Yes, it's fine. How about yours - are you getting along with the bones okay?"

Mowgley thought about bluffing it out, then came clean: "Not really. The prices they charge here, and you have to fillet the bloody thing yourself."

"Would you like me to help?" Without waiting for a reply, she reached over and took his plate. "I enjoy doing it and showing off, to be honest."

He watched as she deftly wielded her knife, removed the bones and put them in a neat pile on the side of the plate.

"Bloody hell, you've done that before. I wouldn't like to get on the wrong side of you in the kitchen."

"I'm a farmer, remember? We see meat before it's put

into little plastic bags and labelled, and I would often do a bit of amateur butchery at home. It's mostly just a knack with this sort of thing and I love fish. But what about you?"

Mowgley glared at a couple on the next table who were looking across and smiling as he took his plate back. Then he regarded the small but very expensive fish glumly and sighed. She reached out and placed a hand on his.

"Would you rather have something else?"

"I don't think they do a chicken phal here. To be honest, I'd rather be somewhere else than have something else."

"Thanks very much."

"No, I mean this place is not really my style. I'm more of a curry man. I don't like paying ten times what the food cost just to have some waiter make me feel like a pratt because I won't pretend to like sun-dried tomatoes."

"Actually, sun-dried tomatoes are off the menu in posh restaurants now. They fell out of fashion years ago."

Being careful not to dislodge her hand, Mowgley laid down the fish knife as he could feel himself going into rant mode. Predictably he ignored the warning signs. "That's exactly what I mean. What I can't understand is how food can be in or out of bloody fashion. Ten years ago, all those poncy telly cooks were telling us that we had to eat *nouvelle cuisine* and they spent most of their time apologising to the world for English cooking. Now they've done every possible bloody programme about the grub from every other country, they've started bollocking us about not appreciating traditional English cooking and acting like they invented steak and kidney pudding. Can you bloody believe that? And another thing, why are they all so bloody thin?"

"Who?"

"These celebrity chefs. If they really like food as much as they crack on about it, they couldn't stop themselves eating it, could they? Look at the way they get an erection when they taste their own cooking. How come they're not eating all day and looking really fat like proper cooks?"

"I take it you don't like foodies then?"

"I don't like bullshit and hypocrisy."

She smiled, took a sip of wine and said: "You're not telling me that in your job and at your age you haven't already realised we're all hypocrites to some extent?"

Mowgley took a swig from his glass, scowled at the waiter as he attempted to approach, then continued: "Some are worse than others."

"Anything else you don't like while we're on the subject? Authority, perhaps? I can see you as a rebel with a cause."

"We have to have authority. It's just that the wrong people always have it."

"But what about you?"

"Me?"

"You're the ultimate authority figure, surely? A policeman. Are you telling me you never abuse your authority? Parking on double yellow lines, say? Or do you despise those above you just because they *are* above you?"

Mowgley made a defensive face and summoned another bottle of wine. "This is all getting a bit intellectual. I thought you were a farmer's wife."

"That doesn't mean I don't have a brain and enjoy using it. And don't change the subject. What about your actions. Don't you make people unhappy when you use your authority?"

"Only when they deserve it."

"Ahah." She paused as the waiter arrived at her side and poured wine into her glass. As he moved around the table, Mowgley reached and took hold of the bottle. For a moment, it looked as if the waiter was going to say something, then he let go of the bottle and left.

"There you are," she said, "you just used or some would say abused your authority by having a go at the waiter. He's only doing his job."

"Nobody forced him to take the job. Anyway, most waiters are worse snobs than the people who employ them. I can't see why he thinks he's better than me just because he can make a swan out of a napkin. Besides, he's not hovering around and topping us up all the time because he likes us. I bet you he's told to do it by the management so we'll drink more and they can charge fourteen quid for something you could buy in Bottoms Up for under a fiver."

"It could be that he really is just doing his job. Which is what you would probably say when you arrest somebody who dares to bring a few bottles of that wine back from France."

"No, that's the Customs. I bring loads of wine and baccy back from France all the time. If our government chooses to screw the tax up on small pleasures, why shouldn't people look elsewhere for a better price? That's what they do with supermarkets or buying a sofa. Anyway, I don't get involved with small stuff at the ferryport that doesn't do anyone any harm. I try and keep my job simple and do my best to keep a lid on things. I just don't like people who take advantage of other people."

She raised her glass and looked at him thoughtfully over the rim. "Everybody takes advantage of somebody else. It's called survival. People who can't live with that fact usually go and live in a monastery, which I can't see you doing."

Mowgley realised he had been talking too much. "You seem to have me in a box and all sorted out. What about your views on human nature, crime and punishment and all that?"

"Oh, I'm very simple in my views." She looked at his plate, then up at him and said: "Would you rather leave that and find a curry shop?"

"Not really, After all that work on the fish, you could say I'm fed up with eating - ha ha ha."

Yvonne smiled. "Why do you do that?"

"What?"

"Say 'ha ha ha' in a very forced way when you've made a terrible pun. Is it the verbal equivalent of a nervous tic, or to let people know you've made a gag in case they didn't notice?"

"Hang on a tick and I'll let you know - ha ha ha. Oh shit, there I go again." He looked at her empty glass, then said: "How about another drink?"

"How about another drink at my place?"

"Are you sure?"

She reached out and laid her hand on his again. "Just as long as you promise not to do any tap dancing, ha ha ha. But before we go any further, I have to ask you what those tattoos mean."

He looked down at the faded letters on the fingers of his right hand: "Erm, what do you mean 'what do they mean'?"

"I mean what do the letters stand for?"

"It was sort of the motto of a club I belonged to when I was a kid."

"And what was the motto?"

Mowgley rubbed the fingers of his right hand as if trying to erase the marks. "I think it was 'Anyone Can Be Best' It was an inspirational sort of thing."

"Oh." She looked at him levelly, then said: "But surely, the acronym wouldn't be ACAB? Where I come from, ACAB stands for 'All Coppers Are Bastards.'"

"Ah. Well yes, I had heard that."

"It must have made it awkward when you wanted to join the police."

For the second time that evening, Mowgley decided to come clean: "To tell you the truth, it happened after I joined the police. The evening of the day I got the job, my mates took me out for a celebration, then when I was totally legless they took me to the local tattoo parlour."

"Some mates."

"It worked out alright - I nicked them all when I was on the beat."

"Really?"

"No, not really."

Twenty-three

"Hello stranger."

"That's a funny thing to say, considering I saw you yesterday afternoon. Is that a mark of how much you miss me when I'm not around? Just think what it'll be like when I'm gone forever and you'll bitterly regret all those cruel and hurtful things you've said to me."

Melons yawned and toyed with her first cigarette of the day. "Yeah, whatever."

"Is that the way to speak to a superior officer in the Modern Force? What's up - got the painters in? Now come and sit down and be nice or I'll report you to the Head of PC for using unseemly and inappropriate language to a colleague."

At just before nine in the morning, The Ship Leopard was not officially open, but a dozen ferryport regulars were taking advantage of the facilities. Mowgley was on 3 Across, and in a comparatively good mood. This was comparative to his usual mood at a time when he considered the mean streets of his fiefdom were not yet properly aired. His good mood was partly due to it being a good crossword day, and because he was on his second coffee and calvados. This was one of the few French traditions he thought worth absorbing into British national culture.

Melons sat down opposite him and twisted the paper

round so she could see the clues, and Mowgley handed her the pen and rose to get her a *café-calva*.

"You see, you *have* changed."

He paused and looked back at her. "What are you on about?"

"A week ago you would have gone spare if I moved your paper. Now you hand me the pen. *And* you're going to get my drink instead of sending me or shouting at Two-Shites. It's the new you."

Mowgley smiled indulgently. He liked the way she used what she considered a slightly less vulgar term for their landlord, achieved by simply adding an 'e' and changing the pronunciation.

"Very ladylike."

"What is?"

"Nothing. But what's this about the new me?"

"Since you've been having a regular legover with your Scotch lassie, you've been a much nicer person to know. Mind you, that wouldn't be hard. Everyone's talking about it."

"It's Scots. Scotch is the drink." Then and in spite of himself. "Who's 'everybody'?"

"Just about everyone in the office, Two-Shites... even Dodger Long."

"When have you been talking to Dodger Long?"

"A couple of days ago. I called in to see you, and he said how happy you seemed, especially since you've started sleeping elsewhere most nights."

Mowgley opened his mouth, then decided against going on the defensive and simply said: "I'll get your shant."

*   *   *

An hour later, the Ship Leopard was beginning to fill up, and they were half way through the crossword. Mowgley looked at his watch and put the pen down.

"I suppose we'd better get off to the inquest. Last chance to change your bet. Do you want to swap with me?"

"No thanks, I'll stick with DBM."

"Remind me, what are the other runners and riders?"

"You've got Open, Quayle's got Suicide While The Balance Of The Mind, and Jo got Murder by Person or Persons Unknown."

"And who got the joker and drew Abducted By Aliens?"

"Stephen."

"There's a surprise. How's he getting on with his obbo on Linda Russell, by the way?"

"I spoke to him yesterday, and he said she's doing nothing. She just goes to work and comes back."

"She's not seeing Eddie or anyone else, then?"

"No. Why are you getting Stephen to waste his time like that, anyway?"

"Two reasons. It'll show him how bloody mind-numbingly boring it is to be on obbo. It will also keep him out of our hair in case his dad is sniffing around."

"So what are you going to do if it's Death By Misadventure?"

"Touch you for a tenner to see me through the week, I reckon. Apart from that, don't know. What's the situation with Fulcrum Developments and the Birchall enquiry?"

"Dickie's working on tracking the account. It's not a limited company so nothing at Companies House and no sign of any accounts or tax returns."

"Not even VAT returns?"

"Nope."

"Hmm." Mowgley drained his coffee cup and considered whether they had time to slip in another calvados, then decided against it and put his cup noisily back in its saucer. "So they're not exactly in a big way of business. What about Mr Birchall, the late and apparently unlamented lawyer - have you got a progress report from Cyrano?"

"No chance there. He wouldn't take my calls, so I went to see him and he nearly shat himself."

"Why?"

"He said that Mundy found out that we'd had a drink

and gave him a real bollocking."

"So why would Mundy worry about you having a beer with or weaselling anything out of his toady?"

"Dunno. According to Cyrano, Mundy just doesn't want anybody interfering. It's the usual thing. He wants all the credit until something goes wrong, then he'll be looking for someone to blame."

"When's the Birchall inquest?"

"Don't know that either; Cyrano either didn't have a date or didn't want to tell me."

"Hmm." Mowgley looked regretfully at his empty cup, then stood. "So, as the big fat lady with the small potty said, not a lot to go on, then? Hahahah."

Melons yawned: "So what are we going to do, then? Can't we bring Linda Russell in after the inquest?"

"What do you suggest we charge her with - shagging a person of diminished stature and in possession of an ugly face for personal gain? Suspicion of stealing a letterhead from her employer? Or going on Mundy the Younger's evidence, *not* getting up to no good?"

"But we know there's something iffy going on."

"True, but it's none of our business, according to Gloria."

"When has that ever stopped you?"

"Also true." Mowgley folded and put the newspaper in his pocket. "Come on, I want to see who's won the office sweep."

*   *   *

Borrowing a coin from his colleague, Mowgley broke a general principle and bought a parking ticket.

As they walked to the courtroom, Melons pointed to a new and very shiny Renault next to the barrier of the car park. "That's Linda Russell's motor."

"Well spotted. But where's Young Stephen's? She probably gave him a lift in. I expect he's sitting next to her outside the bloody courtroom."

In the hall outside court number two, there was in fact no sign of Mundy, either close to or distant from his observation target. Mowgley nodded neutrally at where Linda Russell, looking as shiny and expensive as her car, stood talking down to an usher. She half-smiled then looked away. Near the door to the toilets and looking as if he would much rather be on the high seas, Mowgley recognised the French ferry boat steward.

As he continued to look around the marble-floored auditorium, Melons nudged Mowgley in the ribs: "Don't look now - but here comes Aberdeen Angela. Sorry, I mean your significant other."

Mowgley considered reacting, thought better of it, smiled awkwardly at Yvonne McLaughlin and went for a smoke in the toilets.

*   *   *

"Thank you *very* much." Melons took the envelope containing the office sweepstake money from Mowgley, opened it and began counting.

"Have you no sense of decorum, dignity or any other words beginning with 'd' which would suit the occasion?" asked Mowgley.

"I just wanted to check it's all there," said Melons defensively. "I told you it would be Death By Misadventure. By the way, you owe me a fiver for the side bet that Old Mundy would be here."

"No. If you remember, it was me who said he *wouldn't* be here."

"You didn't."

"I did."

"Didn't."

"Bloody did. And no returns."

Melons waved the banknotes in Mowgley's face and said: "I'm not going to bother to argue. I won and you didn't."

"But you just did."

"What?"

"Bother to argue."

"No I didn't."

"Yes you did."

Melons held a hand up again. "Do you realise how childish you're being? A senior police officer, standing on the steps of a Coroner's court after an inquest and having a tantrum to make sure he gets the last word as usual."

"You started it."

"No I bloody -" Melons paused, groaned and then: "Alright. I did."

"I knew you'd see sense eventually. And it was agreed that the winner would buy the loser a good drink out of the proceeds, remember."

"No it wasn't... oh, alright, yes it was."

*   *   *

They stood outside and watched as the witnesses and officials filed out of the building and into the wintry sunshine.

"Have you noticed how people at funerals and inquests react in the same way?" observed Mowgley "They always hang about awkwardly as if they're anxious to leave but don't want to be seen to dash off."

"Usually that's true, but not so with the grieving sister." Melons nodded to where Linda Russell was hurrying away towards the car park. "What did you think of her performance?"

"Excellent. Just the right degree of controlled grief. And she dressed rather well for it."

"Ah," said Melons, nodding towards the doors, "You'll probably want to have an intimate conversation with the chief witness, who I thought also did an excellent job. Came over as a bit of a cold fish, I thought. Perhaps she has hidden depths and deep passions when dealing with great stupid lumps of beef, though. The cows, I mean, of course."

She left before Mowgley could respond, and he smiled

awkwardly again as Yvonne McLaughlin arrived at his side.

"How did I do? Did your coaching work?"

"You were very good. Even better than I thought. Very clear and factual."

"Do you really think what the witnesses say can make all that difference?"

"Absolutely. Together with what the sister had to say, you left him with nothing to make his mind up about."

"What do you mean?"

"Think about it. The Coroner wasn't there at the scene and doesn't know anything about the dead person. He wants whatever facts there are, and the witnesses to point him in the right direction. He's trying to get a clear and accurate picture as to what really happened and why. What he comes up with will make all the difference to whether it goes any further or if everyone goes home and gets on with their lives. Sometimes it can involve a lot of money and pain for lots of people. At the end of it all, the Coroner's got to make his mind up, using a mixture of experience and intuition. People have literally got away with fortunes and sometimes murder because of a Coroner's verdict. In this case, what you and the overboard's sister had to say made his mind up for him."

She reached out and took the cigarette he had just rolled, and waited for him to light it. "Do you think he made the right decision?"

Mowgley shrugged and nearly lost the contents of his baccy tin.

"Who knows what goes on in people's minds and what really happens when you're not there and don't really know what went on before. If you hadn't have been around at exactly the right time, it would probably have been left as an Open verdict."

"And what would that have meant?"

"That the Coroner wasn't prepared to make his mind up on the evidence available. It could have been an accident or suicide. Or even murder."

"Murder? But that would have meant that I was under

suspicion, wouldn't it?"

"Probably. Then it would have been my bounden duty to pursue you relentlessly until I got my man - or in this case, my woman."

She looked at him as if she was not sure if he was joking and moved a little closer. "Is that why you've really been seeing me? Did you think - do you still think - that I shoved her over the side?"

He gave a modified shrug. "Not a lot of point unless you had something to gain by it. Or perhaps you just didn't like her hair style..."

"You still haven't answered my question."

"Which one?"

"About why you've been seeing me."

"Do I really need to answer that?"

"Perhaps not." She reached out and touched his arm. "I just wanted you to know that I've really enjoyed it. Underneath and for all your assumed misanthropy, I think you are a good and caring man. Perhaps you care a bit too much."

Mowgley lit his roll-up, sucked hard and let out a gust of smoke. "Are you giving me the brush-off now that the inquest's over and you've done your bit?"

"No, not at all. I thought it might be the other way round."

"No, and to prove it - what are you doing tonight?"

"Why don't you give me a call?"

"I will. Where would you like to go?"

"To a nice country pub with a real log fire. Or somewhere looking out over the sea. Anywhere except the Ship Leopard or the Midnight Tindaloo."

"What about the Dogs?"

"What dogs? Has George got hitched?"

"I meant *the* Dogs. What about a night of sophisticated splendour at the greyhound stadium?"

"That sounds exciting; I've never been to the dogs."

"I've been going to them for years."

"Ha-ha-ha." She reached out and touched his arm

again. "I suppose I'd better not kiss you?"

"Better not. I might be accused of interfering with a witness."

"Anytime." She looked up at him for what seemed a long moment, then turned away. "Take care of yourself, Jack. Catch you later."

"Yes" he said to himself as he watched her walk away, "I'll catch you later."

*   *   *

"That's funny."

"What is?"

Melons nodded at the empty space next to the car park barrier.

"Linda Russell's gone, but still no sign of Stephen or his car. And unless he's getting very good at undercover work, he wasn't outside the courtroom, waiting for her."

"He could have been that hippy selling copies of *The Big Issue*. Or that bird on the game by the steps. Or more likely, perhaps he's been watching the wrong person for the past week."

"No seriously, I've got a funny feeling about this. I tried his mobile while you were talking to your... friend. No answer again. He's very fussy about keeping it with him."

"So what do you want to do about it?"

"Don't know. You're the boss. But I'm starting to get really worried..."

Twenty-four

Detective Constable Stephen Mundy's car was parked neatly in the long-stay car park at the marina village, but there was no sign of its owner. Mowgley noted that the mooring for Eddie Barnes's luxury cruiser was empty. The *Wet Dream* had gone.

"What do you think?" asked Melons.

"I think we should stroll along to Pathetic Heights and call on Miss Russell," said Mowgley.

*   *   *

"What's our excuse?" Melons rang the bell again, and Mowgley winced as the opening bars of 'A Life on the Ocean Wave' wafted through the door.

"Well, we could try the old 'we just wanted to thank you for attending the inquest' ploy, or we could just come straight out with it and ask her if she's seen our undercover detective. She's probably got a better idea of where he is than he does."

Mowgley gritted his teeth and pressed the bell-push again. The tune had changed to the main refrain of 'What shall we do with the Drunken Sailor'.

Melons looked along the corridor, then said: "What about getting in for a look around if she's not here?"

"Kick the door down and effect an entry, you mean?"

"I've got my credit card."

"What for - to pay for the damage? Have you ever tried opening a locked door with a credit card?"

"No, but I've seen it on the telly."

Mowgley looked to see if she was serious and tried the bell again. This time it was a hornpipe.

"I thought you said she had style," said Melons.

"It's not her fault. She only rents the place."

As they waited, Melons took her mobile phone from her handbag and pressed the recall button. "Probably get a good signal up here" she said as Mowgley began to walk towards the lift. "It's ringing."

"Big deal. So what?"

"It may be a coincidence - but so's the phone in her flat."

They looked at each other, then Melons pressed the stop button. The fluting tone coming faintly through the door stopped. She pressed the recall button, and, after a pause, it started again.

"Have you got that credit card?" Mowgley held his hand out. "Thanks," he said, "mine's over the limit."

Slipping the card into his pocket, he stood back and kicked the door very hard.

"Shit." He massaged his foot, then tried again.

"Try kicking it near the lock instead of in the middle," said Melons encouragingly.

Mowgley kicked out again, and the door crashed open.

"How did you know?" he asked as he limped across the threshold.

"I've seen it on the telly."

*   *   *

In the lounge, they found Stephen Mundy's phone in his jacket, which was draped across the back of a chair. His trousers were on the floor. On the table were an empty wine bottle and two glasses.

"Well," observed Mowgley, picking up a man's shoe, "he

can't have gone far. But she's done a runner."

"How do you know?"

"All the bits and bobs have gone. There were some pictures over there. Like this -" He reached into his coat and pulled out the photograph of Linda Russell with Eddie Barnes. "I thought it might come in handy, somehow," he said defensively, "I borrowed it on my last visit."

"Never mind the fucking photograph," said Melons sharply, "what about Stephen?"

"Mind your fucking language if you please, and I haven't got a photograph of him," said Mowgley mildly, "I know what he looks like, though."

"You bastard. What if he's..."

"Run off with her and Eddie to be their cabin boy? Streaking around the marina? Trying to beat the record for swimming to the Isle of Wight whilst pissed? Don't panic. Just listen." He pointed at the door to a bedroom, from where a regular thumping noise could faintly be heard.

"From my limited experience in these matters that's a bed head hitting the wall," observed Mowgley. "You wait here, Sergeant. Whatever he's doing, he's probably doing it on his own, and we don't want to embarrass the boy, do we?"

*   *   *

Mowgley looked glumly at his glass, then observed: "Nearly three quid for a pint. No wonder they call this place Happy Jack's. At these prices, the owner must be fucking delirious. Do you realise, all these people are sitting in a shop unit pretending to be a waterside bar in New Orleans on a former rubbish tip pretending to be a Californian marina and paying loads of money for the pleasure when they could get exactly the same thing for half the price at Two-Shit's. People are funny, aren't they?"

"I've just called his office, and Eddie's there."

"I think that's what's called a non-sequitur" observed Mowgley. "I don't know what a sequitur is, though."

"I'm sorry, sir." Stephen Mundy looked as if he were about to cry.

"Don't worry, lad." Mowgley patted the young detective's freshly-clad knee. "I bet you not one person in a thousand knows what a sequitur is. It's never come up in the Telegraph crossword, and I've been doing it for nigh-on twenty years. I bet there's professors of English who couldn't tell you what a sequitur is."

"You know what he means," said Melons sharply.

"Yes," agreed Mowgley, "I know what he means."

They had found the young constable spread-eagled naked on the bed, his arms and legs tied to the uprights in each corner with black pure silk stockings, and a pair of crutchless knickers over his head.

"What I want to know," said Mowgley, after taking a deep draught of his Export Strength Premium Lager Beer, "...is why you kept your socks on?"

"She said she wanted to play a game," Mundy answered miserably.

"What, you mean like Monopoly or Scrabble?"

The constable looked at Melons for support, then persevered.

"She came up to me while I was sitting in the car yesterday evening and asked if I could help. She said she couldn't make the key to her flat work. I didn't like to say no, and she'd already seen me anyway. So I went up with her and it went in easily."

"I expect it did, hahahha."

"She asked me if I'd like a drink," continued Mundy, "and I thought it would be a good way of finding things out about her. One thing led to another and she said she liked to tie people up and be on top, so I went in to the bedroom and -"

"And she tied you up," Mowgley said encouragingly. "Yes, we guessed that, but can you cut to the chase? What we really want to know is, what happened then?"

"She pulled my underpants down and-"

"Yes, yes." Mowgley ignored his sergeant's glare, lolled

his tongue out and rolled his eyes theatrically. "And what happened then?"

Mundy looked even more miserable: "She laughed and said she didn't like cocktail sausages. Then she left. She said she'd phone you in a couple of days if she remembered."

"Bloody cow." Melons looked at Mowgley. "What are we going to do now?"

"Have another drink. You've called her car and description in to the fun factory and other appropriate locations?"

"Of course. At least we've got something to charge her with now."

"What's that - not liking cocktail sausages?"

She sighed wearily, then handed her glass and a ten pound note to Mundy. "Get the drinks in, Stephen."

As the young detective left, she said: "Can you be serious for a moment? I know you're trying to make him feel better with a bit of manly ribbing, but where does all this leave us?"

"In the shit, basically. But as you said, we've got something to charge her with now. As soon as Quayle comes up with the details on Fulcrum Developments, we may have something more." He narrowed his eyes, put on his execrable Humphrey Bogart voice, and drawled: "But that's about it, blue eyes. That's all she wrote."

"So run it all past me again. We've got a woman going overboard and a verdict of Death By Misadventure. We've then got her husband committing suicide."

"Apparently."

"Apparently: Gloria says it was because of grief, but he would say that just to keep us out of what was really going on. We think It's more likely Birchall killed himself - if he did kill himself - because he was being investigated for lending a client's money to a development company we don't know anything about to buy the client's property, both without her knowledge. His wife could have jumped over the rail because she knew what had been going on and her lovely new lifestyle was all going to fall to bits shortly. At least, that's what I think we think, don't we?"

Mowgley made one of his Chinese faces. "He might have done himself in for both reasons."

"What do you mean? His wife going over the side might have been the final straw?"

"His wife going over the side might have been the worst thing that could have happened, or the best."

"You think she was involved in it in some way?"

"Maybe, baby."

Melons lit a cigarette, handed the tin back to Mowgley, and continued: "Anyway, we know - or we think we know - that the sister was involved in it all in some way or another. She was knocking off with Birchall -"

"Probably." Said Mowgley mildly.

"After catching her in her nightie coming down the stairs at his place, I would say more than probably. Linda Russell was also knocking off with Eddie Barnes, and she worked for him and the council and was the best person to have got hold of that memo about planning permission for the property which you say was definitely a fake."

She paused for approval and Mowgley nodded gravely. "Correct."

"Now she's done a runner."

"Also correct."

"But if she's behind it all, why would she run for it now; why wait until after the inquest if she was going to go anyway?"

Mowgley stroked an imaginary beard: "Pay attention, child, and I will mark your card. If she'd not turned up for the inquest it would have looked very dodgy and we would have had something to go after her for. The Coroner would probably also have adjourned the sitting or come up with another verdict if she did anything to stir it up and give us a reason for digging deeper. She would have been worried when she found the photograph gone after my visit. That's one of the reasons I took it. When she saw Young Gloria hanging about, she'd have been even more worried. I think she was waiting for something to happen here quite apart from the inquest, and whatever it was has happened, and she was free to go. The photograph missing and Stephen hanging about just made her mind up for her a bit quicker."

"That's why you put Stephen on to it, wasn't it. You knew she'd suss him and that it would make something happen. You crafty bastard."

Mowgley stroked his imaginary beard again and nodded as if in scholarly acceptance of high praise: "That's why I always finish the crossword before you. To get the answer, you have to understand the question, and the person setting it."

"So what *is* the answer?"

Mowgley looked up as Mundy returned with the drinks, gave a restrained shrug, then said: "I don't have a fucking clue. Yet. But we're getting there, aren't we? I think we can all agree that the game is most definitely afoot." He took his drink from Mundy, then said: "About time too, young'un."

"Sorry sir, there was a crowd at the bar. And I had to wait for the barman who's doing our tab on your credit card."

Melons looked sharply at her superior: "I thought you said your card was duff."

"Elementary, my dear Watson. I gave him yours."

Twenty-five

For the second time that day, Mowgley waited at a front door. At least, he thought, the bell on this one had an unirritating if unimaginative buzz. He pressed the button again and looked at his watch. Yvonne had said just after eight, and he was only an hour late.

"Hello? Did you know she's gone?"

An elderly woman was waving her stick at him from the forecourt of the house next door. There was a Neighbourhood Watch sticker in the bay window and a slight gap between the net curtains. She had obviously been on obbo.

"Beg pardon?"

"She left just after lunch."

"I see. Did she say when she'd be back?"

"Oh I don't think she'll be back, young man." This prediction seemed to give the old woman a degree of satisfaction. "The taxi-driver took a lot of bags out. And all her personal things have gone from the front room. She was only renting. Only passing through, you know."

"Yes," said Mowgley, "I knew."

* * *

"Ah, that's it. Got her. Sorry about the delay; she wasn't one of my customers, originally."

Mowgley looked over the young man's shoulder at the screen as Yvonne's name appeared in the top left hand corner. Fingers fluttered over the keyboard and a row of figures and symbols appeared. "Yes, she's been with us for just over six months. She took the lease for a year. The owner's a jolly jack tar and never seems to live there. I expect he's buying the place for the future and letting it out to pay the mortgage. We get a lot of that. It's not strictly in agreement with the mortgage company's requirements, but nobody seems to take any notice nowadays, as long as the payments keep coming." The man smiled archly over his shoulder at Mowgley. "But I don't suppose you're going to arrest him or me for that, are you, Inspector? If you do, I promise to come quietly."

Mowgley scowled and instinctively stepped away from his close proximity to the man's tightly sheathed buttocks. He also made his voice deeper when he asked: "What about another address for her?"

After more fluttering on the keyboard, the man straightened up and shook his head. "Can't help with that. Apart from the owner's details there's nothing but her name and the banking record. Are you sure she's actually gone? She's a month in advance, and there's her security deposit and no instructions on her leaving. Perhaps she's just gone away somewhere for a break or something."

"What about references? Surely you must have taken some details about her when she wanted to rent the house?"

"Of course, but, as I said, she's not one of my customers. I've never met her."

"Then can I speak to whoever fixed it up in the first place?"

"I'm afraid not, unless you've got a ouija board. Whoops, sorry about that, not at all funny. The arrangements were made by a lady who worked here part-time until a couple of weeks ago."

Mowgley suddenly felt very tired. "What happened to her?" What was her name?"

"She had a terrible accident. Fell off a cross-Channel ferry. They said she'd been drinking. Margaret Birchall was her name. She was a lovely woman, always immaculately dressed. Wonderful hair and sense of style. She was very good for the company. She seemed to know lots of people in the property business, and had a lot of contacts. I think someone said she was married to a solicitor. She probably only worked here for something to do. When she died it caused all sorts of problems. All her files had somehow been wiped from the computer and there was no back-up. We had to set up new files on all her customers. All the details about references and former addresses were lost. It took a lot of work sorting it all out."

"I suppose she looked after a lady called Linda Russell's flat at Pacific Heights as well?"

"The name seems familiar. I can look her up if you like. But if she was one of Margaret's we won't have much to go on. It's all a bit of a mystery, really."

"Yes," said Mowgley heavily, "it's beginning to look that way."

*   *   *

"What's the matter?"

Melons stood in front of Mowgley's desk, watching as he ate a third Penguin bar with grim determination.

Mowgley opened his baccy tin, saw that he had run out of papers and threw the tin across the room. To make himself feel even worse, he refused one of her cigarettes and snarled. "Haven't you got anybody to arrest?"

"Not at the moment. Are you going to tell me about it?"

"What makes you think I've got something to tell you?"

"I've just seen George in the car and he's looking really miserable, so you must have made him go out for a long walk. You only do that when you're really unhappy. When you came in, Jo says you didn't check the lottery numbers, and you didn't take the piss out of Dickie Quayle or bollock Stephen. And your office door was shut. And you don't like

Penguins."

"Fucking brilliant. You should be a detective."

"What, and have to deal with a load of thieving, inadequate misfits? And that's just the people I'd be working with. Do you fancy going up the pub and getting legless?"

"Why?"

"It's what we do at times of trouble."

*   *   *

"Where are we going?" asked Melons as Mowgley turned into the car park of the public house directly alongside the Port Authority building. "We never come here. They won't let George in. What's wrong with the Ship Leopard?"

Mowgley got out and glared at the hanging baskets of plastic flowers and the sandwich board advertising the day's special of Creole Gumbo. "I want to go somewhere where they'll notice when I'm being a real pain. You got a problem with that?"

*   *   *

After a potentially unpleasant scene when Mowgley demanded reassurance that his second pint and all those following would be served in the same glass, the couple left the bar and settled in a corner seat.

"I suppose you don't want to have a go at the crossword?" asked Melons.

"No."

"Okay. So, are you going to tell me about it now, or when we're so pissed you won't be able to speak and I won't be able to understand you anyway? It's her, isn't it?"

"Yes."

"You've found something out about her?"

"Yes."

"She's still married?"

"No."

"She's got another boyfriend?"

"No..."

"Not a girlfriend?"

In spite of the depth of his misery, Mowgley bristled: "Certainly not."

"Then what is it. What's wrong with her?"

"She's gone."

"Oh." Melons reached out and for the first time for two years and thirteen days, laid a consoling hand on her boss's arm. "I'm really sorry. I know I was taking the piss about you and her, but I was really pleased you seemed to be getting on so well, and you were obviously so happy." Then she brightened her tone. "To be honest, I never liked her anyway. She wasn't your type really, was she? Far too... snotty. There's plenty more fish on the beach, as they say."

Mowgley failed to rise to the bait and correct her. "I don't mean she's gone, you silly cow. I mean she's *gone* gone. She's buggered off."

"Without as much as a goodbye?"

"Now you are taking the piss. And it gets worse. This morning I went to see the estate agent who looks after her flat."

"Yes?"

"She didn't tell them she was going, and she left her deposit and just went."

"Blimey - she really must have wanted to get away from you." Melons grimaced and again laid her hand on Mowgley's arm. "Sorry. couldn't resist that one. What about her last address?"

"There isn't one. The woman at the agency who dealt with all that sort of stuff doesn't work there anymore. In fact, she's dead."

"Oh?"

"Her name was Margaret Birchall."

"Blimey again."

"Yes." Mowgley drained his glass and stood up. "I'm going to find the khazi. I hope it isn't unisex."

"No, there's two."

"Good. What am I?"

"You're a Matelot. I was a Jenny Wren."

"My God." He set off towards the door bearing a picture of what was generally supposed to be a French sailor in traditional uniform. "Get 'em in then, and be sure to upset the barman with the fancy hairdo by asking for a packet of pork scratchings..."

*   *   *

On his return, Mowgley found Melons finishing a conversation on her mobile.

"Who was that?"

"Dickie Quayle. He's found Fulcrum Developments. Well, he's found their main account. The manager is expecting him in an hour, and I said you'd probably want us to go along."

"Phone him back."

"Who, the bank manager?"

"No - Quayle. Tell him we'll do it. He can come in here and chance his arm with the Gumbo and the barmaid."

*   *   *

"He's not your bank manager is he?" asked Melons.

After inspecting their warrant cards, the woman behind the counter had shown them into a glass-walled office with a computer terminal, potted plant and a poster telling them how keen the bank was to give them lots of money.

Mowgley frowned, then asked: "Who?"

"This one."

"No, why?"

"Just wondered why you were looking so nervous."

"Don't be bloody ridiculous."

Mowgley sat back in his chair and tried to look as if he was not trying to look relaxed. With some people it was going to the dentist or doctor. With him it was an interview with the bank manager. They were just working for businesses that made a fortune lending you other people's money, and sometimes even your own money, but they always acted as if they were doing you a favour. And it was not as if they had proper bank managers nowadays. In the old days bank managers were always older than you and smoked pipes and were reassuringly free of any awareness of what constituted fashionable clothing. Now, they all looked like the Prime Minister, wore double-glazing salesmen double-breasted suits and went on customer awareness seminars to learn how to fuck you up with a smile. Last week he had got a letter telling him he was over his limit again and that he shouldn't spend money he hadn't got. And telling him they had charged him money he hadn't got for telling him he should not be spending money he hadn't got.

"If you like," said Melons in a stage whisper, "I'll do the talking."

"Why?"

"Because it you talk to him and he gets stroppy, you'll get stroppier and nause it all up. I know how you hate bank managers."

Mowgley thought about it for a bit then nodded: "Alright then. It'll be good practice for you. Just don't cock it up."

"I'll try not to," said Melons dryly.

*   *   *

Some time later, and the manager had arrived, been shown their credentials, made a clearance call to head office, and was doing the familiar fluttering over the keyboard. Just for a change, this one was not a wannabe commodity broker, but a man who had been promoted to the level of his incompetence and thought that made him special.

After not offering them coffee, he had made a point of moving the screen of his computer a further inch towards himself and away from them. Mowgley groaned inwardly. He was one of them. He had information, and did not want to give it away because it was his. It was going to be like drawing teeth.

After further fluttering in response to Melons's question, the manager said that Fulcrum Developments did indeed have an account.

"And how long have they had it?"

More fluttering, then: "A little over four months."

"And who opened the account - I mean did you deal with it personally?"

"Yes." The manager took off his glasses and cleaned the lenses with a small square of cloth he took from the desk drawer. He did so in an almost defensive way, then folded the cloth neatly and returned it to the drawer.

Melons watched for a moment and then nodded encouragingly. "I see. Thank you. And had you had any prior dealings with the company or their representative?"

"No."

"Did they say why they were opening an account?"

After looking at her as if he felt it was none of her business, the manager answered: "The person I dealt with - the company secretary - said that they were in the process of setting up a major development project in France. For various accounting, tax and other - perfectly legal - reasons, they wished to use our local facilities."

"Wasn't that rather unusual? Why wouldn't they use their main account, wherever that was?"

"It wasn't particularly unusual." He put a hand protectively on the top of his computer screen and swung it a further inch away from them and towards himself. "There's no law against setting up a new account in whatever name or location the company chooses, as far as I am aware. As long, of course, that it is all properly constructed, observed and declared."

"Okay. So how did they open the account?"

"In the normal way. Do you want me to go through the procedure?"

"No thanks," said Melons coolly. "So what amount did they open the account with and in what form?"

"What form?" the man repeated, looking at her as if he could not believe that she should need to ask a question with such a simple answer.

Melons lifted her head a fraction, then spoke very levelly and clearly, which Mowgley knew was a sure sign she was copping the needle. "I'll try and be clearer. Did they use their own cheque, cash or bars of gold with swastikas on?"

The manager looked as if he was going to react, then shook his head very slightly and began fluttering again. Mowgley, who had been making an elaborate show of taking notes, scribbled dramatically on a page of his notebook, tore it out and handed it to Melons. It read: *I'm dying for a pint. What a tosser - I bet he's got a small dick.*

She looked at the note, nodded gravely, added a line and passed it back.

He is a small dick.

The manager finished fluttering. "They opened the account with a banker's draft for five thousand pounds."

"And did they make any withdrawals?"

"Not until the second tranche had been put in place."

Mowgley could not resist joining in. "The second what?"

"There was no action at all in the account until last Thursday."

Mowgley smiled and nodded encouragingly, like a primary school teacher helping a pupil to get to the point. "And, what happened then?"

"The company secretary made an appointment and arrived with a second banker's draft."

"How much for?"

The man fluttered again, then said quite calmly: "A half a million pounds."

There was silence for a moment, then Melons asked "Is it still there?"

There was obviously no need for further fluttering as the bank manager said almost wistfully "No. It was transferred yesterday."

"All of it?"

It was fluttering time again, then: "All except for five

hundred and seventy-nine pounds."

"And where did the money go?"

"To the Cherbourg branch of Credit Agricole."

"Surely that's unusual?"

It was the bank manager's turn to look like a schoolteacher dealing with a simple-minded child. "No, not particularly. The company secretary had said that was what was going to happen. We have a reciprocal arrangement with Credit Agricole, and our instructions were to make the transfer at the best exchange rate within a window of three days."

The man looked at the screen and then at them, then seemed to have a brief inner struggle before carrying on: "To be honest, I did think that this instruction was a little unusual - or perhaps unwise would be a better word. The Sterling to Euro exchange rate was not as good as it could have been. I actually advised the company secretary that it would be better to wait as the pound was strengthening, but she was adamant. She said the money had to be in France by yesterday morning."

Mowgley and Melons both started to speak, then he nodded and she asked: "You said 'she'."

"Yes. It's not that unusual for a woman to be a company secretary, especially nowadays."

"And what was her name?"

He looked at the screen then said: "Barnes. Mrs Joanne Barnes."

Mowgley and Melons exchanged glances, then Melons asked: "Can you describe her?"

"She was, I suppose, in her thirties. Smartly dressed and very businesslike. Quite tall."

"Did she have an accent?"

"No, I don't think so."

Mowgley stood up, reached into his jacket pocket and took out a photograph, then walked around the desk. He placed it in front of the manager and pointed to where Linda Russell smiled up at them.

"I don't suppose she looked anything like this woman?"

The man looked down, then shook his head. "No, I don't think so."

"Are you certain?"

For the first time, the man looked uncertain. "No, I'm not. You know how women can look different with their hair done differently..."

"So what did the company secretary look like?" Melons asked.

"Well, quite... ordinary, I suppose."

"And what age would you say she was?" Mowgley interjected.

"As I said, in her thirties or thereabouts, I would say."

Mowgley put the photograph back in his pocket and walked back around the desk. "Thank you for your help."

As he and Melons moved towards the door, he paused and turned back: "Just one more thing; can you get in touch with Credit Agricole in Cherbourg and find out if the money is still there?"

The man shook his head in an I'm-not-sure way: "I can try asking informally, but they don't have to tell me. Banking is a confidential business, and France is a separate state with its own laws. Just because we're part of Europe, they don't have to co-operate. To be frank, I find my counterparts can be rather unhelpful."

"Oh really?" said Mowgley with a level of irony which was heavy even for him, "...it's a shame they can't be more like us, isn't it?"

Twenty-six

The Lada was the last vehicle to cross the linkspan and join the eighty-seven cars, nineteen heavy goods lorries, three coaches, thirteen motor cycles, seven bicycles and a tandem bound for Cherbourg on the overnight crossing.

Mowgley suspected they had been last to be put on board because the loading marshals had been ordered to hide the Lada amongst the livestock and container lorries and other commercial vehicles on the lower deck. Melons thought it was because they had arrived half an hour after the official deadline, and Mowgley had been more than usually rude to the customs officer who had asked them where and why they were travelling.

During the ten-hour voyage, the car ferry would travel seventy-two nautical miles, going slower than during a daytime crossing to ensure arrival at a respectable hour the next morning in Cherbourg, and also to save on fuel costs and give as much time as possible for the passengers to spend as much money as could be wooed from them. While on board, the travellers would, in varying degrees of excess, read, sleep, eat, drink or shag the journey away. Those who could afford it would take a cabin with a porthole through which they would not be able to see the sea, while those on a tighter budget would take an internal cabin. Those on an even tighter budget would attempt to sleep in a reclining chair, sometimes aided with a sleep kit consisting of an inflatable pillow, thin blanket and eyeless mask, on sale in the kiosk at £2.49. Those on an extremely restricted budget or wanting to save their money to spend on more important things in France would stretch out on benches, padded banquettes or even the floor. Before retiring, the passengers would spend an average of £14.97 in the duty-free and gift shop, and much less a head on newspapers, books, maps and sweets in the News Boutique. The bored assistant in the shop selling French fashion garments at more than the cost of a return foot-passenger ticket would be in for a lonely night.

Also before turning in or making themselves half-way comfortable, the fare-paying voyagers would consume a total of 146 gallons of beer, wine, soft drinks and spirits bought at the bar, and 1,234 cups of coffee and tea in or from the cafeteria. There, 187 meals would be eaten, of which just over half would be garnished with chips. Inspector Mowgley would account for a disproportionate amount of the chips and beer.

Melons reached over, avoided her boss's defensive stabbing motion with his fork, and took a chip from his plate. "Are you sure we're doing the right thing?"

"I think so." said Mowgley thoughtfully. "I've parked the car where the loader told me, and left it in first gear. I would have engaged the hand brake if there was one."

Melons deftly stole another chip. "You know what I mean. When we heard the Cherbourg account had been cleared out, we should have told Mundy and let him get on with it. Why do I get the feeling that we are digging ourselves deeper and deeper into the pooh?"

"Because you have no sense of adventure or faith in me as your immediate superior. As I and someone else said before me, the game is now certainly afoot. How can we get this far and then hand it all over to Gloria? If not technically, it's still our job morally, and now we've got this far there's no way I'm going to give up on it just because it's developed from a simple overboard to an international fraud with a couple of possible murders thrown in. You must agree

Watson, it is all getting very interesting. And why do you do that?"

"What, question your judgement?"

"No." Mowgley made another stabbing motion with his fork. "Steal my bloody chips. I asked if you wanted any and you said no, then you take mine. What's that all about?"

"It's about being a woman, so don't even try to work it out."

Mowgley looked as if he was about to enter into a debate on the subject, then shook his head. "I won't for sure. With regard to giving up on this one, what you have to understand, Sergeant, is that the basic requirement for a policeman is an enquiring mind and an unswerveable determination to get to the truth. Whether it's a crossword or a crime, all a good copper wants to do is establish the facts and from there to the truth. He has a bounden duty to himself and the public he serves to follow the winding and sometimes tortuous trail wherever it may lead and despite the dangers he may encounter on the way. Down these mean streets a man must go and all that. As a woman, I wouldn't expect you to understand, but a man's gotta do what a man's gotta do."

Melons cleared her mouth of chips, then said: "What a load of crap. The truth is that you're just a bloody-minded old sod."

"Less of the 'old' if you don't mind. It is true that I may possess a tad of what some people would call bloody-mindedness, but that is another good character trait for a policeman to have. Apart from all that, there's the ancillary consideration that we could do with some more stocks of booze and baccy. Anyway, you're not complaining about a couple of days travelling incognito and away from the fun factory, are you? If we draw a blank at the bank, I promise I'll hand it all over to Mundy when we get back. Is it a deal?"

Melons stole another chip: "How could I possibly object?"

*   *   *

Later, and they sat with drinks and smokes in hands, looking out over the after-rail. There was a faint luminescence on the choppy waters surrounding the boat, reflecting the lights on board. Beyond that it was as dark as a tomb. Without speaking of it, both were thinking what it would be like to be floundering in the water, trying to scream as the huge shape disappeared into the night.

Melons shuddered, threw her cigarette butt over the rail and then asked: "So, what's this Guy like?"

Mowgley took his baccy tin out and opened it: "Which guy?"

"Your friend the French detective. I've not met him yet, remember."

"Bugger!" Mowgley clutched the baccy tin to his chest as a good proportion of the contents was blown over the rail. "He's French."

"Obviously he's bloody French. But what's he like? I mean, what does he look like? Is he tall or short, dark or fair?"

"I dunno; sort of French looking, I suppose."

"Oh. Well, that clears things up then. I'd forgotten all your spiel about how observant you are and how crap the bank manager was at describing what the company secretary was like."

Mowgley did not respond as he finished rolling, licking and lighting his cigarette. They sat looking up at the sky until Melons observed: "Have you noticed how many more shooting stars you see at sea than on land?"

"Erm, could it be because you don't spend your time on land laying on your back and looking at the sky? Well, not when you're with me, you don't..."

More silence, then Melons asked: "I don't suppose you told Mundy we'll be away from the fun factory for a few days?"

"I left a message, and he knows my number."

"Great. So apart from your having to do what a man's got to do, why are we really going over?"

"I told you. To see what the Frog bank manager has got

to say."

"But we already know that the money's no longer in the Credit Agricole account."

"Yes" said Mowgley with exaggerated patience, beginning to roll a fresh cigarette, "but we don't know who took it out, do we?"

"Well, it wasn't Jo Barnes. Even the bank manager wouldn't have underestimated her age by that much. Anyway, it had to be Linda Russell."

"How do you know? Mr Bumptious the Bank Manager didn't recognise her photo. Anyway, It's got to be worth the visit before we give it over to The Fat Controller. The manager at Credit Agricole might be able to tell us something about Mrs so-called Joanne Barnes. He must be able to give us a better description than the Brit bank manager. Being French, he must have taken a better look at his female visitor than Mr Bumptious."

"But we already know that the mystery woman isn't Eddie's wife. I checked and Joanne Barnes has a cast iron alibi for when the company secretary was dealing with the bank manager in Dover. Even if it had been her, do you really think she'd give her real name? Our mystery woman was just taking the piss and letting us know she knew what we knew. it's got to be Linda Russell, hasn't it?"

"Has it? As I said, the twonker in Dover didn't recognise her from the photo."

"That doesn't prove anything. As even the thickie bank manager has noticed, women can change their appearance much more easily than men."

"You always look the same."

"You wouldn't notice if I dyed my hair green."

"You mean you haven't?"

Melons pressed on: "So what about the language difficulty?"

Mowgley nodded reassuringly. "It's alright, I can just about understand what you're trying to say."

She sighed. "The French bank manager; what if he can't speak English? I'm not that good at the subtle stuff, and you're near-useless at subtlety in your own language."

"He will be able to speak English, but he's bound to pretend he can't. It's how educated Frogs get their revenge on us. That's why I've asked Guy to come along. He speaks English quite well for a foreigner, and French as well."

Melons decided to change tack: "Well at least we know what it was all about, even if you do get the sack when we get back."

"Do we?" Mowgley made a doomed attempt to blow a smoke ring, then looked at her: "Is this the bit where you pretend to gather all the suspects together and explain who did what to whom and when and where and why? Tell me about it, then. Was it Mrs Scarlet in the library with the lead pipe, or what?"

"Alright, here we go again. Now, as you like to say, pay attention as I shall be asking questions afterwards."

"So will I," said Mowgley, adjusting the reclining seat. "Go on, then. And be sure to start at the beginning."

"Okay. For sure and certain, we know Margaret Birchall went over the side three weeks ago."

"Correct."

"There was only one witness, and she's done a runner after you frightened her off by getting serious." Melons paused: "Sorry."

"That's all right, you insensitive cow. Continue."

"The sister of the overboard was, we think, sleeping with Birchall and Eddie Barnes at the same time."

"More than probable."

"Linda Russell also worked for Eddie Barnes, and was in a position to knock up that fake memo about planning permission for Didcot House."

"Also correct."

"Robert Birchall was the solicitor who handled the affairs of the old lady who owns Didcot House. She is suffering from advanced Alzheimer's, and he was able to get at her money."

"Spot on so far."

"We know Birchall was naive and a bit slow with

women. He meets and marries Margaret Russell in next to no time. She sets about spending money he hasn't got, and her sister moves down to join in. Linda may even have persuaded Birchall to draw the money out of the old girl's account."

"Wait a minute. Why go to all the bother with the fake memo and the dealings at the bank? Why not just get Birchall to take the money out, then disappear with it?"

"You must have sussed the answer to that. Linda Russell obviously did. It was all about making Birchall think that there was no risk. He wouldn't have the nerve to take half a million of a customer's money and run off with it. He didn't have the guts and it would have finished his career. He needed to believe that they could get away with it and he could go merrily on with enough money to keep both women happy. Linda had to convince him that it could be done with no comeback."

"Keep going."

"With her goings-on with Eddie and Birchall, she must have found out about Didcot House and the old lady being in a nursing home. Perhaps someone really did enquire about planning permission while she was at work. She could have found out that Birchall was in charge of the old lady's money when he went off for one of his regular visits to her. She just had to tell Birchall that she had inside knowledge about the planning permission, and that all he had to do was buy the place, then sell it on to a real building company. Any big company would give millions for a site with permission for all those houses to be built on it..."

"But the big building company wouldn't be fooled by her bit of cut-and-paste creativity with the planning department letterheads."

"As you well know, it was never going to get that far. Birchall just had to think it could and would. Linda would say he just had to use the old lady's money to buy the place in Fulcrum's name, then sell it on, put the money back in the old lady's account, and clear at least a million for their trouble. She may have told Birchall that Eddie knew of a building company which would jump at the chance. She even hooked Eddie Barnes and took him round to show off to Birchall. Birchall would have known how dodgy Eddie is. It was a nice touch."

"Okay. But then why didn't she just get a cheque off Birchall and bugger off?"

"Because even he wouldn't have been green enough to give her a cheque with her name on it. Fulcrum Developments was the credibility icing on the cake. It was another nice touch. As soon as the inquest was over, she could disappear, and she set up the transfer of money at just the right time."

"But if she had the money in the bank, why would she hang about for the inquest?"

"She must have balls of steel, if you know what I mean. By staying on and seeing it through and helping to get a Death By Misadventure verdict, she could slip away unnoticed. If we played by the rules, we would have called it a day with the DBM verdict."

"She gave us a bit of a clue that she was up to no good when she tied young Gloria up, didn't she?"

"As you said, seeing him tagging along must have spooked her a bit - that's why you put him on obbo, you crafty old copper. If Birchall hadn't topped himself and Byng and co not got involved and you had been a normal sort of policeman, she'd have been home and dry. And nobody the wiser except Birchall, who would have had to find a half million from somewhere or face the consequences when the missing money came to light eventually. Perhaps he killed himself because he knew he was going to be stuffed one way or the other."

"And where did the late Mrs Margaret Birchall come in to all this?"

"I don't know - "

"Ahah -"

"- but there are only a couple of choices. Either she was in on it or even started it all with her sister. Don't forget she worked in the estate agents, so she could have found out about Didcot House and Birchall looking after the old lady's affairs. She could have brought her sister in to do the business with Eddie. It could have been her behind it all. When she went over the side, the pooh would have hit the fan as far as Birchall was concerned. He could have killed himself because he thought it was all going to go tits-up on him."

"And the other choice?"

"Erm, okay. Whether or not she just knew about it or was involved in it, Margaret Birchall could have lost her bottle. You heard what the steward said about how she changed and started drinking heavily in the past few months. It could all have been too much for her. Either she got pissed and fell overboard, or she got pissed and decided to jump. Or…"

"Or?"

"Or she was pushed."

"By who - or do I mean whom?"

"You *know* by whom."

"And what about Birchall's death? Did *he* jump or was he pushed?"

"Don't know, what do you think?"

"I don't bloody know, either," said Mowgley irritably. "I'm not bloody Hercule Poirot." He paused and looked thoughtful, then: "I tell you what, though."

"What?"

"If you're right and Margaret Birchall didn't fall off the boat, it definitely wasn't Death By Misadventure."

"So?"

"So it should have been an Open verdict."

"And?"

"That was my bet in the sweepstake. By rights the money should have gone to me..."

*   *   *

Despite or perhaps because of the Abba tribute group, it was quiet in the bar when a group of five men arrived.

"Oh dear." Mowgley sighed and shook his head.

"What's the matter?"

"They are going to get pissed and nasty."

"How do you know?"

"Trust me, I'm a policeman. I know about these things."

*   *   *

Mowgley's intuitive powers were endorsed just under two hours later. He returned from the toilets to find one of the group standing above Melons, offering her a glass of something green and yellow with a small umbrella in it. At the bar, his friends were offering encouragement to her to drink it, and him to give her one. The man, Mowgley noticed, had a shaven head, two earrings, and a bad tattoo of a swift on his very thick neck.

"Hello sailors," said Mowgley in an amiable manner as Melons shot him a warning look, "nice and smooth, isn't it?"

"Piss off," responded the man, who was as tall as Mowgley, at least twenty years younger and probably about the same weight, though most of it looked like muscle. He turned his attention back to Melons: "Come on, treacle. Get your lips round this."

Mowgley looked across at the bar, where the steward was busily avoiding eye contact, and the young man's friends were watching the action with wolfish anticipation. He sighed. The tattoo job would have been almost too much to handle even on his own, and he was not going to get any help. There was no cavalry in the offing. If he'd been pissed he might have considered taking the matter to conclusion there and then, but he was well sober enough to know his limitations without the element of surprise. Or as it used to be called, fighting dirty.

Above all, he did not want to flash his warrant card. The arseholes were pissed enough to not let it deter them, and the procedure that would have to be followed if it all kicked off would mean, apart from a visit to a French hospital, that Mundy would hear about their moonlight flit and why they had gone on it.

"Come along, son," he said mildly, "we're not into all this. Let's just have a nice pleasant crossing shall we? I'll even buy you a beer."

"I said piss off, fat cunt." The man turned again to look down at Melons. "Tell you what, we're in cabin 137. Why don't you come down and give us all a turn?" He looked across at Mowgley. "You don't mind, do you?"

"Just so long as you're not inviting me as well."

As Melons sat very still, the man reached down and cupped her left breast in his tattooed hand. She slowly took a drink from her glass, and put it carefully on the table, looking straight ahead. The man looked up at Mowgley and smiled. Mowgley smiled back. The people at the next table joined the steward in finding something interesting elsewhere to look at. As the tribute group broke into 'Waterloo', two of the man's friends came across and stood behind their friend.

The man jiggled Melons's breast, then said: "Don't forget, cabin 137."

"Melons reached up and gripped his hand, moving the glowing end of her cigarette towards it. As she opened her mouth, Mowgley looked at her, shook his head slightly and said: "We don't want any trouble."

"Course you fucking don't."

The man straightened up, finished his drink and put the glass on the table before pushing his way past Mowgley and back to the bar. "See you later."

"Yes," said Mowgley when he was sure the man would not hear him, "I'm pretty sure you will."

*   *   *

The ferry boat was in safe waters and passing through the Cherbourg breakwater when Mowgley's patience was rewarded and he entered the shower room two doors along from cabin 137. The announcement inviting drivers to re-join their vehicles had already been made, and by now, most of the passengers would be making their way down to the car decks. Mowgley had been standing waiting at the end of the corridor for more than half an hour.

Picking up a bar of soap from the hand basin, he walked over to the shower cubicle and pulled the curtain back. He noted fleetingly that the man was, as he had suspected, mostly muscle, and that he had other tattoos apart from the badly-drawn swift on his neck.

As the man turned towards him, Mowgley smiled encouragingly and held out the soap. Instinctively, the man reached out to take it, and Mowgley let it slip from his fingers. As the man looked down and then up, the Ferry King swayed slightly backwards and butted him in the face. Blood mingled with the water running into the hole in the shower tray as the man slid down the tiled wall. "Just like Psycho, isn't it matey?" said Mowgley pleasantly as he stepped into the cubicle and drove his knee into the man's face. His head snapped back against the tiles, and more blood spurted from the broken nose. Mowgley smiled again and stepped back out of range of the shower jet. Pulling the curtain gently back into place, he left the room, beaming at a woman cleaner as she approached with mop and bucket.

"I should leave it a bit, love," he said pleasantly, "I think there's someone still using the shower."

*   *   *

As Mowgley struggled into the driving seat of the Lada, Melons reached over and touched his hair. "Have you been up on deck?"

"No - why?"

"Your hair's all wet. And that's a nasty bump on your forehead. Don't tell me you had a fight with a shower? I wondered where you got to for the last hour. And you were limping when you came to the car. Did you get stuck in the cubicle 'cos it was such a foreign experience to ablute yourself in the morning?"

"That's a funny word, isn't it?"

"What, 'shower'?"

"No, 'ablute'."

"I think you'll find it comes from the Latin, and was a term referring to a priest's ritual washing of his hands."

"No I won't."

"Won't what?"

"Find out where it comes from as I will not be looking." He raised his eyebrows, smiled, gave a force two shrug and engaged first gear with some difficulty before driving down the ramp towards the open bow doors. A white van was obstructing the lane, and as Mowgley steered round it, Melons pointed to where a group of young men stood by the rear doors, looking up at the steps leading down from the cabin deck.

"That's those bastards from last night," she said, unconsciously touching her left breast. "But he's not with them."

"Ouch," said Mowgley, gingerly rubbing his right knee, "after what he drunk last night, he's probably got a headache and having a lie-in."

"Perhaps," said his sergeant thoughtfully, looking at Mowgley's wet hair, "or perhaps he got stuck in the shower as well..."

Twenty-seven

"It's raining," observed Melons as the Lada limped through the ferryport gates.

"So it is," said Mowgley. "Quelle bloody surprise."

In the absence of wiper blades, he wound down the driver's window, reached out and rubbed his hand across the windscreen and peered through it.

Viewed at dawn and in the mid-winter rain, Cherbourg was not a prepossessing sight. Many visitors and even residents would argue that Cherbourg was not a prepossessing sight at any time of day or year or weather condition.

Hammered by the Allies with not inconsiderable help from the Germans during the D-Day invasion, most of the town had been re-built in the immediate post-war years. Like many things done quickly, the project was mostly done badly. Some surviving gems were buried deep amongst the rows of bleak, square buildings that now lined the quayside, but they were generally as hard to find as a Frenchman who understood the rules of cricket.

But Mowgley liked the eclectic mix of Pre-War Vulgar, Post-War Pragmatic and the odd example of Original Gothic. He also liked the different similarities the town shared with where he worked and lived. Like Cherbourg, his home city had been heavily bombed by the Germans, though not as far as he knew by the Allies. Cherbourg was

French and very different from the other side of the Channel, but because it was a port, not as different as other parts of the country and where France was much more *profonde*.

Leaving the roundabout on which sat the statue of an unhappy - looking woman with a shield and spear, he drove cavalierly across the swing-bridge, giving his Queen wave to the dozen motorists who should have had the right of way. He knew this patronising acknowledgement would anger them much more than a scowl or V-sign. He also knew that the state of the Lada would discourage even a French driver from a jousting match. The local drivers would know that any insurance claim following a shunt with a foreigner would be found in their favour, but they would also know that a car in the condition of the Lada would be very likely to be uninsured. In that, Mowgley thought, they would be absolutely right.

If Cherbourg had a heart, it would be the Theatre Square. Named for the grand building looking snootily down on its surroundings, it was one of his favourite parts of the town; the fact that it featured more bars than shops may have influenced his taste. They had arrived on a market day, and the ornate fountain was surrounded by a jumble of stalls, stands and battered vehicles. Mowgley turned his face towards the driver's window (which he had been unable to wind up again) and breathed deeply. It was times like these when he really knew he had arrived in France. Seagulls wheeled and cawed harshly above, and the pavements were slickly gleaming after the attentions of a squadron of motorised cleaners. Despite their efforts, a reminder of the night before remained with the faint bouquet of urine and vomit. That pungent odour was already being absorbed by the signature smell of this or any French street market, which was a heady combination of freshly baked bread, pizzas, fish not long from the sea but unmistakably dead, very strong cheeses and even stronger French cigarettes.

At this time in the morning, business was not brisk. It was not a livestock market, and nobody much would want to get up early and seek a bargain in farm machinery or three-piece suites, especially wet ones. Most Cherbourgois who were not at work would be along later, and many were now warming up for the day with a *café-calva* in any one of the hundred bars within easy walking distance.

Parking with even less concern than on home ground, Mowgley helped Melons from the Lada, and cautioned her to avoid the prone figure of an English booze cruiser who had not made it back to the ferryport. The detective checked to see the man was still breathing, and that it was not the same person he had stepped over at the terminal during his last visit.

Looking around the sparsely populated square, Mowgley immediately recognised the tall figure of Inspector Guy Varennes. His friend was very French in many respects, and had obviously been working on the way he lounged elegantly against the rim of the giant bowl surrounding the fountain. The collar of his expensive leather jacket was turned up against the driving rain, but he wore no hat. Mowgley noted that even his long, jet-black hair was fetchingly tousled by the rain rather than plastered on his scalp. Perhaps even French rain is fashion-conscious, he thought.

As Varennes waved and started to walk towards them, Melons made a noise in the back of her throat which was a strange cross between a purr and a growl then spoke in a tone that some women would use when describing their favourite cake: "Nine out of ten. Bet he's got a great bum."

Mowgley shook his head: "My God, it's not even breakfast time. And they say men are the hunters."

The two men shook hands and Mowgley introduced Melons. The French policeman gave a little toss of his head as if shaking the rain from his hair but really, Mowgley thought, to display his curls even more fetchingly. He then gave the sort of lazy, full-lipped Gallic smile which Mowgley had last seen worn by Alain Delon in *Le Cercle Rouge*. "Good morning," he said, "you must be Catherine."

"Well it's not Sergeant Quayle or D.C. Mundy, that's for

sure," said Mowgley sharply. Apart from the smile and the hair antics, it irritated him that Varennes was actually speaking with more of a French accent than normal. He took his sergeant protectively by the elbow, and continued: "Guy this is Melons, Melons this is Guy."

D.S. McCarthy shot Mowgley a furious look, then almost simpered as she said, "Hello. It's Catherine. You must be Guy," she added rather unnecessarily, then, "I've heard so much about you."

"Oh?" Varennes ran his fingers through his hair, crinkled his eyes and gave the faintest trace of a shrug, pushed his lips out in a way that would make any British male look ridiculous, then put his head to one side and said: "Not all bad, I hope?"

Feeling somehow outside the conversation, Mowgley harrumphed and led the way up the steps into the Theatre Café. As Guy moved ahead to open the door, the Ferry King looked back at his colleague, put a finger to his open mouth and gagged. She tossed her head, and, it seemed to him, actually simpered at the Frenchman as she sashayed into the bar.

*   *   *

"I wonder if it'll rain tomorrow?"

Mowgley addressed his question to a spot above the heads of his two companions, neither of whom bothered to reply. They sat side-by-side in the booth, shoulders almost touching and engrossed in a discussion about how wonderful they each found the other's countryside, culture and traditions. As Melons eagerly condemned British fashion and cooking and her new friend confessed to a life-time admiration for Marmite, Mowgley did a passable imitation of Fernandel puffing out his cheeks in *Le Blanc et le Noir*, then signalled for the waiter.

Having given their order without bothering to ask what his companions wanted, he slumped back in the booth, feeling even more marginalised as the couple were now speaking in French. As Varennes complimented Melons on her command of his language, Mowgley consoled himself by considering how much more descriptive English was when compared to the limitations of French.

"For instance," he said to Guy after a reflective moment, "there's feeling like a spare prick at a wedding. How would you say that?"

The French detective paused in mid-flow.

"I'm sorry?"

"You will have to excuse him," said Melons, "*Ce matin il est amiable comme une porte de prison.*"

"Wow," said Guy, "I am very impressed that you know even our argot." Turning to Mowgley, he asked: "Did you have a bad crossing, my friend?"

"Eventful," said Mowgley, and then to Melons: "And what's all that about a bloody prison door?"

*   *   *

"Why are you looking so nervous," whispered Melons "Surely your bank manager phobia doesn't affect you over here?"

Mowgley shifted uneasily in his seat: "Just being here reminds me of the day we bought *La Cour*. And don't forget, I still owe Credit Agricole more than the friggin' place is worth."

She nodded sympathetically, then returned her attention to where Guy was deep in a rapid-fire conversation with the Credit Agricole manager. As Mowgley had suspected, the manager insisted on pretending he could not speak English. This was a common affectation with middle-class professionals like estate agents and lawyers who found themselves increasingly doing business with British holiday-home buyers and expatriates. Some cynics said they did so because their Brit customers might give things away if they thought the person on the other side of the desk would not understand their asides, but Mowgley thought it was just Gallic bloody-mindedness.

Whenever a British politician or member of the Royal Family was in France, he or she would at least try and say a few words in French. It did not seem to work the other way around, and he had never heard a French president utter a word of English while on a state visit across the Channel. And this was despite the fact that nearly all French schools taught English to their pupils. On the positive side, Mowgley had often relished the opportunity to say something really offensive about France and the French when one of them was playing the game. He also enjoyed watching the faces of the Gallic audience when Prince Charles made one of his speeches in French, the pronunciation and delivery of which somehow contrived to make it sound as if he were speaking in English.

He pretended to look as if he understood what was being said as he took out his baccy tin. At least he could smoke while his ears were being assaulted by the geese-like gabble. More and more office buildings in Britain were banning smoking anywhere on the premises, and the sight of defiant or dejected people dragging on fags while huddled outside was ever more familiar. It was all part of the rise and rise of political correctness, and went against what he liked to think were the core values of his race. He had read somewhere that the one and probably only aspect of the British character the French admired was a fierce sense of independence and refusal to accept authority. They probably meant the sort of bloody-mindedness at which they excelled. While he found it difficult to admire anything about the French, he had to admit that they were good at not doing what they were told if they didn't think it was a good idea. When the relatively draconian rules banning smoking in bars, restaurants and offices had been introduced, people had simply ignored them and the authorities had not even bothered to try and enforce the law.

As Mowgley lit up, Melons continued to whisper an edited translation of the exchanges: "Guy has just asked if the manager ever met the company secretary woman."

"And what did he say?"

"Yes, he said he met her twice. Once when she came to open the account, and again when she came to take the money out after the transfer from the English bank. He found her very businesslike and pleasant."

Mowgley grunted. "I bet he didn't find it so pleasant when she took all the dosh out." He smiled inanely at the bank manager, then held his hand up, interrupted the dialogue and spoke directly to Guy: "Silly question, really, but can you ask Monsieur if Madame left a forwarding address?"

Guy asked the question, nodded as the man responded, then said to Mowgley: "No. Only the English address of her company."

"Did she say anything at all about why she was taking the money out and what she was going to do with it or where?"

Mowgley jiggled his right leg in frustration as the French detective relayed his questions, listened to the answers and passed them on: "She said her company was involved in a transaction with the government, some sort of contract, and that it was necessary for her to have the money in cash. He understood that more money will be coming over soon. Madame will be calling him to make arrangements."

"I bet she will."

After Guy had passed on some further questions, Mowgley reached into his pocket and handed the photograph of Linda Russell with her sister and Eddie Barnes to Varennes. "Could you thank him and say we would very much like to hear if Madame does return. My colleague will leave a couple of numbers and he can always reverse the charges." He paused fractionally and was rewarded by slight tic-like evidence that the manager had understood the jibe, then continued: "Before we go, could Monsieur take a look at the photo and see if he recognises Madame?"

The manager pretended he needed to listen to Guy, then took the photograph. After a careful scrutiny, he nodded, handed it back to Mowgley and spoke directly to him in French to get his own back.

"He is saying yes," said Guy, "it is definitely her." As Mowgley stood up and prepared to leave, the young detective turned to Melons and smiled: "It is typical of a Frenchman. He says he remembers her smile and her sense of style. He says how well the blue dress she is wearing in the photograph goes with her colouring and her hair."

Mowgley paused, looked at the picture, then walked around the desk, held the photograph in front of the bank manager and pointed at Linda Russell "...but she's wearing a red dress, is she not?"

Without waiting for Guy to translate, the manager shook his head, looked at the photograph again and said to Mowgley in English: "No no, she is wearing a blue dress." He pointed a well-manicured fingertip to where the dead woman sat beside Linda Russell and the councillor. "*This* is Mrs Barnes. I 'ave never seen the other woman before."

*   *   *

"Well," said Melons as they stood on the pavement outside the bank, "that was interesting, to say the least."

"Yes," said Mowgley thoughtfully, "I told you he would be able to speak English if he wanted to."

"You bloody well knew it was her, didn't you?"

"I was, as we like to say in the trade, acting upon my suspicions; like I said on the boat, the first requirement of a good policeman is an enquiring mind and a burning desire to establish the truth."

"But we've got the truth now, haven't we? We now know that Margaret Birchall isn't dead and that she set it all up with her sister and Yvonne McLaughlin. It was a brilliant stroke to have an independent witness to confirm that Margaret had gone over the rail. The whole thing was all a scam to get Robert Birchall to come across with the money. The three witches are probably sitting on the Riviera right now having a good laugh at our and the old lady's expense.

(184)

There's absolutely nothing we can do but hand it over to Mundy to sort out with the Frogs. They'll do bugger all as usual and nothing will come of it. But at least we'll be out of it."

Mowgley turned the corners of his mouth down: "I think you should remember that all it takes for evil to flourish is for good men to do nothing, or something along those lines."

"Who said that, then?"

"I just did," said Mowgley. "Come on, Sergeant, let's go."

"Where to - back home?"

"No way, Pedro. To get over your shock at parting from Guy, I'll treat you to lunch at the Theatre Café. While there, we will plan our next move, and I have a feeling it won't be to the ferryport."

*   *   *

Mowgley buttered a slice of baguette with mustard and pointed his knife at two young women at a nearby table. "Have you noticed," he observed contemplatively, "that nearly all French women are basically pear-shaped?"

"No," said Melons, "I can't say that I have."

"I don't suppose you spend much time looking at women's tits, but it is a universal though not always acknowledged truth that, in general, French women have small top bollocks and big arses. I think the technical term is endomorphic. Anyway, that's why they used to employ only English dancers with big bazookas at the *Moulin Rouge*. Bet you didn't know that, and I bet that's why Guy finds you so fascinating. He's amazed and enthralled at the size of your jugs. Pass the house red, please."

"It's a good job Guy's gone," said his colleague. "You know how proud the French are of their women. And please don't call me Melons when he's around. In fact I would be grateful if you stopped calling me that name anywhere and in front of anyone."

"You're just in a bad mood because he had to slope off.

We're seeing him tonight, so don't sulk."

"I'm not sulking. I just want to know where all this is going. You may be feeling suicidal, but I want to keep my job. You've proved your point and cracked the case, why can't we just call it a day?"

"I told you we'll hand it all over to Mundy and your mate Cyrano when we get back. But first, I think you should give the office a bell and get the address of Margaret Birchall's little *pied-a-terre*. It's no more than an hour from here, I seem to remember."

"Why? You don't really think she'll still be there, do you? What are you proposing - that we give her a call and ask her to wait while we come and arrest her on suspicion of fraud, deception, theft and possibly murder?"

"We could get her on wasting police time at least," said Mowgley defensively. "But you weren't listening. I said get her address, not her phone number. I think we should nip over and check the place out. You never know, she might have left a clue or two…"

Twenty-eight

"Are you sure this is the right place?" Melons inspected the bramble damage to her tights as they stood in front of the neat little cottage.

"Of course it is. Who but a Brit would buy a former cattle byre in the middle of nowhere, then spend so much on making it look like their idea of what an 18th-century peasant's cottage would have looked like?"

"But we don't know that it's hers. It could be another English owner with the same sort of taste. There are lots of them, according to you."

"Also true. But there are other clues if you care to observe them, my dear Watson."

"Go on, then, Holmes, amaze me."

"Well," said Mowgley, puffing on an imaginary pipe, "for starters there's her name and UK address on the twee mailbox on the post at the top of the drive. As I have said so often, when one has eliminated all the incorrect answers, what remains must be the right one."

"Oh. Alright then." Melons watched as Mowgley knocked tentatively on the door, tried the handle, then followed him around the single-storey building as he pulled at the closed shutters.

"She's not in."

"Well spotted."

"So what do we do, leave a note?"

"No, Watson, we continue our investigations inside."

"How? You don't propose breaking the door down? You know how bad at that you were last time."

Mowgley tapped the side of his nose: "Nothing so obvious, my dear. Unless you want to try the old credit card ploy, I'll show you something I learned from a retired rural housebreaker in Cornwall. Very like here, parts of Cornwall. Especially the roofs. When you can't get through the doors and windows, he said, you can always get through the lid."

"You may not have noticed, but we haven't brought a ladder or a full set of housebreaking tools."

"Never mind all that, Sergeant. Just pull the car up tight against the front of the house, stand back and look and learn."

*   *   *

Half an hour later, and Mowgley had removed a number of interlocking roof tiles and dropped them down to his colleague.

"That was very impressive." Melons stacked the last tile against the cottage wall, then shouted: "What's next?"

"Easy. When this place was built, they just overlapped the tiles straight on to the rafters, which were usually branches cut from a handy tree. All I do now is drop down through the gap between the branches into the loft space, then come downstairs and let you in."

"What if there aren't any stairs down or even a loft hatch? I don't want to be a spoilsport, but what if the door's double-locked from the outside?"

"Good questions. In that case it'll be back to Plan 'A'."

"Which is?"

"I get you to kick the bloody door in."

*   *   *

There was a loft hatch, and though the door was double-locked the shutters were not. After clambering through a suitable window and doing further collateral damage to her tights, Melons stood alongside the Ferry King and surveyed their surroundings.

The inside of the cottage had been made into one large room, with a cooker, sink and fridge in one corner. In the opposite corner stood a single bed covered with a patchwork quilt. At the other end of the room, a shabby but comfortable-looking sofa and two armchairs were arranged in front of a wood-burning stove which looked too ornate to work properly. On either side of the stove, two wicker baskets contained kindling, logs and paper.

"Not very grand for someone with her taste," observed Melons after looking around.

"Perhaps she wasn't planning to be here long," said Mowgley.

"What do we do now?"

"Don't you read any detective books? We search the room for vital clues, then make ourselves a proper cup of coffee from that jar of instant."

*   *   *

"So what do we have, Watson?"

"One copy of *A Year in Provence*, a shopping list, and instructions on how to work the telephone answering machine," said Melons. "Not a great result."

"Oh I don't know. She could have been boning up on where to settle, and there could have been a message from her accomplice on the answer phone which would have given us a vital clue."

"The answer phone was blank," Melons reminded him, "and Provence is a big place. The shopping list might be coded, I suppose, but in that case what does 'beetroot' stand for?"

"It's slang for a hard-on in France, I'm told," said Mowgley absent-mindedly.

"It's all been a bit of a waste of time, then."

"Not really. You've forgotten the duty-free receipt in the

kindling basket next to the stove."

"Big deal. All it shows is that she or someone she knows likes Toblerone chocolate and malt whisky."

Mowgley shook his head in mock sorrow: "You see, that's the difference between you and me, and why I'm where I am on the ladder of promotion."

"You mean a rotten rung just above a snake leading right down to the start?"

"Har de bloody har. As it happens, you forgot to look at the date on the receipt."

"What about it?"

"It's the date she supposedly went over the side."

"So what?"

"For one thing, it proves she was here after she was supposed to be dead, doesn't it?"

"Well, we knew she didn't go overboard, didn't we?"

"Just another piece in the jigsaw of compelling evidence if and when the case comes to court, Sergeant." Mowgley reached into his pocket and pulled out a sheaf of envelopes. "Besides, these might come in useful."

"What are they?"

"It's her post. I found them on the mat by the door before I let you in the window." Mowgley held one of the envelopes up: "And this one may come in particularly useful."

"Why?"

"It's her telephone bill."

"Again, so what?"

Mowgley sighed theatrically. "You are determined to be unimpressed aren't you? Roll me a fag and I'll show you something." He opened the envelope, took out the two pieces of paper inside and laid them on the table. "Ahah. Verrry interesting. This one is the bill, okay?"

"Mmm," agreed Melons as she ran her tongue along the edge of the cigarette paper.

"And this," said Mowgley, pointing at the other piece of paper, "is the record of all calls made. It's standard practice with France Telecom -"

"- As it is in the UK," Melons said, handing him the cigarette.

"- As it is in the UK," Mowgley agreed. "I have particular reason to know that frequent calls can be a useful indicator to what people are up to. When my wife was at it with the bloke who lumbered us with *La Cour*, she made an average of seven calls a day to his mobile. That gave me a clue that she was getting more than French lessons from him."

"You mean you went through all her calls? That's not like you."

"You'd be surprised what a bit of marital infidelity can do to a man," said Mowgley heavily, lighting his cigarette. "It's not just bloody women who are sensitive, you know."

He looked at the piece of paper for a moment, then handed it to Melons. "Call me old-fashioned, but I think it would be a good idea to check out where all these numbers are. Besides, it'll give you a good excuse to get in touch with Guy Varennes and ask for help, won't it?"

*   *   *

"Mowgley?"

"Inspector Mowgley, if you don't mind, Sergeant."

"Sorry. Inspector Mowgley?"

"Yes, Sergeant McCarthy?"

"There's a man out here and he's pointing a gun at me."

"Don't take the piss."

"I'm not. Honestly."

Very slowly, Mowgley put his head out of the window through which his sergeant had recently climbed. She was standing by the car, and there was indeed a man pointing a gun at her. He was dressed in green overalls and brown boots and was elderly, but the muzzle of the shotgun he was almost casually resting against one hip was unwavering. Feeling rather self-conscious, Mowgley raised his hands and smiled weakly.

"What shall I do?"

"Well, I could distract him and you could kick the gun

out of his hand and wrestle him to the ground. Alternatively, you could pretend to faint, and I could leap out of the window and wrestle him to the ground. Or, which I think is the better plan, we could both keep very still and I can shit myself while you tell him we are English policepersons pursuing our enquiries."

"I've already tried that and I don't think he believes me."

"Oh. Well, in that case, if you'll excuse me I think I will shit myself."

* * *

Mowgley rang the bicycle bell on the handle of his pint mug and looked around the Bar Normande. "As things go," he said, "it all turned out quite well, didn't it? Quite an interesting day, really."

"If you can call it interesting being held up by a Frenchman with a shotgun then being arrested and banged up in a cell with a drunken tractor driver in a village nick, I suppose it was," said Melons. "If it hadn't been for Guy, we'd probably still be there now."

"I was glad to have been of help," said Guy, as Madame Gilbert arrived to refill their glasses, "I thought that the sergeant was most agreeable."

Madame Gilbert returned with Mowgley's novelty mug, which she had presented to him shortly after he had become a regular. As she said, given the rate he drank compared with the other customers, it would save her legs if he used a litre stein rather than the standard small beer glass. The bicycle bell on the handle was suggested by her bar staff, as it would save their ears being assaulted by his attempts to summon them in French.

Mowgley struggled to remember the French for peanuts, gave up and asked for three bags of crisps in his best mime. "So," he said to Guy, "You'll be able to help us with those telephone numbers?"

"Of course. I have already got someone busy with it. What will you do now?"

"Get the sack, probably," said Melons gloomily. "Especially if Gloria Mundy finds out about us being arrested for breaking and entering."

"Nonsense," said Mowgley, opening his packet of crisps, "we put the roof tiles back, didn't we? And Guy says the paperwork on our arrest will be lost. *And* we got some vital evidence and a lead."

"Which," said Melons firmly, "you will be handing over when you see him, won't you?"

"Of course," said Mowgley reassuringly, "I told you. We're off the case now. Tell you what, though."

"What?"

"French crisps are crap, are they not?"

*   *   *

In the absence of German tourists, the journey back to *La Cour* was uneventful.

As the Lada bumped along the track from the road, Melons looked back for the fourth time. "I can't see his headlights, are you sure he's following us?"

"For God's sake," said Mowgley irritably, "control yourself. He knows where the bloody place is. I don't know why you asked him back. Or rather, I do."

*   *   *

Mowgley stood in the orchard behind the main house, a beer bottle in one hand and what was supposed to be the last roll-up of the day in the other.

All in all, he thought, It had been quite a day. Tomorrow it would be back to the fun factory, George The Dog, The Ship Leopard and a probably eventful encounter with his superintendent. He would hand over all the case-matter to Mundy and let him get on with it. For a moment he thought about the attractions of jacking it all in and escaping permanently to *La Cour*. Would it be so bad to try to live off his wits and the land and spend the autumn of his years getting by on an early retirement pension? He could even learn the language properly, try to find a durable and understanding local widow and get her to set up a bed and breakfast operation. It would, perhaps, be not that bad.

He drained the mug and contemplated the prospect for at least ten seconds. "Oh yes it would," he said aloud, and was about to finish off his beer when he heard a regular creaking noise. It seemed to be coming from beyond the orchard.

Taking a last drag on his cigarette, he walked through the lines of apple trees, out of the gate and into the field beyond. There was a light on in the caravan, and through the net curtain over the window he could see two heads. They were very close together. He thought about breaking up the party, then went in search of a billet for the night. They were both grown-ups and it was none of his business, but he hoped the springs of the caravan were up to a bit of sustained rocking.

*   *   *

The atmosphere in the Lada was somewhat strained the next morning as Inspector Mowgley and his sergeant drove back towards Cherbourg.

Mowgley's mood was not improved by having spent an uncomfortable night in the back of the Lada. Irritatingly, his colleague was aglow with enthusiasm for the Cotentin and its people.

"I reckon," she pronounced as they laboured up the hill to the tiny village of Brix. "I could really fancy living here. The pace of life is so relaxed and the people are friendly once you get to know them. I suppose I could find out about doing an attachment over here?"

"You certainly got attached to the local force last night." Mowgley spoke sourly as he overtook a Volvo estate with British plates. "He must have been showing you police procedures for hours in my bloody caravan."

"That's none of your business."

"No, but it's my sodding caravan. You've probably done more damage to the springs in one night than its had in the last twenty years."

They drove on in silence down the hill from the Auchan roundabout, and Mowgley pulled on to the sloping car park of a bar displaying a sign advertising English tobacco.

"I'm going to get some baccy - are you coming in?" he asked uninvitingly.

"No thanks. I'll wait here."

"Please yourself, Sergeant." He applied the handbrake that didn't work, elbowed open the driver's door and walked in a very pointed manner into the bar.

*   *   *

She found him sitting in the corner of the bar, playing with a lighter in the shape of a pistol which came as a free gift with bulk orders.

"I'm just finishing my coffee," he said, "I'll be out in a minute."

"I think you'd better come out now," said Melons, "somebody has just run into the car."

Outside, two men were trying to disentangle the back bumper of a Renault van from the near side wing of the Lada.

"They backed into us," explained Melons rather unnecessarily, "they say it was all their fault and they will have it fixed. They own a garage."

"What are they trying to do - drum up business?" Mowgley winced as the van backed away, taking the whole rusting wing of the Lada with it.

*   *   *

Several hours later, and they were sitting in the bar of the Mercure hotel, watching as the boat they should have been on steamed through the Cherbourg breakwater.

"Well," said Melons brightly, "this is nice isn't it? We get a free night in a posh hotel while they repair the car."

"I'd have rather had the money and left the car," said Mowgley. It would have been cheaper for them to give us the scrap value and call it quits. In fact, I wouldn't be surprised if you didn't organise it all just so you could have another night over here."

"Don't be ridiculous, why would I do that?"

"I wonder. Are we going into town for a few beers or what, then?"

Melons coloured slightly and fiddled with her mobile phone. "Actually, I've got a few calls to make, then I thought I'd have an early night."

"I expect you need one." Mowgley put his glass down and stood up.

"I'll have to have a wander on my own then." He got as far as the door to the foyer, then looked back as Melons put the phone to her ear. "You do know you don't need a code for Varengebec from here, don't you?"

"Yes thank you."

"Don't mention it."

*　　　*　　　*

By midnight, Mowgley had visited seven bars and was leaving the eighth when he was accosted by a woman leaning against a hamburger van.

She walked over and touched his arm, then spoke in heavily accented English: "Are you looking for a good time?"

"No," said Mowgley, "I'm looking for a curry shop. But failing that..."

*　　　*　　　*

Back in his room, Mowgley opened the mini-bar and peered inside. "Do you want scotch, brandy or gin?"

"I am not fussy."

"No, I can see that."

He took the drinks over to the sofa and sat beside the woman, who had taken her coat off to reveal a pair of very long legs and a short skirt. Mowgley passed her one of the glasses, and was encouraged when she took his hand and put it on her thigh.

"Do you like me?" she asked, reaching towards his trouser fly.

"I think you're a very nice girl," said Mowgley, leaning back and preparing to surrender himself to what seemed to be the inevitable outcome.

"Do you like something... different?" his guest asked, spreading her legs wider and moving his hand beneath her skirt.

"As long as it doesn't involve animals or ice cream," said Mowgley, beginning to explore the possibilities now open to him.

The woman groaned and leaned further back, arching her back and resting her legs on the coffee table. Mowgley leaned over towards her, moved his hand further up between her legs, and then groaned louder than his prospective partner. Reclaiming his trouser fly, he stood up and pointed a shaking finger at the door:

"Look mate, I know you've got a living to make, but I forgot to say I draw the line at shagging people with bollocks. Especially when they're bigger than mine."

Twenty-nine

The *Hampshire Pride* moved fairly smoothly into its UK berth, bearing its typically eclectic mix of passengers and their vehicles, including Mowgley's freshly restored Lada.

"Looks a bit funny with a new wing, doesn't it?" He held his fingers in the shape of a square in the way film directors do, then squinted through it at the vehicle as they walked across the car deck. "That must be the colour the rest of the car was once. Nice of those garage blokes to take the trouble, though."

There was no response. Although the crossing conditions had been calm, their passage together had been stormy. As well as Guy Varennes being at the breakfast table, Mowgley had not been pleased to discover that the whole hotel appeared to know about his adventures with the transvestite prostitute.

"She/he is quite popular in the town," Guy had remarked over coffee, "...and she is said to give very good value for money if you like that sort of thing."

The unintended implication that Mowgley did like that sort of thing had been savagely rebuffed, much to the French detective's amusement. "I don't know why you are so worried about what people might think," he had observed, "In France, we do not think such things are important."

Mowgley had reacted by pointing out that any nation

which ate horses and snails and had come second and had to be bailed out in the two and only world wars was hardly likely to worry about such things, but Melons had sided with Guy in the ensuing debate and comparisons of culture. The news that Guy had brought details of the calls Margaret Birchall had made from her Normandy cottage in the past month had done little to ease the situation, and Melons had remained distant throughout their return.

On board, Mowgley and his partner had had a long and increasingly hostile conversation, covering aspects of their relationship that he had not realised even existed. The discussion had ended when Melons said she had been thinking about asking for a transfer, and Mowgley had said it sounded a good idea.

As soon as she had left the table in the bar and gone up on deck to cool down, he thought how much he wished he had not said some of the things he had said, and just how much he would miss her if she left him. It was one of those not infrequent times when Mowgley thought how useful a remote control for Life would be. Just like with a video-recorder, he would be able to press a button and go back to just before an unpleasant event, and do things differently the next time. He would even be able to fast-forward through the bits he knew were going to be boring, and erase some of the bad stuff. He would also be able to press the pause button and put his life on hold. Thinking about it, he got that effect by having a session at The Ship Leopard and then sleeping it off, which was the best reason for a session he could think of at this or any other troubled time.

*   *   *

The Ferry King lay in his bunk, counting the rivets in the overhead bulkhead. Unsurprisingly and slightly reassuringly, the tally came to the same number as the last time he had counted them.

Through an open porthole he could hear the steady roar of traffic throwing itself furiously from the surrounding areas into the bottleneck of the main road into the city. In mid-afternoon it would start all over again, with twenty thousand drivers trying to escape from the neck of the bottle, just like ants trying to get out of a real bottle. That, he thought, was a really bad metaphor - or perhaps it was a simile - but he was far too knackered to think of a better one.

With an indulgent groan, he swung his legs over the edge of the bunk, stood up carefully and shuffled to the galley, keeping a weather eye open for overnight deposits from George.

Looking in the mirror above the sink unit, he noticed that the rash was spreading. Soon, he would have to wear his collar around his forehead to hide it. At the rate they were multiplying, perhaps all the spots would join together soon and he would just look sunburned. A bit hard to explain away in November, though.

He stood on tiptoe and peed into the sink, remembering to run the tap for decency's sake, then washed, thought about cleaning his teeth, and plugged the kettle in instead.

A little later, he found George hiding in the chain locker and persuaded him to come out for breakfast. When it was made clear that there was no immediate threat of a walk, George joined him to see off the remains of last night's takeaway from the Midnight Tindaloo. As he divided the contents of the silver cartons onto two plates and put one on the floor, Mowgley said: "There you are, mate; a real dog's breakfast. Looks great to begin with, and you end up with the leftovers. A bit like life, really, isn't it?"

Heartened at the depth of this philosophical observation and the improvement on his metaphorical structuring and perhaps even influenced by the aftertaste of the curry, he decided he would clean his teeth after all.

Outside, Mowgley was pleased to note that the submarine next door was still afloat, but puzzled to find his car missing. Then and even above the traffic noise, he heard the grinding machinations of Dodger's car crusher.

"Oh shit," he said to George The Dog, "I hope I didn't leave anything important inside."

*   *   *

At the gun-turret office, he found Dodger hard at work on the company books. There were two of them, one labelled THEIRS and the other MINE. Mowgley observed that the unofficial record of the scrapyard owner's fiscal dealings was far fatter than the official company accounts.

"You could have told me about the Lada," he said reproachfully.

"What about it?" said Dodger, looking up from his labours.

"You've bloody crushed it, haven't you?"

"No. Just warming the machine up, that's all."

"Well, it's not where it should be."

Dodger sucked his pencil and then his teeth: "That's not exactly unusual, is it?"

"I wasn't drinking last night," said Mowgley defensively. "Well, only a couple. I remember distinctly parking it in the usual place."

"Perhaps someone's nicked it."

"Are you taking the piss?"

"Yes."

Mowgley was not in the mood for badinage, so pressed on. "Have you got another one I can use?"

"Only if you fancy a half-track armoured troop carrier. Might be a bit dodgy if someone spots you haven't got any tax on it." Dodger laid down his pencil, sucked his teeth again, stretched and said: "Want a bit of bad news, by the way?"

"No thanks. I've got plenty to be going on with."

"The council's trying to get me out. They say that the place is an eyesore."

"Surely not."

As he already knew, sarcasm was wasted on Dodger, who continued: "They're offering me money to go. If I do, you'll be out of a lodging."

Mowgley gave what he hoped was a hollow laugh: "That's the least of my worries; the way things are going I could be out of a job."

*   *   *

After persuading George to walk to work, it was an hour before Mowgley arrived at the fun factory. Melons was at her desk, her back firmly turned towards him. He considered apologising for his part in their row on the previous night's crossing from Cherbourg, then decided against it. Leaving George in his favourite spot under her desk, he walked through the aisle of desks to find his office door closed and an anxious-looking Stephen Mundy hovering outside. Through the glass panel in the partition, Mowgley could see the blurred outline of a figure seated at his desk.

"Oh blimey," groaned Mowgley, "It's happened already. Just tell me it's not Dickie Quayle whose got my job."

"Actually," said Mundy the Younger, "it's my father."

"That's not your fault, son. He had to be somebody's" Mowgley patted the young man on the shoulder, straightened his tie and his back, and walked into his office.

*   *   *

An hour later, Chief Superintendent Mundy and his bag-carrier left the office, Inspector Byng with a large box file carried meaningfully in both hands as if in evidence of what could be Mowgley's final fall from grace. The pair and the file were followed a little later by the Ferry King, who walked across to the coffee machine, kicked it, then limped over to where Melons was regarding him steadily.

"Do you want a hand?" she asked in a more sympathetic tone than when they had last spoken.

"What with?" asked Mowgley, massaging his foot.

"Clearing your desk."

"Already done," he said, loosening his tie then self-consciously pulling his collar higher. "Gloria has taken all our stuff on the case. For your information, he was kind enough to tell me that we have been dealing with and merrily traipsing along the trail after a pair of probably psychopathic and clearly man-hating killers."

"Beg pardon?"

"While he was dealing with the Birchall investigation, Cyrano thought it would be a good idea to run Mrs Birchall and her sister through the national computer, like what we would have done when we got around to it. Given all the MO hints, clues, matches and fiddly bits, the machine came up with a couple of ladies who the Jocks are very keen to interview on account of a dead solicitor in Glasgow with coming up for half a million pounds missing from his clients' accounts. He was supposed to have been killed in a hit-and-run job. The girls have obviously got a taste for it, now. That's just one of the reasons Mundy wants us off and him on the case. He finds the sisters McGrimm and gets all the credit."

"Oh, I see. Actually, what I meant about clearing your desk was have you got the bullet?"

"How thoughtfully put. No, I've not got the bullet though I had to bite it a couple of times ha ha ha, but we eventually saw sort-of eye-to-eye. Broadly, Mundy is sending Cyrano over to liaise with the authorities in France, whatever that means, and to continue the investigation. We are off the case. I am on an official warning, but am still, until further notice and as you will no doubt be happy to learn, your commanding officer."

"Shit."

"Thanks very much."

"I meant shit that we are off the case. It's not fair."

"Don't panic. You'll still get the chance to talk to Frog One. In the meantime, I have a job for you."

"What's that?"

"Take me down the pub. The Lada's been nicked."

"You jest?"

"No. It must have been the new wing making it so attractive to an international team of quality car heisters. Or not."

*   *   *

Melons returned from the bar and put the glasses on their table. "I still don't know how you get away with it."

"What, getting you to buy the first round so it'll be your turn to buy the last? All these years and I thought you hadn't noticed."

"I tumbled that stroke a long time ago. Nobody needs to go to the toilet straightaway every single time they go in a pub. What I meant was how you get away with it with Mundy. You must have something really good on him."

"Not as much as you've got on me."

"You don't think I'd ever use it, do you, in spite of how horrible you are to me?"

"Perhaps not."

"What's that supposed to mean?"

"Nothing."

"Bollocks to nothing." Melons reached down and patted George, then stood up: "Either we have this out, or I'm putting in for a transfer. I can handle just about anything from you except this betrayed boyfriend act."

Mowgley looked into his glass and said nothing.

"Well," said Melons, sitting down again, "Are you going to tell me? What's your problem? It's all about me and Guy isn't it?"

"All that stuff is nothing to do with me," said Mowgley, "it's just that -"

"What?"

"You know."

"No, I don't."

"Never mind. If I've upset you I'm sorry. Just been a bad time, that's all."

"Don't start crying; you'll embarrass George."

Mowgley smiled half-heartedly, then said: "You know you're the only woman I've ever trusted, don't you?"

"What about your mother?"

"I never knew her. She ran off with a seafaring man when I was still a baby."

"Are you sure?"

"Of course I'm sure. It's not the sort of thing you forget, is it?"

"It's just that last time you mentioned her, you said she was killed in a knife-throwing act in a circus when you were twelve."

Mowgley hardly missed a beat. "Ah. You're thinking of my stepmother."

"I thought she was the one who was awarded the *Legion d'Honeur* for being parachuted into Occupied France and assassinating the mayor of Vichy. That's what you told Guy."

"The bastard. I told him that it was still on the Official Secrets List. Anyway, are we mates again?"

"Only on four conditions."

"Name them."

"The first is you go to the doctor about that rash."

"And the second?"

"You give me the rest of the week and the weekend off and don't call or come round and see me until at least next Monday morning."

"Why?"

"I'm going somewhere and seeing someone."

"But you've just bloody well got back from over there. Now let me see, let's work out the attraction. Three letters, and he gets stuffed and burned to a crisp every November the Fifth?"

"Cut it out."

"Alright, I give in. What's the third?"

"You stop doing that ludicrous non-laugh when you think you've made a gag."

"Why, it makes you gag, does it, ha ha ha? Okay, don't hang up. What's the fourth condition?"

"You stop calling me Melons. Especially in front of Guy."

*   *   *

The phone rang as Mowgley was composing his numbers

for that week's National Lottery syndicate entry. Against strong opposition, he intended selecting the first six numbers on the entry ticket. In the first place, he had pointed out to the other members, there was statistically just as much chance of them coming up as any other combination. In the second, it was obvious that nobody else would be crackers enough to choose those numbers, so if they came up they wouldn't have to share the jackpot with anyone else.

Finishing the job as the phone rang, he picked the receiver up.

"Hello, Madge's Massage Parlour?"

"It's me, Catherine."

"Sorry, you must have the wrong number."

"Har de har."

"Where are you, Mel - *Mizz* McCarthy? - I need your vote on the Lottery numbers."

"It'll have to be a phone vote."

"Why?"

"I'm still here. In Limoges."

"Lim-what? Where's that? Anywhere near where my aunt lives in Brighton?"

"You haven't got an aunt in Brighton, and you clearly weren't listening in the hotel last week. Three of the calls on Margaret Birchall's phone bill were to Limoges - to a hotel near Limoges. It's in France, as you bloody well know."

"And?"

"Guy checked it out and she stayed there twice in the month before she was supposed to have gone over the side of the boat."

"How do you know? You're not telling me she used her real name?"

"Of course not. Guy sent a copy of her passport photo to a friend in the force down here. The receptionist recognised her. So we thought we'd come down for a look around. We wanted to go somewhere nice for the weekend anyway."

"I'm glad to hear you've been on the job while being on

the job. Ha-ha-ha."

"Watch it, you know what we agreed. That's a yellow card."

"Sorry. Couldn't resist that one. So what turned up?"

"Quite a lot. The receptionist remembered helping her out with some numbers for local estate agents. She said she was looking for a place to rent."

"So you went house-hunting?"

"Not yet. There's more."

"You sound like Jimmy Cricket."

"What?"

"Never mind. A truly great comedian, too soon forgotten. So what more is there?"

"Cyrano Byng's here as well."

"What?"

"Mundy must have done the same homework as us when he got the telephone bill from you with all the rest of the gubbins. Or more like he had someone with more than his half a brain cell go through the paperwork. Anyway, Byngabong's been staying at the hotel since last Friday. And the bad news is that the receptionist gave him the estate agent details before us."

"I hope he doesn't know you're down there. That would drop me right in the shite, as you would say."

"I don't know if he knows about me being in town, as he's not at the hotel."

"I thought you said he was staying there?"

"He is... or has been. Nobody's seen him for a couple of days. His rooms still got all his stuff in it, but he's not around, and he didn't say anything about when he was checking out."

"Oh," Mowgley said thoughtfully, taking a new lottery entry form and beginning to tick the boxes above the last six numbers. "Is there an airport in Limoges?"

"Yes, I think so. Why?"

"I'll give you a bell when I'm due to arrive."

"Are you sure? Mundy will not be best pleased."

"Sod Mundy. I'm not letting The Fat Controller, Cyrano,

the bloody Frogs or even you take the credit for all my hard work."

"But whose going to pay for all your dashing around?"

"You never know, we might get lucky. I've got a good feeling about the lottery."

Thirty

"You spotted me in the crowd alright, then?"

"Yes, sort of." Melons looked at Mowgley's rumpled suit, complimentary airline ballcap and the Safeway carrier-bag containing his change of clothing, and shuddered.

"I was in a rush," he said defensively. "I didn't have a chance to pack properly."

"Really?" She led the way out of the terminal building to where Guy was waiting in a car. Before getting in, Mowgley took off the cap and offered it to a passing child. The little girl looked him up and down in much the same way as Melons had, then ran off and grabbed her mother's hand.

*   *   *

As they drove along the RN 147 in the direction of Bellac and the hotel at Magnac Laval, Melons told Mowgley about developments since they had last spoken.

"We called the four estate agents in the area that the receptionist told Margaret Birchall about. One didn't recognise her description, and another said someone looking like her had been in but they hadn't been able to help her. A woman in the third place we called said they gave her some details of suitable places, but she hasn't been back to them yet."

"What about number four?"

"Don't know yet. They said they remembered her but the person dealing with her was out of the office. He's expected back later today."

Mowgley nodded, then sat back and concentrated on the passing countryside, gradually releasing his death-grip on the arm rest as he became re-acquainted with his French friend's style and standard of driving. "Funny old life. isn't it?"

"What do you mean?" asked Melons.

"Just a few weeks ago we'd never heard of Mrs Margaret Birchall. And you'd never heard of Guy Varennes. Now here we are all sitting in a car in the middle of France on the trail of a couple of well-likely murderesses, if that's the plural of 'murderess'."

"Well, it's better than being in the pub with nothing to do, isn't it?"

"Hmmm," said Mowgley dubiously as he put two fingers up at an overtaking motorist who happened to be overtaking on their inside, "I think that's worth a debate. In a pub, of course."

*   *   *

The hotel at Magnac Laval was, as provincial French hotels go, quite smart, surprisingly efficient and almost welcoming. After learning that Inspector Byng had still not put in an appearance, they booked Mowgley in, with the detective making an effort not to ask if they were in separate rooms.

After unpacking by upending his carrier bag on the spare bed, he examined the bathroom, put the complimentary soap and shower gel into the Safeway bag and went down to join the others in the bar.

*   *   *

It was another two hours before the missing estate agent returned to his office. Guy spoke to him from the hotel lobby, then returned to where they were sitting at the bar.

"Well," asked Mowgley, "has the eagle landed?"

"I'm sorry?"

"Forget it. What news?"

"I think we are getting somewhere. The man said that he showed an English woman answering our description around several properties at the end of last week."

"And which one did she take?"

"None of them, yet."

"Shit," said Melons, then and to Mowgley's extreme disapproval, looked apologetically at Guy.

"But," continued the French detective, "she is interested in two of the places, and was waiting to see what her sister thought."

Mowgley stopped tearing his beermat into small pieces and looked up with renewed interest. "And...?"

"So, he left her the keys. It is quite usual in rural parts. Both houses are unoccupied. She is staying, she told him, in a small *auberge* at La Bazeuge - it's not far from here - and I have the addresses of both the properties to which she has the keys." Guy paused, looking quite pleased with himself.

"Good Boy. And did you remember to ask about Inspector Byng?"

"I did. The man said that an English policeman had been to see him two days ago, and he gave him the same information."

"Well done." Melons looked at Guy as if he had just done something particularly clever. "So all we have to do is drop in on Madame Birchall at the inn."

"As long as she's there," said Mowgley.

"Where else is she likely to be?"

"At either of the two places she's been looking at. Have you got your car with you?"

"Of course not. We came down in Guy's car."

"Then this is plan 'A'. You go with Guy to the inn, and if she's not there, you hang on while Guy looks at one of the places she has the keys for. She hasn't met you, so don't try anything clever and just give us a bell if she shows."

"What about you?"

"I'll get a cab to the nearest place she looked at. If they do cabs around here, that is."

"I am sure that the whole of Magnac Laval can boast at least one taxi company," said Guy a little huffily.

"Then we have a plan. You can give me a call on the mobile if you find her first, and I'll do the same."

He tossed the remains of the beer mat on the table and stood up. "Exciting isn't it? An international operation to track down the suspect in her lair. There's only one thing that worries me."

"What's that?" asked Melons.

"What if Cyrano has already got her?"

"He'd hardly bugger off back to England without checking out of here, would he?"

"You know what a rotten detective he is. Perhaps he can't find his way back here."

*   *   *

Following Mowgley's instruction, the taxi drew up at the top of the lane leading to the cottage. He showed the address to the driver again, and the man nodded impatiently, pointed vaguely out of the open window, then looked pointedly at the note Mowgley had given him.

"What's up,in " asked Mowgley innocently, "have I given you too much?"

Following a Gallic glower and a shrug at the higher end of the scale, the driver and his cab roared off in the direction of Magnac Laval, while Mowgley began walking towards the cottage.

*   *   *

Although the afternoon was well advanced, there were no lights showing through the windows of the old farmhouse, and no sign of a car outside. Regardless of these indicators, Mowgley thought it imprudent to knock at the front door, and made his way around to the rear.

Seeing nothing of interest through the windows on either side of the back door, he turned his attention to the outbuildings. Through the deepening dusk, he could see a ramshackle shed with no doors, and a more substantial, barn-like building beyond.

His search of the shed resulting in no more of interest than a wheel-less wheelbarrow and a rotting cider-press, he made his way across to the barn and went gently through a hole once presumably filled by a door.

He stood for a moment in the darkened building, listening to the sound of his own breathing. Then, as he flicked his lighter on, a sudden movement above his head caused him to drop it. On his knees, he ran his hands across the rough earth floor. He found the lighter easily enough, and also something wet and sticky to the touch. He re-lit the lighter and looked at his hand.

"Oh shit," he said, and it was.

*　　*　　*

After climbing the loft ladder and further disturbing the family of rats, Mowgley decided he was wasting his time.

Walking back towards the door of the barn in complete darkness to conserve the fuel in his disposable lighter, he slipped on something soft and almost fell. "Oh shit again," he said aloud, and lit the lighter to look at his shoe and confirm his suspicions.

In the flickering pool of light, he could see what looked like a small and dirty sausage. He picked it up, then dropped it again when he saw that it looked very much like a human finger.

*　　*　　*

The beam from the headlights of the car moved across the kitchen wall as Mowgley sat in the dark. A door slammed and he heard footsteps approaching the house. He lit the lighter, burned his finger again and then looked at the cigarette he had been trying to make. In the small pool of light he could see his hands were shaking. Bloody Melons, he thought, she was supposed to give him her phone. Or to be fair, perhaps he had forgotten to tell her his was charging itself in the fun factory.

As he put the badly-rolled cigarette to his mouth and lit it, the kitchen door opened.

"Bonsoir," he said pleasantly, "Fancy seeing you here."

Surprisingly unsurprised and even more surprisingly unabashed, she walked in and stood by the table.

Before speaking, she looked at him in what seemed a reproachful but affectionate way. Then she spoke in an evenly modulated tone: "Would it be too much to ask how you found me?"

"Not if you make me a cup of tea and tell me where your sister is."

"She's back at the hotel, packing. It'll have to be coffee, I'm afraid."

"That'll have to do, then." He took a long draw on his cigarette. "You forgot the phone bill. At your place in Normandy."

"Of course. I called the hotel at Magnac Laval a couple of times, didn't I? That was stupid."

"Nobody's perfect. You've done pretty good up to now."

"Obviously not." She picked up the kettle then put it down again, laughing melodiously as Mowgley sat more upright in his chair. "Don't worry. I wasn't going to brain you with it. And I don't know why I said coffee anyway, as there's absolutely nothing here." She took her coat off, hung it on the back of the door and sat opposite him at the table. "I suppose you want to know why and how we did it."

"I know at least half a million reasons why. But I am interested in how you did the boat bit."

"Make me a cigarette and I'll tell you."

She watched as he put tobacco in a paper and rolled it, then took the cigarette and leaned forward for a light. "Quite like old times, eh?"

"Yes. So what about the boat?"

"Nothing very dramatic or clever, I'm afraid. I just took turns going over every month as Mrs Birchall and Yvonne McLaughlin. It wasn't very hard getting hold of another passport."

"I've seen *Day Of The Jackal*. And on the night of the overboard, you went on as both?"

"That's right. Me as Margaret drove on as usual, and me as Yvonne was booked on for a cabin as a foot passenger. When I'd parked the car at the kiosk and checked in as Margaret, I just walked over to the terminal, changed to Yvonne in the toilets, and got my ticket. Then I changed again, went back to the car and drove on. They never check that all the foot passengers have actually boarded the boat."

"And what then?"

"After I'd claimed my seat in the overnight lounge as Margaret, it was off to the toilets for another quick-change, and then I took my cabin as Yvonne. It's surprising how quick I got at it after a bit of practice. I still can't believe how easy it is to make people think you're someone else just by playing about with a bit of make-up, a wig and glasses and a change of dress code and accent. I suppose they see what they want to see. Anyway, after I'd made a scene as Margaret and had a conveniently memorable run-in with the two louts, I went down to the cabin and changed to Yvonne for the last bloody time, thank God."

"So plan 'A' was for you and Linda -"

"- it's Bridget, actually."

"- for you and Bridget to work on Birchall about the old lady's property, then panic him when his wife fell over the side?"

"That's right. We thought with Margaret dead and her sister gone, he'd just have to sort out the missing money himself."

"But he killed himself, didn't he? Or didn't he?"

"That was ...sad. We didn't know it was going to happen."

"What, you thought he might be conveniently killed in a hit-and-run instead?"

"Oh." She inhaled deeply, then dropped the cigarette on the slate floor and stepped on it. "So you know about Scotland?"

"Yes," said Mowgley, "I know about Scotland. And -" he reached into his pocket and took out the finger, "- I think I know about Inspector Byng as well. This just came off in your hand, did it?"

She looked at the finger for a moment, then sighed and stood up. "That wasn't me."

"You mean he did it himself?"

"Bridget can get a bit carried away. It was an accident. He tried to grab the carving knife. That's why I came back when I noticed…"

"Charming. So what's become of the rest of him?"

"Oh, he's... around."

Mowgley shook his head, dropped his cigarette on the floor, and put his hands flat on the table to push himself up. As he did so, she put her hands over his and leaned forward across the table. "I don't suppose you'll believe that I really liked you."

"Oh, *please*. Can't you do better than that?"

"It's true. I think perhaps you're a little bit like me."

"Which bit? The thief, the liar, or the enthusiastic accessory to murder?"

She smiled. "You want something else out of life, don't you? Something more? It's what you said before. There's plenty of money now…"

He groaned and began to pull his hands from hers. "You're not really asking me to run off with you and the money and start a new life together?"

"Why not? You're in a position to do exactly what you like, aren't you? I've got the money and you've got me. One way, you get the arrest and the glory and go back to sleeping on a redundant lightship and running your little empire and scraping around to make ends meet. I go to jail. The other, you can go anywhere and do anything you like for the rest of your life. And I don't go to jail."

"But I'd have to spend the rest of my life looking over my shoulder, wouldn't I? And counting my fingers. Or rather, my legs."

"Your legs?"

"Don't you remember when you told me about the female tarantula?"

She looked into the recent past, smiled softly again and said: "Oh yes. Of course."

Mowgley disentangled himself and stood up.

She looked up at him with what appeared to be genuine unhappiness. "Is this where you read me my rights, or whatever it is they call it nowadays?"

"No. I was going to ask if you've got a mobile phone."

"No, but my sister has."

"Oh yes, and when can we expect to see her?"

As he reached for his tobacco tin, something hit Mowgley very hard on the back of the head, and he fell down. He lay on the floor, legs kicking impotently rather like, he thought, a new-born foal trying to get up. He knew from experience that when something or someone hit you very hard, it was not easy to concentrate on what to do for the best. It happened most noticeably when someone got a really good dig in a boxing ring. The brain would be sending out signals, but the bits they were sending them to didn't get the message, or got a distorted one. At the same time, the mind was usually off elsewhere and often thinking almost dispassionately about other things. It could be a bit like sleepwalking or trying to make a dream work out as you wanted it to. Almost idly as he tried to make his limbs do what they were told, he wondered if comparing his legs with a new-born foal was a metaphor or a simile.

His vision started to clear, and he became aware that the woman he had known as Linda Russell was standing over him. She was holding a copper saucepan in her left hand, and there seemed to be a good deal of blood on the heavy base. More was dripping from it. Then Mowgley felt something sticky and warm moving slowly down his face as he tried to sit up, and conjectured that it was probably his.

While he thought about this and what to try and do next, she hit him in the face with the pan. When he started to pay attention again, he saw that Linda Russell had a short kitchen knife in her other hand. With some interest, he watched it and how the blade caught the light of the drop lamp above the table as she raised it to shoulder height. It seemed to Mowgley that this was all taking a very long time, then as the woman bent towards him their eyes met and she smiled. He was thinking whether he should smile back when a hand came into his field of vision. It took hold of Linda Russell's wrist. After a bit more thinking, Mowgley realised the hand must belong to Yvonne, as both his hands were at the end of his arms and not doing much. Then he watched while a grunting, swaying struggle took place, and it reminded him of some hen-nights he had attended when a uniformed bobby.

Eventually, it seemed to him that it would be a good idea to try and restore order, so he kicked out at Linda Russell's boot-clad legs. Not surprisingly, his aim was bad, and his foot hit the wrong shin. The hand holding Linda Russell's wrist let go and there was the sound of a chair overturning on the slate-tiled floor as Yvonne fell out of the picture.

Beginning to think a little more clearly, Mowlgey reached out and held on to the seat of the chair he had been sitting on, then managed to get another hand on the table edge.

As he began to pull himself up, he felt a blow above his left shoulder blade, and thought it was just as well that most women couldn't even punch their weight. Finally on his feet, he found himself once more looking into Linda Russell's eyes. She was still smiling that funny smile, and he thought how perfect her make up was, and how red her lips and white her teeth.

Then he noticed she was holding the heavy-based copper saucepan in both hands, and wondered where the knife had gone. He twisted his head and saw that the handle was sticking out of his shoulder. He was obviously not going to be able to reach it with either hand, so he took them off the table and grabbed hold of the lapels of the raincoat she was wearing.

Their faces were no more than a foot apart, and it occurred to him that it was like one of those movie scenes where the couple who had been at each other's throats for most of the film suddenly kissed passionately. As the copper saucepan came his way, Mowgley thought that a kiss would probably not suit the occasion, so head-butted her instead.

Linda Russell's head snapped back and she reeled away from him, the force of her departure ripping the lapels of her coat from Mowgley's grasp. With things still moving more slowly than he thought they probably should, he stood and swayed and watched as she spun almost balletically around and then down, the saucepan flying into the air as her head hit the corner of the wood-burning stove sitting in the marble fireplace surround. In spite of the luxuriant thickness of her hair, the crunching sound of the contact seemed unnaturally loud.

Then, with urgent matters attended to, Mowgley's legs stopped working again and he fell forward onto the floor.

It was a curious feeling to find himself lying alongside and facing the woman who had been trying to kill him. Once again they were face-to-face, but he saw that she was no longer smiling. The long blonde hair on one side of her face was as lustrous and full as before, but on the other side it was matted and almost completely red, dotted with small, uneven shaped pieces of white and what looked like a squidgy lump of grey-ish stuff. As he looked again into her face, he saw that she wore an expression of faint surprise, and her eyes were wide open. She appeared to be looking at him, but it was clear that she was not.

Mowgley lay still, and thought it might be a good idea to try and get some sleep. As he drew his legs up and closed his eyes, he thought about George The Dog, Melons and whether his numbers had come up in the lottery on Wednesday. It would, he thought, be a bit of a shame if they had, and he was not there to enjoy the winnings.

Epilogue

"What's the French for 'Someone bring me a bloody ashtray'?"

"It's a non-smoking area. Anyway, you said yesterday you were going to quit."

"I have. I give up smoking after each fag. That way I'm a non-smoker more than I'm a smoker, so everyone can stop nagging me about it." He smiled craftily. "No good getting older if you don't get smarter, is it?"

"If you say so." Melons shot a concerned look across at Guy Varennes, then laid a hand on her boss's shoulder. "How are you feeling today?"

Mowgley shifted uncomfortably in the hospital bed and raised a cautious hand to his bandaged head, then groaned and used the other hand.

"Do you really want me to tell you?"

"Only if you feel up to it."

They sat in silence for a moment, then Guy said, "I cannot help wondering why Madame McLaughlin let you go."

"Let me go? You make her sound like an employer giving someone the sack."

"He means why she didn't finish you off before she went," said Melons. "She had nothing to lose after Byng, maybe Birchall and probably the bloke in Scotland. And you had just done for her sister -" Melons broke off and flushed deeply. "I mean, her sister had died in the fall."

Mowgley winced and took his hand away from his head. "She said she liked me."

"Well, that's something to be grateful for, I suppose." Melons ignored the reproving look of a passing nurse, lit and handed over a tailor-made cigarette. "She must have thought something of you to use her sister's phone to call for an ambulance before she skipped. I suppose there's no accounting for taste."

The patient shook his head in irritation at not being able to come up with a snappy rejoinder, immediately regretted it, then turned slowly towards his French colleague. "I suppose there's no chance of your lot picking her up?"

"Perhaps. She had a good start, but we have a description. Unfortunately, she has plenty of money and seems quite good at making a disguise of herself, and I do not suppose she is using the same name and passport as before."

"No, I suppose not as well." Mowgley drew deeply on the cigarette, then handed it back to Melons. "So haven't you got any good news for me?"

She shook her head. "Not really. We didn't win the lottery, so I suppose we'll have to go on with the job for a bit longer."

Mowgley nodded and again regretted moving his head. "I could have taken early retirement but I fancied keeping my legs."

Melons frowned. "Do what? 'taken early retirement'? 'Keeping your legs'? Are you feeling okay? Perhaps you're still a bit delirious?"

"Delirious? Oh yes, I'm obviously bloody ecstatic to be laying in a Frog hospital with a hole in my back, a splitting headache and looking like the Elephant Man." He reached out for the cigarette and turned again to Guy. "Have your blokes found poor old Cyrano yet?"

"I am afraid not, but they are checking every unoccupied building in the area, and even the pigstyes..." It was Guy's turn to break off and flush.

Mowgley was silent for a moment and then asked Melons: "Have you heard from Mundy since yesterday? Did he say when he was arriving with the grapes and flowers?"

"He called this morning and said he wants to see you as soon as you're a bit better. Amongst other things, It's about the Lada."

"They found it, then?"

"Customs found it while they were doing a tail on a car full of known Frog importers. They followed them to the scrapyard, and picked them all up after they took your car to a lock-up in the city and started working on it. By the time the collar had happened, the wing of the Lada was off and they saw it had been packed with loads of bags of top quality coke. When you think about it, it did seem funny the way those blokes in Cherbourg were so keen to take it away and repair it. They've been doing one a week for more than a year, and it really is - or was - as foolproof as it gets. They bash into a Brit on his way back to the ferry, apologise and offer to fix it. Then they take the car away, fill the damaged bit or any conveniently out-of-sight niche with the class 'A' flavour of the month, mend the damage and give the motor back, then follow it on the ferry and nick it from wherever the owner leaves it. If the stuff gets found on the way through customs, they're in the clear. Bet they'd have had a fit if they'd known you were on the job."

"So why didn't Customs tell us this thing with pranging cars was going on?"

"They say they did. You've had six briefings, according to them. And just to prove it they've sent the date-delivered copies to Mundy. That's another thing he wants to see you about."

"I bet he does," said Mowgley gloomily. He took a final draw on the cigarette, then picked up a hand-mirror, looked into it and smiled.

"What is it, Jack?" asked Melons.

"I've just realised," said the Ferry King, running a hand down the side of his neck, "my rash has gone. And it's my birthday today..."

Glossary

For reasons discussed at the beginning of this book, Portsmouth has over the centuries developed its own language. As with all such words and expression, the origins of those listed here will depend on whose claim you choose to believe. By definition, street-talk can have no conclusive provenance. The entries are in alphabetical order and I have included some which do not occur in the book. For obvious reasons, I have spelled these non-words phonetically.

Bok:

From the Romany language and simply meaning 'luck', but used in Portsmouth in a negative form to mean the act of bringing bad luck or the person who brings it. My dad claimed my sailor uncle was a bok for Portsmouth FC as they always lost when he was in port and went to Fratton Park.

Brahma:

There are various spellings but only one pronunciation for this word, which can be used as a noun or adjective. Broadly, it means something or someone of outstanding quality, as in 'What a brahma Ruby' (see below) or 'She's a right little brahma.' Unlikely, I would have thought, but it may have some connection to the impressive bull of that name. One of the three major deities in the Hindu pantheon bears this name, which may also have some bearing on the matter.

Cushdy:

Another Romany expression, broadly meaning 'good'. You might make a cushdy bargain, or say that someone has made a cushdy result. Sometimes the word is used on its own in reaction to hearing of someone's good fortune, as in 'Did you hear about Baggy? He's moved in with that brahma-lookin' nympho widow who owns a pub.' An appropriate response would be: 'Yeah? *Cushdy*...'

Dinlow:

Fool, idiot. Often used in the short form of 'din', and can also be used as an adjective as in 'You dinny tosser.' I am told this is yet another Romany word with common currency in Portsmouth.

Iron:

A gay man. One half of the rhyming slang 'Iron hoof' for 'poof'. Other and seemingly limitless non-pc allusions include shirt-lifter and turd burglar. Lesbians may be referred to as muff-divers or minge-munchers. There is a well-loved if apocryphal tale that, in the 1970s, an anonymous wag took a small ad in the For Sale section of Portsmouth's daily newspaper. The clearly naive young lady who took the call duly typed it up and it appeared next day as follows: *For Sale: One muff-diver's helmet. Only slightly used*. The lovely thing was that her bosses could not reprimand the staff member who took the call for not knowing such an improper expression.

Lairy:

This is a very common way of describing an irritating general attitude, as in 'he's a lairy bastard.' Alleged to originate from mid -19th century cockney 'leery', and said to be common to south of England, particularly coastal areas.

Laitz:

A state of absolute rage, as in 'he went absoloootly laitz, didn't 'e?' NB. Another London-esque linguistic custom in Portsmouth is to end statements with a question, as in 'I've gone down the road to see the mush, 'aven't I, and he's only done a runner, 'asn't 'e?' Origin unknown.

Muller:

To murder, but used mostly in a benevolent setting as in 'I could muller a pint'. Allegedly, the expression derives from the name of one Franz Muller, who committed the first murder on a British train when he killed and robbed Mr Thomas Briggs, a banker, on the Brighton Railway in 1864. Muller was hanged later the same year in one of the last public executions at Newgate prison in front of a mostly drunken crowd said to number 50,000. The murder resulted in the introduction of corridors to link railways carriages and the establishment of emergency communication cords. Again, the expression is said to be common to the South coast.

Mush (pron. 'moosh'):

An address to any male friend, stranger or enemy, to be used as in 'Alright, mush?' to a mate, or 'What you looking at, mush?' to someone you would quite like to hit. Again said to come from Romany, and is now somewhat dated and generally being replaced with greetings to friends and strangers by 'mate'. 'Mater' may be used with a particularly close friend. 'Matey' has more or less disappeared, but was for hundreds of years reserved for people who worked in the Naval Base, as in 'Dockyard matey.'

Oppo:

A naval term for a close friend. According to the most likely source, it is short for 'opposite number' and referred to the man on board who did the same job as you during another watch. It paid to become friends for all sorts of reasons.

Pawnee:

Rain. Corruption of Romany *parni* for 'water' and *pani* for 'rain'. Allegedly also from the old Gujarati word for water, picked up then corrupted by British troops in the early days of the Raj.

Ruby:

Fairly modern and universally popular rhyming slang for 'curry'. Derived from Ruby Murray (1935-96), a husky-voiced Belfast-born songstress at the peak of her fame in the late 1950s.

Scran:

Food. Credited generally to the RN via Liverpool or Newcastle, but also said to derive from Romany.

Shant:

As with skimmish (see below), a noun or verb referring to ale or beer. Some Scots claim it as their own, others attribute it to the Royal Navy.

Shoist:

Free, gratis. As in 'How much was your car?' 'Shoist, mater - I nicked it.'

Skate:

Any Royal Naval rating. The term allegedly comes from the 18th century practice of nailing a fish of that name to the mainmast on long voyages for use by the crew in the absence of any obliging females on board (The genitals of the skatefish are said to be very similar to those of the female human).

Skimmish:

Alcoholic drink but usually confined to beer. Can be used as a noun or verb as in 'Fancy a skimmish?' or 'He was well skimmished.' Apparently originated in and peculiar to Portsmouth, but derivation unknown.

Spare:

Apart from the obvious, this word has two main uses. A 'bit of spare' is an available single female. To 'go spare' is to lose one's temper in an explosive manner.

Sprawntzy:

Smart, well turned-out and confident-looking. Origin not known, but 'sprawny' is Polish for efficient of self-assured.

Squinny:

Once again, a word which can be used as a noun or a verb or adjective. You can squinny or *be* a squinny. Basically it means whinge or whine about something in particular, or to generally be a moaner. According to academic sources it is a derivative of the word 'squint' and came into common use in the Middle Ages, but I am not convinced.

Wheee:

According to decades of research (by me) this word/expression is absolutely unique to Portsmouth. As 'Well I never' might be employed in more erudite circles, 'wheee' is brought in to play as a reaction to any piece of information or gossip from the mildly surprising to the truly shocking. Thus it would be used in the same way but with a different level of emphasis if someone said their bus was late that morning, or the next-door neighbour had formed a satanic circle and taken to keeping goats in the back garden for sacrificial and other purposes. I have asked people from all across the county, Britain and the world to try it out, but they can never replicate the depth, subtlety and variety of meaning conveyed by a true Pompeyite saying ' Wheee...'

Yonks:

A long time. Like so many other examples, apparently imported into Pompey *lingua franca* by the RN. Some respected etymologists claim it comes from 'donkey's years', but I think that's a load of cack...

Deadly Tide

If you enjoyed *Death Duty*, you might like a look at the first two chapters of the second book in the Inspector Mowgley series. For more information, visit www.george-east.net or www.amazon.co.uk

Part One
January 1st, 2000

One

The sound of the shot echoed flatly across the open waters.

With no more than a surprised grunt, the body rolled over and slipped beneath the surface, leaving only a spreading stain of red to mark its passing.

On shore, the man straightened up, took off his headphones and looked out to where a fishing boat chugged towards a reluctantly rising winter sun. He had heard that some professional fishermen carried shotguns on board and shot any seals they spotted. There was a colony on the other side of the harbour entrance, and he had read that each one could eat up to ten percent of its body weight in fish every day. It didn't seem a lot, but an adult seal can weigh in at more than five hundred pounds. Whichever way you did the sums, that was a lot of fish. You couldn't blame the fishermen for protecting their livelihoods, but the animal rights brigade would be up in arms if they found out.

He reached down and patted Alfie's head and thought how sentimental humans could be. It was fine for the boat's crew to catch and kill thousands of fish every day because people liked to eat them. But even quite logical people would be horrified at the idea of shooting an inedible - unless you were an Eskimo - seal.

He put the 'phones back on and started the next sweep. He'd been over this stretch of the beach every day for the past week and this would be his last trawl. It was unlikely at this time of year that he would find any recently mislaid money or valuables, but more historic shallow-buried and detectable coins, jewellery and other items worth picking up might lie in wait. This was because these hidden treasures were constantly on the move as a result of heavy seas or even modest tidal changes. The incoming tide also brought small and non-floating objects lost at sea in to the shore.

So far he had not won enough from sand, sea or stones to do more than cover the cost of his detector, petrol for journeys to and from the beach and the odd pint at the Legion. But he had convinced himself that there was some really good stuff down there, and it would make all his efforts a waste of time if he chucked it in and stopped looking. He had been hunting on this beach and coastline for more than a decade, and knew something really worthwhile was waiting for him to turn it up. Of course, all beachcombers and metal hunters thought that, or they would not do what they did in all weathers and times of day and tide. But it was undeniable that there were some very rich pickings for the lucky ones.

Finds along this part of the coast over the years included ancient coins and rings and other ornamental pieces which were sometimes made of gold. Once, a guy with a detector had literally stumbled upon what the papers described as a priceless Celtic figurine. When it had been declared treasure trove, the finder had made nearly fifty grand, and something along those lines would do him nicely. If, or rather when it happened, he would buy a state-of-the-art machine and take a long break in some suitably exotic location where pirates had done their best business. The experts said that there never had been any such thing as buried treasure, but the odd mislaid doubloon or piece of booty would be quite enough to keep him going. Somewhere in the Caribbean would be nice, but until then, life was a beach on the rarely sunny and often shitty south coast.

The man half-smiled at his bad pun, then frowned as a middle-aged woman walked past with her cocker spaniel on a lead. She was not a problem, but the annoying thing for any hunter was that most of the really good stuff was found by people walking their dogs or taking an early-morning stroll. But it was about time his luck changed, and the start of a new century was a very suitable time for him to strike gold. Or anything else worth a good few bob.

He breathed deeply and set his shoulders like a warrior preparing for the fray, checked his settings and switched on the finder.

Almost immediately, a strong signal came through his headphones.

He took them off, pulled the mini-trowel from his belt, sank to his knees and began to probe the shingle.

Unsurprisingly, his search turned up nothing more exciting than a strip of metal foil and half a dozen ring-pulls. Beer or soft drink can ring-pulls were the most common cause of a signal, but if you set the machine to discriminate against them, you were also discriminating what could be much more valuable items, including gold. He shrugged resignedly, put the handful of junk into his gash bag so he would not find it again, and stood up. Perhaps now the tide was right, he would try a bit of wet sand sounding. It looked really strange, but people did not understand that you could use a metal detector in water as long as it did not reach up to the box, and shallow waters could be the happiest of hunting grounds.

After lighting a cigarette and having a good cough, he was on his way down the beach when he saw something floating in the water. It was black and bulky and seemed about the right size, so at first he thought it was the body of the seal. Then he put on his distance glasses and felt his heart quicken. It was not a dead seal, but some sort of bag. Not a bin liner, but a proper bag. It was floating high on the gently moving surface, but showed no sign of coming in to shore.

He looked round to where Alfie was worrying a strand of seaweed encrusted with slipper limpets, and whistled. When the brindle Staffie arrived at his side, he pointed at the bag, threw a stone at it and made encouraging noises. As he had suspected, Alfie regarded the bag coolly, then put his head on one side and looked at his master as if doubting his reason. Some dogs loved the water; others like Alfie did not. In fact he clearly thought it undignified to go chasing off anywhere after something uninteresting and inedible just because his master thought it was a good idea.

Keeping his eye on the bag, the man switched the detector off and laid it carefully down on the sand well beyond the reach of the incoming tide. He thought for a moment about taking his shoes and socks off and rolling his trousers up, then saw that the bag appeared to be moving slowly away from the shore in spite of the tidal movement. Its height and square shape was probably giving it the properties of a sail, with the action of the wind helped by the slight undertow. Without bothering about his state of dress, he splashed into the shallows.

As he got closer, his heart rate upped again and his heavy breathing was caused by more than the effort of wading through the icy water. From this distance, he could see that it was no ordinary bag. It was black and roughly the shape and size of a small cricket bag, with large, looped handles. The flap was secured by two strips of leather, their stylised brass ends held in place by an ostentatiously ornate brass padlock. The bag had a crocodile skin texture, and given its overall quality, he would bet it was the real thing and not a knock-off. He was no follower of fashion, but knew that this sort of designer handbag cost a fortune. They were a very upfront way of showing other women that you or your man could afford to spend more on a handbag than a lot of people paid for their cars. Also, the sort of women who owned bags like this one did not usually use them to keep their sandwiches in. If genuine and empty it could be the best find for many a month. If not empty, it might contain something worth even more than what it would make at the weekly boot sale.

He stopped, took a last draw on his roll-up, dropped it in the water and breathed deeply to try and calm his racing pulse. The reason his heart was trying to get out of his chest was that he had fantasised about a situation like this for years. Some people dreamed of winning the lottery or having sex with a supermodel. He dreamed of being presented with a valuable gift from the gods of the sea.

He was waist deep now and within arm's length of the bag. Reaching down and taking hold of the handles, he realised it was not empty, and that whatever was in it was quite heavy. Rather than try and heft it from the sea, he turned and waded back to the shore, towing the bag by one handle.

Onshore and completely unaware of the effect of the icy wind on his wet legs, the man pulled the bag from the sea. He looked at the small golden lock, then reached for his belt and the screwdriver he used to fine tune his detector.

*   *   *

A little more than a mile away and on the other side of the harbour entrance, a yacht was heading for the shore. Enthusiasts would have recognised it as a Westerly Centaur, and real yachting anoraks would have known it was a little over twenty-one feet in length and eight foot five inches in the beam. The Centaur was a popular and enduring model which had been designed and launched with a suitable fanfare at the 1969 London Boat Show, and this one had obviously been well looked after. The sails were furled neatly and it was running under the power of its MD2B 25HP Volvo diesel engine at a cruising rate of around five knots. In the cockpit, the large chromed wheel was unattended and moved slightly from side to side as the vessel came in at almost a right angle to the shoreline of the deserted beach.

The keel hit bottom as the water depth dropped to less than half a fathom, but the impetus of the boat and the continuing thrust of its propeller pushed it on for another yard before the *Daydream* juddered to a stop. It sat upright in the shallows for a few moments, then slowly toppled over to one side. The engine laboured on for a little while, then coughed and stalled. Then, the lapping of the small waves against the hull was the only sound breaking the calm of the day and place.

*   *   *

The elegant padlock was obviously more for show than protection, and surrendered meekly to the screwdriver. Turning the swivel catch, the man separated the strips of leather and lifted the flap. It was full light now, and he could see a layer of rectangular, plastic-wrapped packages close to the top of the bag. The plastic was opaque, so he could not see what it was covering, but when he took one out it seemed solid and quite heavy. Unfortunately, it was clearly not as heavy as a gold ingot would be. He put it down and gently lifted another block out, and then another and another until there were nineteen packets ranged neatly on the sand. Their removal revealed another layer of packages. These were narrower than those in the top layer, and the shape and size was immediately familiar. The plastic was also fairly translucent, and what he saw through it caused his heart to beat even more strongly.

He had never owned a Euro note, but he had seen them featured on the wall of his local post office since it had become a Bureau de Change as well as issuer of stamps and tax discs. The sandwich board outside showed a selection of notes, and one of them had the same size, shape and stylised number 50 that he could see through the plastic wrapping. At a very rough guess, there would be around a hundred more notes in the packet, and there was a whole layer of packets.

As he began removing them, he realised that Alfie seemed as interested as he was in the bag's contents. The dog had begun to scrabble at the side of the bag, and was making a low, keening sound his owner had not heard before.

As he continued to empty the bag, the man became aware of a slight but distinctive odour. He thought for a

(237)

moment what it reminded him of, then remembered. His regular drinking partner at the working man's club was a butcher, and though apparently quite fastidious in his dress and matters of personal hygiene he gave off the same faint, almost sweet smell.

The odour grew stronger as he removed the last of the packets and the layer of plastic sheeting he found beneath them. Alfie was now so anxious to get his nose into the bag that the man had to grab and hold his collar.

Leaning closer, he felt what he accepted to be a completely unjustifiable flutter of disappointment as he saw there appeared to be no more money in the bag. All that remained was another plastic-wrapped package, this time almost as long as the bag and roughly oval in shape. He pulled it out and, holding it up clear of Alfie's frantic scrabbling, peeled off a length of brown duct tape.

As he did so, the sickly smell increased and he instinctively turned his head away. Removing the final strips of tape, he opened the packet and saw what was inside. Then he gasped, stumbled backwards and felt a rising warm tide in his throat as he dropped the object on to the sand.

Alfie showed no such signs of aversion, and with a somehow triumphant growl he opened his jaws wide, took a firm hold on his prize and scampered away up the beach. He was a mostly obedient dog, but nobody was going to deprive him of several pounds of slightly decaying but still fairly fresh meat.

*   *   *

As the log book would confirm, the triple-nine call from the beach hunter was made at 8.49 a.m. As per procedure and after being taken at Netley Control Room, it was transferred to area control for Havant. As a result, the nearest patrol car to the beach was despatched on Priority One to locate the caller, detain him and tape off the immediate area of the beach where the bag had been found.

The nearest senior CID officer had been about to enjoy his first breakfast of the new century in the canteen at Cosham, but felt duty-bound to abandon it and was at the scene not long after the patrol car officers had cordoned off the beach at Sandy Point.

The Scene of Crime Officers - a middle aged male and a younger female civilian specialist- had also come from Cosham, and the man was finishing a bacon sandwich as their car pulled up by the entrance to the narrow concrete strip leading to the beach. In the next hour, the white-suited pair would carefully examine the bag and its contents, and take a number of photographs of the items where they lay. Using her dual credentials as a forensic officer and fashion-conscious woman, the female half of the SOCO team declared the bag to be a genuine Hermes Birkin, valued new at around £6,000. Had it been the version with its handles studded with diamonds, she informed her bemused colleague, it would have been priced at around £30,000.

Regardless of its value, the bag would be labelled and packaged and sent for more detailed forensic examination at a central laboratory in Aldermaston. Before a sweep team was called in to conduct a fingertip search of the beach, the packets of banknotes and those containing an unknown substance would also be examined, photographed, tagged and bagged ready for despatch. The same treatment would be given to the human arm which Alfie had been persuaded to release, and also the one still in the bag. Both would be taken with all speed to the Pathology laboratory at the Queen Alexandra hospital, some five miles and fourteen minutes away, with the driver of the patrol car relishing the opportunity to use his siren and flashing lights to good effect.

TWO

The woman parked on yellow lines and walked across the road towards an alleyway which ran alongside an Indian restaurant. All was quiet, she noted, in spite of the advanced morning hour. It seemed almost as if the city had woken up, taken a look at what the new Millennium had to offer, then decided to have a lie-in.

Sidestepping a brownish, lumpy pool of what could be curry sauce, vomit or worse, she shuddered slightly, pushed the unlocked back door open and walked up the stairs, her heels clacking on the uncovered staircase. One of the doors leading off the landing was ajar, and looking through she saw a young Asian man standing by the foot of a bed. He was naked, and their eyes met before she moved on. As she climbed the steep stairs to the attic, she reflected that he had not looked embarrassed, angry or lustful; rather, his expression had been apprehensive, even fearful. Perhaps, she thought, he was not supposed to be in the building, or perhaps not in the country.

The smell of curry farts, stale rolling tobacco and unwashed socks welcomed her as she opened the door to the attic room. The curtains on the small dormer window were open but the glass was so filthy that she could only just make out the mound on the bed. But she could hear a rhythmic creaking and panting, so coughed loudly.

"Happy New Year. If you're busy I can come back."

The creaking stopped abruptly and a bedside lamp was switched on, revealing a figure sitting up in bed with a blanket around its shoulders. Detective Inspector John Mowgley held a spoon in one hand, and a large foil container in the other.

"It's alright, I was just trying to soften up this lamb bhoona. It's set solid."

Of all people, Sergeant Catherine McCarthy should know of and be inured to her colleague and immediate superior's little ways, but she still winced when confronted with some of his grosser excesses. He saw her expression and paused mid-spoonful. "What's up? Lots of people have breakfast in bed."

"Yes, but not cold curry."

"Are you not being a teeny-bit racist, Sergeant? Millions of people around the world eat curry for breakfast. Anyway, for some reason I was not in a state to eat it last night and it would have been a waste and an insult to Bombay Billy to chuck it away. He left it on the stairs after closing as a New Year's present. At least that's what I hope it was left there for..."

Mowgley laid the container down, stretched, yawned, sucked thoughtfully on and then scratched himself with the spoon in an area thankfully hidden by the blanket, then asked in his best hopeful little boy manner : "Have you come to take me down the pub for a recovery session?"

"Maybe later. I'm afraid I've come to take you to work first. I did try to phone, but a strange man answered."

Mowgley ran a finger around the inside of the foil container, licked it clean, then nodded as he remembered. "Ah yes. That would be King Dong. We had a bet in the khazi at the Leopard and I lost."

Melons shook her head, reached in to her handbag and took out Mowgley's phone. "I know, I stopped off at the docks to pick it up on the way here. You owe me twenty quid. I won't even ask what the bet was."

"Good Idea. Not to ask, I mean. Put the money on my account, will you, Sergeant?" He reached out and took the phone, looking at it resentfully. "So why have you come to take me to work on a national holiday?"

"Crime never sleeps. They've found something nasty on the overnight boat from Caen."

"Well, it's a French boat, isn't it? What do you expect? Have they started putting snails and that tripe stuff on the menu again?"

"Not as far as I know. But I don't think Senora Maria Assumpta Sanchez expected to find what she did in the cabin she was about to clean."

"What, a couple having it away? Someone having a poo with the curtain not drawn?

"No, a man's body."

"Oh." Mowgley swung his legs over the side of the bed and got down on all fours to begin a fingertip search of the floor for his smaller items of clothing. "Well, it happens, doesn't it? . I read somewhere that a statistically disproportionate number of men die of a heart attack when they're on holiday. Was he getting on a bit?"

"Don't know, there was no passport or any means of identification in the cabin."

Mowgley gave an unconcerned shrug. "So what? Surely a detective of your years and training can tell from a bloke's face roughly what age he is."

Melons reached down, picked up a sock and handed it to her boss. "Not if he doesn't have a face."

"You mean someone had bashed his face in?"

"No, like I said, he didn't have a face, or rather he didn't have a head. Nor any arms or legs."

*   *   *

Mowgley continued dressing in the car on the way to the ferry port. Although the grisly find was interfering with his plans for a leisurely day at his local, it was, he conceded, an interesting start to the new Millennium. A handful of people died on cross-Channel ferries each year, and there were procedures in place to deal with such an event in a dignified and unobtrusive way. Normally, it was someone expiring from age or with a chronic medical problem.

Much less commonly, a death on board was the result of an accident. Even more rarely was it a manslaughter brought about by a fracas, and murder on board only happened in Agatha Christie whodunnits. There was the occasional death-related event of interest, as when a woman tried to smuggle the body of her elderly husband on to a ferry bound for England. He had conked out in Cherbourg the day before the couple were due to return, and she had left him in the car overnight. At the check-in she had claimed he was sleeping, but she had neglected to close his eyes. When questioned by the French police, she had said they had not taken out insurance cover for the mini-break, and she knew it would have been a lot of red tape and expense to ship him back or bury him on the wrong side of the Channel. Besides, she said candidly, he hated the French and it would have been unthinkable for him to spend eternity in their country rather than his own.

"Bugger."

Melons glanced at where he was struggling with his shirt. "What's the matter?"

"The bloody thing's shrunk in the wash. I can't do the buttons up."

She gave a scornful grunt. "Shrunk in the wash? You have to wash clothes for them to shrink. Unless you were laying about in the rain outside the pub last night, perhaps? Otherwise I have to tell you that the reason your shirt will not do up is because you have got quite porky since moving home from the scrap yard to The Midnight Tindaloo. And it can't be good for you to live on curry."

"You're verging on being racist again, Sergeant. If you don't mend your ways I might report you to our Gender Equality and Diversity Awareness Officer."

"Erm, that's me, actually."

"Who says so?"

"You did when that journo from the local rag asked if we had one."

"Oh. Okay then. Make a note to have a word with yourself."

He gave up the struggle with his shirt collar as they reached the entrance to the ferry port. Melons drove under the giant goalpost and took the lane alongside a long line of cars waiting at one of the check-in booths. An illuminated screen on top of the booth was repeatedly apologising for the delay but, Mowgley noted, did not explain that the reason the punters were being held up was because a major body part was occupying one of the cabins.

He gave a regal wave and smug smile as they sped past the row of glum and fractious faces, then sighed reflectively. "Why oh why do they do it?"

"What?" asked his colleague.

"Spend a fortune to be banged up in a car for hours with the kids screaming and the dog being sick, then be herded on to a rusty old tub and fleeced for hours, before having two miserable weeks being ripped off in a place where the natives can't even be bothered to pretend they appreciate the billions the Brits bring over the Channel and leave in their country."

Melons shrugged. "Having rows and being ripped off is what going on holiday is all about."

"That's my point. They could have had twice as much fun and saved shedloads of dosh by having their rows in the comfort of their own homes."

*   *   *

Having shown their warrant cards to an over-fussy uniform guarding the gangplank, they made their way to the main deck and its information bureau.

Being a modern French ferry, this part of the ship looked like a cross between a set in a 1970s science-fiction film and the stage area of a Eurovision song contest hosted by a minor country determined to make up for what it lacked in status and Gross National Product with a total overkill of bad taste. For not the first time, Mowgley looked around and wondered how the French were generally acknowledged as being such good designers when they were clearly so crap at it.

It was difficult to appreciate the true awfulness of the area, he thought, as it was athrong with people in various stages of frustration, irritation and bubbling rage. All the banquette seating having been taken, some passengers were sitting on their suitcases, while other mostly younger travellers sat or lay stretched out on the floor. Some of the seasoned voyagers who were more accustomed to unexplained delays browsed in the shops, while dozens of clearly unhappy passengers were milling around the information point as if looking for someone to blame.

"That's another thing I can't understand," said Mowgley as they approached the spot where Detective Sergeant Quayle was clearly failing to ignite a spark of interest in the aloof young blonde woman on the other side of the counter.

"You mean why Dickie Quayle works so hard to pull women that are obviously not interested in him?"

"No. Why they call it an Information Point when the one thing you can guarantee you won't get there is information."

"Yes," said Melons, "I suppose that's an oxymoron."

Mowgley looked across at a huge abstract sculpture in stainless steel at the foot of the heavily chromed winding staircase. "Is it? I thought it might be a rearing horse or a French fireman climbing a ladder."

"No, I mean calling it an information bureau is an oxymoron. It's a contradiction of terms, like 'sensitive man'. And talking of insensitive men..."

Quayle straightened up as they arrived. "Ah, you've arrived, then...Sir. As you can see, it's a right faux pas here."

Mowgley noted the fractional but significant pause before Quayle had tacked the 'Sir' on, and that the least popular officer in the Fun Factory had deliberately pronounced the French words as if they were English. That would be meant as a bit of revenge on the bored blonde. Nothing Quayle said or did lacked a purpose.

Clearly picking up his superior officer's irritation and

almost showing his pleasure at it, Quayle went on to explain the situation. All commercial drivers and more than half the car owners had driven over the linkspan and quit the port before the alarm had been raised and disembarkment stopped. The foot passengers and coach parties were, as he could see, still on board and would be held until they had been interviewed. The Spanish cleaner had serviced all the cabins which had been officially in use and were on her list, and had only looked into the Gauguin Suite to check it was all in order.

"The what?" asked Mowgley.

"The Gauguin Suite, Sir. As well as the two and four-berth cabins, there's a handful of fancy ones. They're much bigger and there's a proper bed and a telly...and a complimentary set of bath stuff and chocolates. They cost about the same as a room in a four-star hotel so aren't that popular - unless someone can afford it or has pulled on the crossing and doesn't want his style cramped by a single bunk."

Quayle smirked as if to indicate he himself had taken advantage of the facilities, and drew a scowl from his superior.

"So how did the body- and whoever put it in there- get into this 'suite'?"

"It's quite usual for people to take a cabin although they haven't booked one, and they often turn up at the desk at some time during the crossing and pay cash. The experienced travellers know that they can get a spare cabin cheap just by waiting."

"But there's a list ?"

Quayle made a wry face. "Sort of. The person behind the counter just takes the money, hands over a card key and makes a note of the cabin number."

"But not of whose taken it?"

"Yes, Sir."

"Yes they do make a note of the name of the booker, or yes they don't make a note?"

"Yes they don't, Sir."

Quayle went on to explain that the member of the crew who had given out the key to the cabin where the body was found was waiting in the purser's office; the cleaner who had found the unexpected occupant was also there, and in a bit of a state.

"Fancy that," said Mowgley with what he knew was wasted irony, then asked for directions to the cabin.

Leading the way through the crowd, he looked over his shoulder and asked his sergeant to be sure to put Quayle's name in the Punishment Book.

"I would if we had one," she said, "but what's his offence?"

"Being himself will do for starters. You can't get much more offensive than that."

"Fair enough. I'll get a book tomorrow."

*   *   *

It was not hard to locate the Gauguin Suite as there was a large uniformed constable guarding the door. In a way that implied he was suggesting the Inspector did not enter, he said that the Scenes of Crime team were inside.

"Team?" responded Mowgley with no small degree of irritation, "having a game of cricket, are they?"

As he reached for the handle, Melons' phone rang once then stopped. She moved around the corridor, then shook her head and said "Rotten signal. It's from Stephen and he never calls unless it's important. I'd better go up on deck."

Mowgley grunted. "Any bloody excuse to avoid looking at a body." He turned away so that his sergeant would not see him take a deep breath, then pushed the handle down and opened the door.

*   *   *

"So what was it like?" Melons asked.

"Quite comfortable, really. The bed was well-sprung and the free chocolates were okay if you like the poncy dark kind. There was one of his crappy paintings on the wall. I think it was *Still Life with Flowers*. As I'm sure you know, after his marriage broke up, Gauguin joined a collective of American painters at Pont-Aven in Central Brittany. They got up to all sorts of naughtiness in the woods between splashing stuff on canvas, and Gauguin invented Synthetism. The idea was that the artist should paint what he saw and not what 'was'. Just an excuse for not being able to paint very well, I reckon."

"But I thought you were a big fan of Van Gogh and Impressionism?"

"I am. But Vincent was genuinely trying to break new boundaries in art and capture the moment by painting what he saw. Besides, he died in absolute poverty like an artist should. And he was really potty. Gauguin just pretended to be."

"I see." Melons exhaled a feathery stream of smoke. They were leaning on the rail of the main deck and looking out across the ferry port towards their office and local pub. "Actually, I meant what was the body like?"

"Oh, you know," said Mowgley with studied nonchalance, "once you've seen one headless and limbless torso, you've see 'em all."

"So how many have you seen before?"

"Well, none, now I think of it. I was speaking figuratively. Boom-Boom. Funny enough, it was sort of not as bad as seeing a proper body which has been messed about with. Having no arms and legs and head, it looked more like something in the back of a butcher's shop. It was just a big lump of meat and had no real...humanity."

"I bet you still honked."

"Only a bit," said her boss defensively," and I got to the toilet bowl in time. But I think SOCO were not happy with my contaminating the scene."

Melons aimed the butt of her small cigar at the narrow gap of water between the ship's side and the jetty. "So what does the passport tell us?"

"Not a lot. There wasn't one. Nor a bag or any clothes.

The scratch 'n' sniff pair were a couple of foreigners from Southampton and not at all helpful. But they did say they'd had a good look and there was nothing in the room but the torso. No bag, no clothes, no nothing. There was a load of blood though, so they reckon he was cut up in situ."

"So it was male, then?"

"Yep. At least they'd left that little appendage. Well, not so little, really."

"At least we know where his arms are- I think."

"How do you mean?"

Melons held up her mobile. "The call from Stephen. He said that a bag has been found on the beach at Hayling Island. Looks like it had some Class 'A' stuff in it, and a load of euro notes. Oh, and a pair of arms.

Printed in Great Britain
by Amazon